THE CHILDREN'S HOUSE

Also by Alice Nelson

The Last Sky
After This: Survivors of the Holocaust Speak

ALICE NELSON

The CHILDREN'S *House*

VINTAGE BOOKS
Australia

A Vintage book
Published by Penguin Random House Australia Pty Ltd
Level 3, 100 Pacific Highway, North Sydney NSW 2060
penguin.com.au

Penguin
Random House
Australia

First published by Vintage in 2018

Addresses for the Penguin Random House group of companies can be found at global.penguinrandomhouse.com/offices.

A catalogue record for this book is available from the National Library of Australia

NATIONAL LIBRARY OF AUSTRALIA

ISBN 978 014379 118 8

Cover photography © Getty Images: image of little boy by Robert Westbrook, Blend Images; brownstone house by iStock
Cover design by Louisa Maggio © Penguin Random House Australia Pty Ltd
Internal design by Midland Typesetters, Australia
Typeset in 12pt Goudy Oldstyle by Midland Typesetters, Australia
Printed in Australia by Griffin Press, an accredited ISO AS/NZS 14001:2004 Environmental Management System printer

MIX
Paper from
responsible sources
FSC® C009448
www.fsc.org

For Danny Shub

There is remembrance, and communion, altogether human and unhallowed. For families will not be broken. Curse and expel them, send their children wandering, drown them in floods and fires, and old women will make songs out of all these sorrows and sit in the porches and sing them on mild evenings. Every sorrow suggests a thousand songs, and every song recalls a thousand sorrows, and so they are infinite in number, and all the same.

Housekeeping, Marilynne Robinson

Truro, Cape Cod
December, 1997

Feed my lambs, Jesus said. She murmurs it to herself as she holds the bottle to the child's mouth, trying for the lilt she remembers in the voice of a long-ago pastor. My lamb. The wind at the glass takes the sound of her voice and tosses it away like a scrap of fabric. Winter in the sky, the cold a tiny stab in her bones. Outside, these strange trees that throw their leaves away. A flock of birds rises up above the marsh, a dark arrow pointing the way.

The child's eyes are on her as she lifts the end of the bottle higher. Wary, watching, drooping now with the rhythmic suck of his mouth against soft plastic. They told her that he was past the time of milk-drinking, that she should stop now with these bottles. Those soft lips. Never at her breast since that first day when someone's hands had placed him, shuddering with blood and breath, against her, guided his gaping mouth to the right place. She had wailed then, in a way she never has since. No nourishment for him there. Hard to believe that she was able to sustain him inside her for so long. To bear the jab and turn of him against her ribs as she lay awake in a narrow bed in the refugee camp in Gisenyi. A foreign creature, she had felt him to be, a slippery lake fish swelling her body.

She sits beside the child for a moment. The marsh fills the window behind her. The old glass wavers the shifting fields. Flooded ground, this house was built on. Truro, Cape Cod. Even the name of the place sounds strange to her. A long way from Rwanda, though there were marshes in her country too. And birds, with their songs of praise at dawn. Soon it will be light enough to leave the house. She has her coat on already, encased in the heavy puffiness of it. Her canvas bag is tucked under the bed. It is Christmas Day; still very early in the morning.

The child will not close his eyes. He is always fighting sleep and she knows no ways to coax him into it. No song, no whispered words. His hand is curled in a fist against his cheek like a small shell. Gabriel, he is called. It is not a name from her country. A Congolese pastor in the camp gave it to him. She had another name under her tongue, but the pastor said that the child needed the name of an angel. That it was a good name for a boy who would grow in America. So she said nothing and let him choose the name he wanted. The last name was wrong, too. They did not know, the people who had written on the papers to come to America, that in Rwanda each child had its own last name. A name from their language, chosen with a special meaning for that child, not something shared with others in the family. On the papers for the baby they wrote her own last name, the one her mother had chosen for her alone. Nsengimana. 'I pray to God', it meant. An answered prayer, a child of faith, she was, the first to live after two born dead. She had been sure that her own baby would be born dead too, or would be something monstrous.

2

She had not seen that they had written the wrong name for the child until the two of them were in America and she lined up the plastic cards she had been given – one to buy food in the stores, one to show to the doctor at the clinic. It was too late then, to change it. It was easier, they had told her. Easier for them both to have the same last name. It was the way it was done in this country. Families were knitted together with the same name.

The child is sleeping at last, his head making a shallow dent on the white pillow. In the city, before they had met Marina, the little boy had cried and cried. She didn't know where he found the energy for so much crying. If she stepped into the other room and shut the door against him, the noise would eventually become a low whimper. Other times he would wail until he fell asleep, and she would find him curled up under the table, his cheek against the floor. If it was cold she would put her winter coat over him and in the morning he would be wrapped in it, like some small bird in a nest, staring up at her as she moved around the kitchen. As though he were afraid of her, that look. As though she were something to cause him fear.

It still surprises her sometimes, when she looks at him sleeping, that he could have come from her. That he could really exist in the world. And yet here he is. All the times she took him to the clinic in the city to be poked and touched and measured, to be given medicine or needles, it was in her mind that they would not give him back to her. That they would say it was enough now, would know she was not to be trusted with him. But they did not. Just gave her a bottle of medicine or a bright candy for the child and that was it, a smile and the door opening, someone else walking through as she lifted him on to her back in the waiting room and tied the wrap under her breasts. That was one thing she had remembered, after all – the folding and tying of fabric. The way to carry a child.

She places the empty bottle on the nightstand and presses the blanket in around his chin. Always watching her, this child, following her from room to room as soon as he could pull himself across the floor. And yet she cannot look at him. Slides her eyes away. 'Utabazi' was the lost name she chose for him. It means 'he belongs to them'.

So small he looks, folded under the heavy blankets. She knows the weight of him, has carried him tied to her back through the streets of the city. But now he will grow without her. How long until her body forgets the heft of him against her, the damp heat of his cheek through the fabric of her wrap? Soon he will be too heavy to carry, he will walk holding someone's hand. She bends to pick up her bag from under the bed. She needs to be far from the house before the others return.

On the blanket beside the child she places the two plastic cards with his name on them, the little booklet from the health clinic, the travel paper with the stapled-on picture. In the photograph he is only a tiny baby and his face is all wail and tears. Her hands are there in the frame, holding him up into the flash of the camera, her fingers against the white of his too-big shirt.

At the door she looks back at the bed for a moment, then steps out into the hallway, turning the latch softly. The house is still and dim, all the curtains left open to let in the light when it comes. There is nothing else she has to leave behind for the child. She cannot write a letter, does not own a string of beads to place around his neck. Better that there is no memory of her. Better to let herself dissolve in him without a trace. He is too small for remembering.

4

The morning is pungent, rain-wet. A stand of trees leaning over the path. Beyond them, the shapes of the town shimmer mistily, as if under waves. She walks away from the house, past the covered bins and the wooden letterbox to the road. More light will be in the sky soon. She stands still, staring at the rows of silvered fences, the gardens smoky with fine rain. Then she sets off along the side of the road, her feet leaving dark shapes on the wet grass.

Harlem, New York
June, 1997

Marina often found herself wondering when the first murmurs of Constance's plan had begun to stir in the girl. Whether it was something she had calculated from the beginning, an agonising scheme with a coiled heart of mercy in its reasoning, or if it had been pure desperation, slipshod and hasty. In the years to come Marina would travel back in memory, trying to order the strange unfolding of that summer. Sometimes she believed that the seed was sown on that first day on the street in Harlem; the small rehearsal of intimacy with the little boy. That Constance had simply been biding her time through that summer and the fall. Surely there had been hints of what the girl had intended, which Marina had failed to see, as she had failed to see so much that summer.

But perhaps we know nothing with any certainty. Jacob would tell the story differently. He would say that it was her own need blossoming that made it possible for the girl to loosen her grasp on her child. That what happened was more Marina's doing than anyone else's. And Constance? They would never know how she would tell it because she had cast herself without a trace into the wind, to be carried off with all the disappeared, the wanderers and the unhoused. Constance was gone, but they would forever-more be forced to consider her. Her life, however little they knew about it, was now inseparable from their own.

Those first summer months in Harlem ran together in Marina's mind into one long spell of raw, roiling heat. The swelter and noise of the streets, the dazed shimmer of the afternoons, the thick balmy fog of evening. Hot blasts of air rose up through the subway grates; the rumble and clatter of the trains below them seemed louder than in other parts of the city. It was hard to imagine that fall would ever come.

In the neighbourhood a strange sense of solidarity formed with the heat; a feeling that they were under siege. Conversa-tions were full of marvelling at the unreasonable extremes, the persistence of the heatwave. They were united, all of them, in the surrender it required. Sometimes consolations were offered, hopeful observations that the temperature seemed kinder today, that the weather might break soon.

Everything about Harlem was extraordinary in those first months. The men from the Caribbean holding out their wares to passing traffic on Second Avenue, the *curandera* with her painted windows and strings of herbs, the old Italian women sweeping their steps, the foragers and can-collectors, the beggars yawing their way up the subway steps with their paper cups held out in front of them, the young Mexican women selling tamales on the street corners. All seemed foreign and magical. These unimaginable lives, the lost streets, the shopfront churches, the tenement buildings scaffolded with fire escapes – everything seemed to contain a story. 'Hey, Romeo. Hey, Juliet,' the panhandler who sat near the gate to Mount Morris Park called out to her and Jacob every time they walked past. 'Spare any nickels? Dimes?' The same refrain, every day of the summer, and the sharp jingle of his cup. Marina gave money often and haphazardly, sometimes a handful of coins, sometimes a ten-dollar bill. It was like a tax on her presence here, she felt, in a neighbourhood that belonged to others.

She and Jacob had bought the brownstone on 120th Street the previous winter. Since she had first seen the tall, narrow house on the edge of Mount Morris Park, something about it had burned in her. The crumbling façade, the curved bay window, the wild, shady square of garden with its ruined grotto – it all seemed so enchanting. The house had been owned by a small order of nuns who had lived there for half a century until the last of them had grown too old to manage and they had moved to a retirement home upstate. Before she and Jacob repainted the house, Marina had collected the wooden crosses that had been left hanging high on the wall of each bedroom, mementoes of the devout old women who had knelt each morning on the hardwood floors and slept in narrow iron beds. She liked the idea that it was a hallowed space. That it was possible to live in a state of grace. She imagined the nuns drifting down the stairs, dipping their fingers into the small brass bowl of holy water that was attached to the doorframe when she and Jacob first came to see the house.

Eight nuns had lived here, the real estate agent told them. Before that, several Italian families, dividing up the four floors between them. With just Marina and Jacob and his son, Ben, the house felt oddly unpeopled. It was the largest place Marina

8

had ever lived. Originally they had planned for Jacob to move his psychiatry practice here and see patients in the room below the level of the sidewalk, the one with its own door tucked under the front stoop. The nuns had held soup kitchens and prayer meetings there, so it would be perfect for his secular ministrations, Jacob joked. The compromised light could be fixed with lamps, the room would be suffused with a dim, intimate softness. They chose a long linen-covered sofa, a new leather armchair, and printed and framed a photograph that Jacob had taken of the pale spread of clouds above the ocean.

But after they moved in Jacob hesitated. Living here now, he was no longer sure that his patients would be comfortable coming to Harlem. Marina knew it was not just that. The brownstone on 22nd Street in Chelsea where he worked was an enormous part of his life. It had been his own analyst's practice for nearly half a century, the lease passed on to Jacob like a kind of baton when she retired. He loved the ease of the brief walk from his office to NYU, where he taught in the School of Psychiatry two afternoons a week; the park bench by the great arch of Washington Square where he ate his lunch when it was not too cold; the café on the corner where they knew his order. So much of his life took place in that room, so much of his thinking was framed by that view from the bay window, the sun playing over the stone faces of the houses across the street. When the time came, Jacob could not bring himself to give up the practice in Chelsea. They could afford the rent – it was not a question of money, he said.

What was it a question of, really, Marina had wondered, staring around the beautiful room they had prepared together for him in Harlem. She could not help thinking that part of Jacob's clinging to the practice in Chelsea was so he could keep something that was purely his own. A private sanctuary away from the life of their household. Marina knew that some days he lingered at the practice long after he had finished with his patients. He would lie on the leather sofa, his legs draped over the arm, a book in his lap. He liked to feel the silence of the room, he had told her once, after a day full of talking. It took at least an hour, he said, after his last patient had left, for the echoes of the voices of the day to stop sounding. For his mind to feel uncluttered. Marina could hardly begrudge him this: her writing was a secret room, too; a place she retreated not wanting to be followed. It was hard for her to surface sometimes after a day of work, for the real world not to feel thin and elusive.

Even after nearly a decade of marriage there were elements of her husband that were still a mystery to her. In spite of all the things they knew about each other, small and large, there were depths that had not been plumbed and perhaps would never be. Sometimes Marina felt that they had both consented unconsciously to be their best selves, to maintain a graciousness in their intimacy that might have fallen away much earlier in other relationships. A marriage can't stand too much trouble, someone had once said to her, and she believed this to be true. For her and Jacob, this love was an unexpected bestowal of grace, a rare and miraculous second chance. They knew this and it made them careful with each other, and careful with their love. It was to be cultivated and tended. They paid attention to it in a way they might not have, had it not come after considerable sorrow.

Each morning Jacob left early to catch the subway downtown, Marina standing on the steps watching him walk to the end of their block and wait to cross Madison Avenue. He was, she thought, like a kind of exiled prince who had succumbed to living in Harlem because she had wanted it so. Dignified but slightly bewildered as he stepped out among the throngs on the street each morning. She watched Jacob standing on the street corner among a small knot of people: an old man pushing a shopping trolley, two boys exchanging an elaborate, wordless handshake. The wind swept some plastic bags towards the fence of the park behind them; they looked like torn white flags against the chain-link. Jacob nodded kindly to the old man and the boys, reaching his hand out to steady the shopping trolley as they crossed the road. There was such enormous goodwill to her husband, Marina thought. He was mannerly to a fault, but it was something more than that. He had a readiness to believe the best of people, an enduring faith in their goodness. She was not sure how this could be so when he spent his days listening to the profound and endless ways in which people failed themselves and each other. He should know, Marina thought, just how much to expect from mankind, but there he was, always hoping for the best. Greeting a homeless man and two neighbourhood boys with the same mild politeness he would show a colleague at the university. He was such a good-hearted child, Jacob's mother, Rose, had told Marina once. It struck her as a strange turn of phrase, but an apt one. To have a good heart. It was no small thing.

'Earl Grey fumé,' Jacob had said with a flourish when he had brought her a cup of tea earlier that morning. They had become part of the currency of their marriage, these carefully made cups of tea. He leaned over and kissed the top of her head, his hands on her shoulders. 'How did you sleep?' Jacob asked this every morning, with the same slightly perturbed look of concern.

'Fine,' she said, trying to disguise the trace of impatience that crept into her voice at the question. 'I got up early because I wanted to get started on some work.'

'At four?'

'You know me. Mornings are my best time. It's harder to feel hopeful about the book in the afternoons.'

'Why don't you have a sleep after lunch?'

'Perhaps I will.'

Even when she had not slept well, Marina did not confess this to Jacob. He saw it, she knew, as a symptom of the things that had harmed her, had compromised her happiness. She took a sip of her tea and looked at him standing in the doorway in his checked linen shirt, sleeves rolled up, his hair still damp from the shower. One of his buttons was hanging from a thread; she should mend it for him. This lovely man who believed in people's fundamental goodness, who cared deeply and earnestly about whether she had slept well or not. She still swelled with gratitude, and amazement, too, at her great and narrow escape from an entirely different kind of life. Everything between them still felt so pure and definite that summer. It was baffling to her sometimes, the immensity of her love for him, the impossible good luck of their marriage.

As he walked away down 120th Street, Marina could just see the small coin of baldness among Jacob's dark curls. It made her feel curiously tender, this circle of pale, unprotected skin.

For nearly eight years they had lived on the Upper East Side, on Park Avenue. It was Jacob's apartment, bought after the end of his first marriage. Marina had always felt like an imposter among the genteel stone buildings with their bottle-green canopies and gleaming brass doors. The streets were full of doormen and dog-walkers, women in fur coats slipping into sleek black cars, dark-skinned nannies pushing blond children in strollers. On every corner brightly coloured daisies sprouted from carefully tended planter boxes. There was a dreary uniformity to it all that Marina hated, a cold sort of nowhere feeling. The neighbourhood felt so removed from the heart of the city that they might as well be in one of the smug suburbs. In the mornings the laundry room of their building was full of maids chattering in Spanish as they folded clothes. The help. Marina was the only one in that building who seemed to do her own laundry. At night the empty streets felt like an apocalyptic scene; the strange, pallid light on the buildings and the sense of furtive life all around her. There were no hidden lanes, no boarded windows, nothing derelict or mysterious.

Marina wondered if it was her desire for camouflage that had brought them to Harlem. She had spent the first years of her life in Israel, never away from the kibbutz where she was born. That distant childhood had displaced her somehow, and since she had come to America she had courted foreignness, always more at ease in neighbourhoods full of forsaken worlds, the ghosts of other places hovering above the streets. El Barrio was to their east, Black Harlem beyond their strip of brownstones on the edge of the park. Marina took comfort in knowing that even the locals were once strangers here. A railroad ticket and a suitcase, and you could be transplanted from a cornfield to the 125th Street station.

In their first week in Harlem, caught in a sudden downpour, she had ducked under the awning of one of the small Pentecostal churches. Three old women in fur coats stood beside her, purses clutched under their arms. The rain blurred the street beyond them and they recited the names of their hometowns for her. Scotland Neck, North Carolina. Yazoo City, Mississippi. Tiger

Bend, Louisiana. The names sounded to her like charms. Afterwards she wrote them down in her notebook; the private core of a memory, words she might come back to one day.

At times in that first summer, with no classes to teach, Marina did not leave Harlem for days in a row. Old men in their undershirts sat around plastic tables playing dominoes, and people congregated on street corners, outside the bodega or the liquor store. She came to recognise certain faces, a half-smile or a particular stare as a group parted wordlessly to let her pass. In the mornings she walked along Second Avenue, turning down streets at random. A window box full of dusty geraniums, a thin dog leaping out of sight behind a fence, a young Mexican woman waiting in a doorway, the smell of frying. All these half-lit lives. She would often walk as far as the East River and stand staring out at the factories across the water, streaks of cars flashing past on the expressway, the rumble and hiss of trucks loud in the blazing morning. Sometimes there were fishermen casting lines out into the brown water. It seemed improbably hopeful to fish in such a river.

After Jacob left for work in the mornings Marina would sit on the front stoop, drinking her cooling cup of coffee, the morning sun glinting off the silver filigree of the mezuzah on the doorframe. It was ornately worked with birds and leaves, the Hebrew letter *shin* nestled into the stamen of a flower. The design was based on a Scroll of Esther from nineteenth-century Poland, the woman in the silver shop told them. This pleased Jacob. His father was born in Poland; his aunt's name was Esther. He bought a second mezuzah for his mother, saying the blessing for her after he hammered the tiny nails into the doorframe of her apartment. He was full of these small kindnesses; a lovely solicitude for all of them. Late at night poring over one of Ben's calculus textbooks so he could better understand the new language his son brought home from college.

'A deep-cut ellipsoid algorithm,' she remembered Jacob musing once. 'Have you ever heard of one of those?'

'It sounds like a weird kind of poetry.'

'It does. Ben always says there's a poetry to pure mathematics.'

She had come to depend on Jacob's care, Marina realised, as she had once depended on her brother's. Her husband's hand against her cheek as he brought her a cup of tea in bed on a Sunday morning, strong and smoke-tinged, tea leaves carried back from the Mariage Frères teahouse in Paris. All these clues to the life they shared: the shining black canisters like secret talismans, the knowledge of precisely how long to steep the leaves, the pale blue of the deep Limoges teacup she loved. 'Marriage tea', Jacob called it.

A strange word, marriage. A clipped sound, stern and serious, no quiet sibilance to it. Strong casing, the proper shape of it around them. Her cream silk dress, a clutch of peonies, Ben's little blue blazer, his serious young face. The ring-bearer, he had appointed himself, so solemn between his grandmother and his aunt under the flag at City Hall. Their cluster of five, arms linked as they walked to a restaurant for lunch afterwards. It was unfashionable, really, the regard in which they held each other, the closeness they had nestled into, their delight in the raucous games of canasta around the kitchen table in the apartment on

15

the Upper West Side where Jacob had grown up and his mother still lived.

Marina had stepped tentatively into the circle of Jacob's family, expecting suspicion. She was so young. She had no family. Surely his mother would disapprove. But she was befriended in a way that was both mysterious and welcome to her. Within a few months there were kitchen conversations with Rose, a circle of old photographs or a recipe book spread out before them. Weekly lunches with his sister, Leah, who would walk up to Columbia to meet her on her day off from the social service agency in East Harlem where she worked. 'Little sister', she called Marina, conspiring with Rose to tend to her. Flowers sent to Marina's office every week of the winter semester after she had once said she needed a clutch of yellow jonquils to see her through the grey four o'clocks of January. Every paper she published, every book review, clipped and catalogued, sent to Rose's friends and relatives in Israel, Delaware, Miami. The joke among them that Rose was her greatest publicist.

Marina submitted happily to their kindness. No one had ever made her chicken soup when she was unwell, or knitted sweaters for her. At first Marina thought that their love must come from their relief. Jacob's first wife, Leni, had left him and Ben when the boy was only three years old, moving to London with a colleague of Jacob. 'On Jacob's dollar,' Rose told Marina mournfully. It was the disaster she had predicted from the first day Jacob had brought Leni home, this terrible wounding of her beloved son. It had become a dark thread through the family: Leni's unsuitability, her inadequate mothering, her unforgivable defection. The shamefulness of it, Ben's confused grief, the greyness that had crept into Jacob's skin. And then, after nearly three years of absence, Leni's return to New York and the court battle that led to a joint custody arrangement.

Jacob only managed to communicate all this to Marina as a kind of shadow play, a shaky and unsatisfying recounting. He kept his sadnesses at a distance – from her and perhaps also from himself. It was Rose who told her the terrible details of Jacob's first marriage. The catch and sob in her son's voice on the end of the telephone on the Sunday evenings after he dropped Ben at Leni's house, his misery at the empty stretch of hours, the silent apartment, the childless week ahead. The clattering house of Jacob's heart.

On the day of the wedding, Rose held Marina's face between her hands and kissed her solemnly on both cheeks, like a formal bene-diction. Marina remembered the moment so clearly; the smell of Rose's powder and the violet perfume dabbed above the collar of her paisley silk blouse, the crepey softness of her cheeks. The world was offering her the figure of a mother at a time when she thought she had stopped looking behind her for what had been lost. Gizela, her own mother, lost. But absence still feeds, Jacob would say. All those damaged children he worked with, the wounds festering through the years, his own son searching for a mother in the terrible months after Leni had left. Three years old, four years old and calling every nursery teacher 'Mommy'.

The doorman in their old building insisted on calling Marina 'Mrs Kaufman' after the wedding, beaming as he rushed to hold open the door for her, to take whatever packages she carried. The whole production made Marina uneasy: his starched uniform, gleaming epaulets and white gloves, the absurdity of this elabo-rate costume of service. 'Yes, ma'am,' his voice calm and sweetly lilting. It seemed unkind, churlish, to point out that she had not changed her last name. The doorman was from Trinidad. Once, he had shown her a photograph of his wife and son. He wanted to bring them to New York, he told her, but his wife was from a small village and was terrified of the city, was sure that she would be robbed or murdered there. One day he would convince her to come, he said. One day.

No doorman in Harlem, just the wide stoop and the curving black trellis of the fence on to the street. In the spring semester she would set off early for Columbia. It was only a few blocks west and a walk through Morningside Park to the university. It soon became a ritual, those ten minutes immersed in the craggy wildness of the park, the unexpected rush of the waterfall down the cliff face, the fretted shadows of the trees. Marina would stop to drink a takeaway coffee on a bench in the park if she did not have an early class or a student expecting her, peering anxiously through the small glass window in her office door. She hated that window, the feeling it gave her that she was constantly on display. For some reason it made her think of Schumann locked in his cell in the asylum in Bad Godesberg, the mind that had produced all that sublime music unravelling profoundly. She had read that when Schumann's wife, Clara, came to visit her husband towards the end of his life, she was only permitted to look in at him through the small window in the door of his cell. It seemed such a poignant story – that the only thing left to Clara was to watch Schumann from behind a closed door. Marina often imagined the young woman standing at the door, her husband's suffering something her love could not touch. She wondered if the act of looking at him had brought Clara any solace. She could not imagine so.

There were panels of glass in the dormitory doors in the Children's House on the kibbutz, too. The nurses on night duty would peer in to see if the children were sleeping. So many nights Marina lay awake staring up at that small, illuminated square, closing her eyes when she saw a nurse's face looming at the window. Sometimes it was her brother's face. He calculated the times the nurses carried out their checks and knew when it was safe to slip down the hallway to see her.

She and Dov never shared a dormitory. On the kibbutz children were grouped according to their age, and Dov shared a room with several older children. Late at night he would sit on the edge of her bed and tell her stories: fairy tales recounted in a whisper, or narratives of his own invention. So many years later Marina could still remember the hushed sound of her brother's voice whispering to her on those late nights, the other children around them sleeping. All the stories he wove for her under the palest skin of early morning while their parents slept in their own room far away on the other side of the kibbutz.

'Dova'leh', she had called her brother. Little Bear. They spoke to each other in Hebrew in those days. It was the language of the kibbutz and of the country, but it had slipped away when they came to America. Marina could barely recall it these days. It was a strange thing, to feel the language in which you had first known yourself to be gone from you. But in so many ways the child she had been in Israel was like a figment of a dream. The little girl who had waited anxiously to see her brother's face at the window seemed as far from her as the language in which she had called out for him. In New York they had reinvented themselves in English, as their mother had when she was taken away from her own country.

On the mornings of their first spring semester in Harlem, Marina would sit on the bench in Morningside Park and look down at her

19

watch, allowing herself just a little more time before she resumed her walk to Columbia. Some mornings even the thought of delivering a lecture or meeting with one of the graduate students she supervised felt like an insuperable obstacle. The measure of impersonation involved seemed too monumental. She did not love teaching in the way Jacob did, did not believe she had his skill for making people feel they had been allowed into the secret room of his imagination. Her students were mostly clever and conscientious, but they required so much of her. Patience, kindness, a considered display of interest in their lives. And a need to be entertaining, captivating, to inspire and amuse. It was not enough simply to impart knowledge to them. Many students signed up for her classes because of the small circle of fame her first book, on the Romani people, had brought her. She had become known as the 'Gypsy scholar', the very name conjuring up some sort of glamour. A mystique or foreignness was expected from her, as if she might come to class with gold coins braided into her hair.

'They're all in love with you,' Jacob said once after she had been complaining about the relentless neediness of her students.

'Oh, hardly.'

'I would fall in love with you if I were an angst-ridden undergrad.'

'Would you? I think you would have found me bookish and boring when you were nineteen.'

'Bookish and beautiful.'

Perhaps students were drawn to Marina because they saw her as someone who contained secret histories, a translator of sparse and hidden knowledge. They thought her mysterious. The success of the Romani book beyond the academic world had coaxed her out into the open, and the festival appearances, a *New Yorker* article, the interviews and the invitations to speak at conferences had made her position at Columbia possible. Universities loved a small circle of fame, the promise of prestige. Her friends from graduate school had been offered jobs in North Dakota or Ohio, been forced to travel to some distant prairie town for a tenure-track position, or scramble for sessional work in the cities. Professor Hirsch. Still the sound of it was strange to her. It made her think of stately chambers and cut-glass inkwells. A respectable life, orderly and faintly smug. Something far from a barefoot young girl standing at the edge of a field.

If Marina naturally migrated away from the fray, for Jacob it was the opposite. Despite his natural reticence, he loved the world's embrace. Like hers, his real work took place in secret, but over the years he had become a public figure, feted and admired. Resented, too, and subject to the small cruelties and envies that fame, no matter how minor, brings. Already when she had met him a decade earlier in California he was being heralded by some as a rising star in the world of child psychotherapy, criticised by others for his lack of scientific rigour. Jacob said that he saw psychoanalysis not so much as a science but an art, that the abstractions and certainties of science were contrary to the complexity of the human being. He trusted his unconscious to supply the idea that could be fashioned into a way of treatment. A kind of working blind. And there was the success of his clinical work, the undeniable success of it. All those children.

Because Marina was so much younger, and because of a certain hesitance in her nature, people assumed that she had been seduced by Jacob. A younger woman caught up in the slipstream of his success, his charisma. But it had not been that way. Marina had seen Jacob and hunted him down single-mindedly, tempted by nobody else. Often she returned in her mind to that first day, a lecture he was giving on grief and psychotherapy at Berkeley, where she was a doctoral student. He was a visiting professor, there for a semester from New York. The talk was open to the public and the hall was full and clamorous. Slipping in late she had found a place standing against the wall at the side, not far from the stage. She could see Jacob's dark curls against his pale jacket, his elegant profile in the dim light of the lecture hall. He allowed a long silence to settle before he started to speak, and then he began, unexpectedly, with a line of poetry. 'The same loneliness that closes us/ Opens us again'. A hush settled over the crowded theatre, Jacob descending into his lecture like a diver, slow and precise, surfacing briefly to look up from the lectern, a small pool of light from the lamp around him. Whispers spread through the room, all those women staring up at him from the front row, sitting up taller. Just let me be alone with him, she remembered thinking, everything logical in her suddenly unfixed. *Just let me be alone with him.*

Some nights that first summer in Harlem, Marina would slip out of the house for a late walk, the moon hanging hazily above the skyline, the briny smell of the river coming at her on a sudden wind. She would circle around their neighbourhood, arms crossed over her chest, slowing down to read the posters and notices papered in a haphazard collage over the walls of the corner bodega. On these walks she felt an old wildness again, something reckless and shadowy rising up in her. She and Dov had walked the streets of Brooklyn at night like this when they were children. Sometimes because their mother had locked them out of the apartment, on other nights from a need to escape the tiny flat, their mother's closed bedroom door. They would put on their coats and set out together, weaving up and down the streets of Crown Heights, often walking as far as the Botanic Garden on the edge of Prospect Park. There was something hushed and magical about the gardens at night, a wild and secret quality that was never there in the daytime. One winter they climbed through an unlocked window into the tropical conservatory and stayed there all night, in the ripe warmth of the palms and ferns. It was like being lost in the jungle. They felt like children in a fairy tale, alone with the dark mystery of the night. A gardener found them early the next morning, sleeping on their spread coats, and chased them out. The windows were always locked after that, but they still came back to the gardens at night, pretending they were wild children lost in a forest, camping out under the night sky. The stars could barely be seen in the city, even in the middle of the night, so Dov made a map for her. White buttons sewn carefully on to a dark square of silk stolen from their mother's closet. Marina had it still, folded away among her letters. Even after twenty years it felt unimaginable to her that Dov was dead. She wondered if anyone but her still remembered him.

Walking home along the edge of Mount Morris Park, Marina would look for Jacob's silhouette in the light of his study window. Sometimes she would stop in the street and stare up at him, his head bent over a book. His beauty never ceased to surprise her. In the early days of their marriage she had harboured a sadness that she had not known him in his youth. She had only shards and rumours from those years; legends and stories that came to her from other people. A photograph of a young man leaning against a white car. Old medical textbooks with his name printed on the flyleaf. But something about the faint vulnerability of him now made her more fiercely tender. His hair faded to the colour of ore, the deepening eye sockets, the shadows and marks on the body, the paleness of his ankles. It would be enough, Marina thought, looking up at Jacob, just to be permitted to stay together quietly. To live unexceptional lives and not to have to unstitch or amend the replete, singular existence they had created. But permanency could never be assumed. She knew enough to know this.

Upstate New York
December, 1997

Later in the morning the sway of the bus as it follows the curve of the highway makes Constance feel sick. She can feel the hum of the road in her bones. So different, this smooth glide along a paved surface, to the jolting lurch of the rare truck or car of her childhood in Rwanda.

It is nearly midday but the light is so pale it could still be dawn. A dim, grainy glow at the window. In her own country grey cranes were the first to say that the night-time was over. Then the turacos like big green parrots. If you looked close you could see the long-neck storks and pelicans slipping through the morning mist. Oh, it was something.

This country, America, has its own bird talk but it is a different thing altogether. She does not know the names of any birds here. How can they survive this white time with no leaf on any tree, and the cold so strong that even one small square of bare skin can send it deep into you? Still, there are birds. She has seen them on the shore below, coasting on the cold waves. And back in the

25

city there were clouds of them, rising up against the buildings. Once, a brown bird flew into the window of the apartment – she felt the sickening slap of it against the glass. She didn't dare to look down at the courtyard below, for days avoided the place the bird might have fallen. She wonders if she will ever know what the birds here mean. Which are the ones to say that sunrise will not be long now. Which ones circle a grave or call out when the rains are close.

She pulls a small knife out of her bag and uses it to slice apart an apple. It's a habit she fell into with the child, passing him a piece of fruit that he would take from the blade. Sometimes he would reach for the knife and she would slap his hand and he would cry loudly so that she would have to turn away from him and cover her ears. She would walk out of the apartment and close the door and crouch down in the hallway, her head against the wall. His roar would grow terrible then, because he thought she was gone. He did not know that she was always there, just on the other side of the door. She would count all the numbers she knew in English before she went back into the apartment. Sometimes the chant of numbers felt like a prayer.

Before they moved away from the city, the Catholic nuns who lived in the big brown house by the park had told her often that she must talk to the child. That otherwise he would be a lonely little boy. She thought of the mamas carrying their little ones in her village, but she could not remember any words she could say to the child.

She has not spoken one word of Kinyarwanda since she came to America. If she has to speak, she uses the English words she has learned. 'Apartment'. 'Coffee'. 'Diaper'. 'Appointment'. 'Late'. 'Rent'. 'Shoe'. Sometimes men she passed on the streets of the city tried a few words of her language, or a low hiss of Swahili.

She ignored them, turning her head away and walking faster. She would never go among her own people again, not to listen to each one start to tell again what he saw, to travel in memory. The little boy didn't know how to speak in any language. No word ever came from his mouth, though he was past the time of talking. Perhaps he would never speak. He cried though. Oh, he could cry.

The nuns had told her that she should pray, too; pressed prayer cards with pictures of saints into her hands. Once, they gave her a string of rosary beads made of something carved and white like a fine bone. She buried the cards and the necklace in Mount Morris Park, at the top of the hill that rose up in the middle of the park. She dug a shallow hole with the end of a stick, watching as Jesus' pale face on the card disappeared under the dirt. Over the weeks she added Saint Claire with her lamp, Christopher crossing a river, Ignatius kneeling in prayer, Francis and his tiny birds. She placed a stone over them to keep them safe. Gabriel the Archangel with those feathered white wings she put away in a drawer in the apartment. An angel's name given to the child back in the refugee camp. For protection. The name of an angel and sweet prayers to Jesus were what he needed to live and to grow well, the pastor had told her. But he did not grow well, the child. She could see that. She had given him her fear, and something even worse than fear. A great cold hollow. Even she could see that.

On the first nights when they were hiding in the marshes, people would gather together to pray to Jesus, even those who had no habit of prayer. But it had not lasted long. After so many weeks people had no will left for it. No strength or faith or memory of what words could be said. Constance would not pray again. Counting English numbers when the child was

27

wailing was the closest thing she would do. At times her mind wanted to whisper names instead, but it was best not to. It was like a dark pool, she thought, one you could step into and disappear forever. The water would close over your head. When the names rose up she pushed them down. The best thing was to let a great emptiness fill her mind, as if everything had been scoured away.

After the nuns moved out of the brownstone, Constance would walk through the park and climb the steps to the great rise of rocks. She liked a high place. There was never anyone at the top of the rise and she would sit, chin in hand, without counting the hours. Sometimes, peering down into the park below, she saw the white woman, Marina, with Gabriel, on the path near the playground. The summer was finished by then and brown leaves were everywhere, great piles of them in the small squares and parks of the city. Very soon the winter would come. All that white, leafless cold for months. Everything before and after just a dream or a memory of warmth.

She hadn't thought of the little boy as a child someone could want before she met Marina. In the morning she would bring him to the tall brown house where the nuns used to live, buttoned into his new red coat. Marina was always so happy to see him. The first thing she would do was bend down to pick him up so he could put his arms around her neck and press his head into her shoulder. This woman knew what to do with him, even though she had no babies of her own. There was the older boy, but Constance knew he was born to another woman. All of them in that family – the grey-haired father, the tall son, Marina, the aunt and the grandmother – they meant each other well. She could see that from the very start. They meant each other well.

One day from the rock on top of the hill Constance watched Marina and the child playing in the leaves. She could see Gabriel's red coat, the bright flash of him diving into the piles of leaves, his hands reaching up to Marina as she pulled him out. So small, the two of them looked down there. Both of them laughing. She couldn't hear it, but she could see their faces twisted into the shape of it. Her own face, she thought, had forgotten how to do that. She tried to make the shapes of a laugh, opening her teeth and trying for the sound to see if she could remember it. Her voice sounded strange to her. When she had to speak she thought that her voice had become that of a ghost. It was not the new language; it was to do with her throat. Perhaps one day she would find she could not speak at all. Constance stood up and walked down the hill and left the park from the far gate, careful not to let them see her.

She leans her head against the window of the bus, the chill of the glass sharp through the knitted cap she wears pulled down around her face. In the pocket of her coat is the paper for this journey and the words that will take her to the right place. It's like a puzzle she has to solve, finding the right way to go. If she breaks it down into parts it is easier. This morning she pushed the piece of paper across the counter to the woman selling bus tickets, tapped her finger against the name of the town and slid some bills under the glass partition. And now this bus is flashing past so many towns, the sea already far behind her. When she reaches the next place she can find someone else to ask. Another bus, or a walk, if her legs can make it, although walking is harder because only the first few parts of the way they tell her ever stay in her mind and she has to keep stopping and asking which way next.

Another bus would be better. Perhaps a bus that never stops, coasts forever through a white morning.

Harlem, New York
June, 1997

Marina stepped out of the house, pulling the front door closed behind her. It was early but the heat was already hovering over the street like a dense fog. She sat down on the steps, a teacup in her hands. There was the world. The veer and bustle of it. New York in all its intricate, ceaseless motion. Garbage trucks, slamming doors, the squeal and hiss of a bus lurching in against the sidewalk. There was a small cluster of commotion on the corner, too far away for her to unpick. A mob of starlings rose up above the brownstones, a dark scattering against the unexpected blue of the sky.

Earlier, she had poured a cup of coffee in the silent kitchen, looking out at the last curve of night. The spread of time just before sunrise was when she did her best work. Drifting straight from sleep to work she felt that something from her dreams was still strong in her. And then these moments on the steps, weighing what was already written, that feeling of the day stretching comfortably out before her. The summer was ahead of them – the long, hot weeks when the whole city seemed to unfurl; their usual month in the beach cottage they always rented on Fire Island. And beyond that, her long-awaited sabbatical. A whole semester to work on the new book, her chronicle of the Hasidic movement in the country. Not a cool academic study or a conventional history, but a looser, more creative investigation. Conversations with hundreds of cheerful young emissaries sent to remote and unlikely outposts, reflections on the relentless proselytising zeal, the passion for bringing Jews back to their faith. Just one mitzvah, enough to draw the Jewish soul a step closer to God. God's sales force, a young rabbi had once called the movement. An odd choice of subject, most people thought. Such a shadowy, secretive world, so suspicious of outsiders, so arcane and unfathomable. You should choose something more glamorous, one of her colleagues said to her. Less religious. But most of what she wished to know was in a way linked to strangers, to worlds she did not yet understand. And the Hasidic families she and Dov had lived among as children in Crown Heights had been kind to them. Invited them in for meals, sent them home with containers full of food and warm loaves of challah. After Dov had died and her mother had gone, it was an Hasidic family who had helped her, even though her brother could not be buried in a Jewish cemetery.

From the top of the steps she could see her stepson, Ben, riding slowly down the street on his bicycle. She had never liked the word 'stepson'. It sounded like something cold and formal, a gulf between them, a relationship somehow in opposition to another more valid one. When, at fourteen, Ben came to live with Jacob and Marina permanently, Leni railed against Marina, blaming her for Ben's refusal to return to her house. Marina manipulated Ben, she claimed, lured him into turning against her.

'You don't have your own child, so you want to play at being mother to mine,' she said. 'You are not his mother,' she wrote in an angry letter. The years Ben spent shuttling between his father's house, and Leni and her partner Michael's loft on Bleecker Street, had caused Jacob enormous grief. He hated the way that a large share of his son's life was secret from him. Ben's other bedroom with the bunk bed and the constellation of glow-in-the-dark stars that Jacob never saw; all the meals around the dining table with Leni and Michael; the trip to Disneyland of which there were no photos; all the tremors and echoes of that other home that would never be known to Jacob. His small consolation was that there were no other children. Children of Leni and Michael, half-brothers and sisters, would have seemed too much of a claim staked on his son. Even an unfamiliar sweater or a new pair of winter shoes could make Jacob feel queasy with loss.

Ben wheeled his bike through the gate off the street and smiled up at Marina. He had just finished an early shift stacking shelves at the supermarket and he looked exhausted. He came to sit beside her. The boy had the most graceful beauty, the kind that made you want to stare a little too long. He looked uncannily like his father at the same age. Not even a slice of his mother in him. He was given to long, thoughtful stares like Jacob, to the same close, attentive listening, the same lovely solicitude. How strange it was to have this earlier, freshly minted version of her husband beside her.

She had been worried that Ben would need to swerve away from her and Jacob in adolescence, that their closeness might shatter and have to be reconstructed as something else later on. There were so many horror stories. Her friends with tall, truculent boys, teenagers full of rage and contempt, their adolescence a stage of siege. It had not been like that at all. Ben remained resolutely himself, pensive and steady, never anything awkward or unlovely about him. Still the clear, serious person he had been when she had first met him at ten years old.

But something had happened to Ben that year. A kind of muffled sorrow had taken hold of him, an inexplicable and disabling mantle of grief. Although grief was not really the right word for it. It was quieter. Something flat and detached, and far more unsettling. He had announced to them just before the spring semester that he would not be returning to Brown to finish his third year of college. That he had decided to take a hiatus.

'A hiatus?' Jacob had asked incredulously. 'To do what?' Even from across the room Marina felt the quiver of panic in Jacob, his struggle to collect himself. His love for Ben had always encompassed something hovering and anxious, a deep fear that somehow Ben had been compromised by his mother's defection all those years ago. A part of Jacob had been waiting all along, Marina realised, for a disaster to come to pass. And here it was, just when they thought they had reached safety.

He would rather not be at college right now, Ben said simply, providing no other explanations. No, nothing bad had happened; yes, he still enjoyed his studies. *He would rather not.* It became like a refrain, the same words offered up again and again. He would rather Jacob not organise a summer internship with a biologist colleague at NYU; would rather not come to Fire Island with them that year; would rather not see the therapist that Jacob had found for him. He abruptly broke off his relationship with his high-school girlfriend, Isabel. The stricken girl turned up at the house one day when Ben was out, her lovely face blotched and swollen with crying. She had caught the bus down from Sarah Lawrence College because Ben was refusing to answer her phone calls.

Marina made her a cup of tea and Isabel folded her head into her arms on the table and sobbed, her slim shoulders heaving dramatically. Marina had often privately thought that Isabel was too sweet and guileless for Ben, but sorrow had swelled her into someone fiercer than her previous mild self, had given her a new authority, and when she raised her ferocious, wounded face and sat up to drink her tea, Marina couldn't help feeling faintly afraid of her. She barely dared to put her arm around Isabel.

'We're just as baffled as you are,' Jacob said, pulling up a chair at the table beside the girl. 'We don't understand it either.'

This only made Isabel weep again, her face in her hands. She had come to them seeking an answer, some explanation for the swift discarding that had befallen her. She wanted comfort and they could offer none. Marina had looked up at the clock on the wall above Isabel's head. She had been deep in her work when the girl arrived; for several minutes she had not realised that the doorbell was ringing. A book never exerted a stronger hold on her than when she was wrenched away from it. The beginning of a project was an anxious time for her. There was always the certainty that she would falter. That whatever she wrote would not be enough. She wanted to steal away and return to her work.

'That's the worst thing,' Isabel said at last, wiping her eyes with the back of her hand like a small child. 'There's no reason. If there were a reason it would be easier.'

Marina watched the screen of Jacob's professional self lower across his face, his wise and considered listening posture clicking in despite his own confusion. Sometimes he looked at her like that, his chin resting on his hand. Attentive, interested, all-knowing. How many hours of his life had he spent sitting in hushed rooms listening to people's private sorrows? Didn't he grow weary of it, Marina wondered, watching him speak calmly to Isabel. He never complained about his patients as she did about her students. Where did he find the energy to be so endlessly patient? Perhaps that was one of the widest differences between them. Kindness for her was a rush of feeling, impetuous and often unplanned. For Jacob it was something to be carefully dispensed, within reasonable limits. Something sensible and measured.

Isabel left a letter for them to give to Ben. For days it sat on the hall bureau unopened, like a sad remonstration.

'Write back to her,' Marina said finally to Ben, handing the letter to him as he left the house one afternoon.

Ben took the letter and stared down at his name on the envelope. Whatever future awaited him was far grander and stranger than one that contained Isabel, Marina thought to herself.

'What should I say?' Ben said quietly, looking up at Marina.

'Something consoling. Tell her that she will always be your first love. Be kind.'

The next morning Ben asked Marina to post the letter he had written to Isabel. She sat at the kitchen table with the envelope in her hand. Ben had printed his name and address carefully on the back. It reminded her of the solemn way that he used to sign all his drawings with his full name as a child. Marina still had a pencil drawing he had made for her of a chemical reaction, appalled by her lack of knowledge in that arena. The combustion of propane and oxygen, resulting in carbon dioxide, water and energy. Every molecule was coloured and named, a flaring yellow sun labelled 'heat and light!' to represent energy. At the bottom of the page he had signed 'from Benjamin M. Kaufman'. The drawing still hung on the wall above her desk.

What had Ben written in the letter to Isabel? The envelope felt very light; there couldn't be more than two pages inside, possibly only one. Had Ben explained himself to the girl? Was he even capable of wrapping words around what was happening to him? Marina listened for the fall of the letter as she slipped it into the post box.

Three months later, at the end of the spring semester, Marina ran into Isabel's mother at the Whitney. Marina had taken a group of students there to see the Edward Hopper paintings as part of a new graduate seminar she was teaching on loneliness and the city. They had been reading Simone Weil on the silence of all great painting, the desire to see a landscape as it was when no soul was present in it. No paintings, it seemed to Marina, were more scoured clean of the burden of human presence than Hopper's cityscapes. Clustered around one of the paintings in the busy gallery, trying to talk loudly enough for the little knot of students to hear her, she had not unfolded her ideas as lucidly as when she was writing notes for the lecture. She could sense a ripple of boredom in the students. It was the last week of classes; they were fractious, distracted. Half of them hadn't even bothered to come to the museum. She conquered the desire to close her notebook and walk away, walk back across town to her quiet study and her own work. 'Let's go and fortify ourselves in the café and continue this discussion,' she said to them.

Turning from the paintings, Marina had taken a moment to place Isabel's mother. She stared at the neat blonde hair, the diamond earrings, the expensive handbag. She remembered her, of course, as soon as the woman began to speak.

'Ben broke her heart. I know, I know – the inflamed passions of the young. But that's the only way to describe it: heartbreak.' Isabel's mother pressed her hand to her heart as if she could feel her daughter's pain in her own body. She had the same green eyes as Isabel, Marina noticed, a sparkling marine colour.

'It absolutely destroyed her, the way he cast her off like that,' her mother said, lowering her voice. 'She could barely finish the semester. We had to take her to a psychiatrist in the end. She was practically suicidal by the time we got her there. She had to be medicated. The whole thing was terrible for all of us.'

There was a heavy air of reproach in her voice. Ben had harmed her child and she wanted something from Marina. Contrition, an apology.

Marina reached out and touched Isabel's mother's slim shoulder. 'I'm so terribly sorry.'

The woman stared down at Marina's hand. 'There's no denying he behaved disgracefully.'

'No.'

Isabel was much better now, her mother said. She had just left for a study-abroad program in Paris. And she had met a lovely boy, a law student with excellent prospects. A little stab between the ribs, that word 'prospects'.

Ben's strange abdication from the world made Marina think of Bartleby in the Herman Melville short story. He had weighed all the possibilities and chosen simply to do nothing. There might be a strange liberation in it, she thought, for this boy who had so far done everything that was expected of him. Perfect grades at Calhoun, chess medals, tennis championships, the scholarship to Brown, plans for a medical degree. He had brought them no trouble. Perhaps there was a radical sort of calm in swerving his life away from its carefully planned course; his other, rejected future unfolding somewhere without him. To decide not to try anymore. There was an odd sense to it in a world so sullied and catastrophic. But he would not discuss any of this with her or Jacob. She had always felt a solitary inner core in Ben, but now he had slipped completely out of their grasp. His misery, whatever its cause, was kept carefully from them.

Sitting beside him on the steps of the brownstone, Marina leaned her shoulder against Ben's. Once, when he was a little boy with a fever, she had sat up late into the night with him, sliding a cool cloth over his forehead, whispering stories. When he finally fell asleep, a tremble had moved through him, as if he were trying to contain some secret sorrow. Just when she thought she could leave him and return to her own bed, his small hand reached out for hers. Nurses tended sick children in the dormitories on the kibbutz. Marina could not remember a single time that her own mother had sat beside her when she was ill. Her brother, yes, but never her mother.

Ben patted her arm gently, as if she were the one in need of comfort, and rose to his feet. 'Don't stay out here too long. You'll melt,' he said.

There were so many things she wanted to say to him. Sorrow passes, she would like to say. I know this.

Marina stayed sitting there on the steps after Ben had disappeared inside the house. An old Mexican man walked past pulling a wooden cart and turned into Mount Morris Park. In the summer the streets were full of these carts selling cups of flavoured shaved ice, soda, candy, husk-wrapped tamales. A grey cat weaved along the fence and dashed across the road. The animal looked terrified, as if it had escaped from a wholesome and clean place into this chaotic and improbable world. Marina thought she could sit for hours like this, suspended, watching the life of the street.

From further down the block she heard a loud wail. It was the sound of a child, but louder and more frantic than any child's cry she had ever heard. She walked to the bottom of the steps and looked down the street. A few houses on, a small African child was lying on the sidewalk, every limb stiff and splayed out, his face contorted with fury. His legs thrashed against the fire hydrant, kicking so violently that a blue sandal arced through the air on to the road. A young woman wearing a patterned wrap tied around her waist stood a few feet away, clutching a plastic shopping bag. The girl made no effort to comfort the child, just stared at the ground while he continued to scream wildly, his back arching and tears streaming down his face. Surely the girl couldn't be the hysterical child's mother. She seemed so separate from the little boy.

Marina couldn't help feeling that she was transgressing, witnessing some private moment. There was such a frightening wilfulness on display, more than a child's angry tantrum. This crying was nothing that could be appealed to. Just then, the girl turned and fixed Marina in her gaze, huge eyes glaring out of her sharp face. How old was she? She looked no more than seventeen or eighteen. But those eyes. Marina wondered if she should approach them, but there was something daunting and guarded about the girl. What could Marina possibly offer them? A glass of water, a piece of chocolate to bribe the child?

Suddenly the girl walked swiftly away from the child, past Marina and west towards Lenox Avenue, her shopping bag banging against her legs. She did not glance back once at the little boy, who remained on the sidewalk screaming. Marina stood up and hurried down the steps towards him. He was in a frenzy. Grief was the only word she could summon for it. Such a serious word for such a small child, but it felt to her like pure, raging sorrow. An adult kind of desolation. His contorted face, his furious flailing, the toneless wail coming from him. She picked him up and set him on his feet, her hands around his tiny ribs, his chest hot and damp through his shirt. The little boy stared at her, still crying but stunned for a moment out of his frenzy. She had never seen such enormous eyes in a child's face; they were almost too large. He was very beautiful, fragile and baby-like, but there was something fierce and nascent about him too, something not of the child at all. Dark whorls of hair grew neatly around his shining forehead. He was older than she had first thought, perhaps two years old.

The child watched her warily, his body still heaving, his tiny shoeless foot on the hot concrete. She retrieved the plastic sandal from the side of the road and pushed the boy's hot, dusty foot into it. The buckle was missing.

'Come on,' she said, taking hold of the child's hand. 'We have to catch up to her.' He was quietening now, and walked along readily enough beside her. He stared up at Marina, his cheeks wet and flushed.

The young woman was standing on the corner, waiting for the light to change. Would she have crossed? Marina wondered about it afterwards. Would she have walked across that road? When they reached her, the boy slipped out of Marina's grasp and ran and pressed himself against the woman's legs, his face turned into her thigh. She did not acknowledge Marina or speak to the child, simply shifted her shopping bag to the other hand

and took the boy's arm. She did not hold his hand, Marina noticed, but circled her fingers around his wrist. The two of them crossed the street and walked away, the little boy trying to keep the broken shoe from slipping off his foot.

Back inside the house Marina stood in the kitchen waiting for the kettle to boil and staring out at the green square of the garden, at the climbing jasmine that covered the high mesh fence. The jasmine always made her think of rich, riotous abundance, of untarnished hope. How extraordinary that it had grown so quickly. From a hook on the fence the old brass bird feeder swung heavily in the wind. It was something they had found in India. It was supposed to hold oil lanterns but Ben had decided it should be a bird feeder, pouring seeds into the tiny brass cups that had once held sacred oil in some distant temple. Jacob worried that the birdseed would attract rats, that the garden would become infested with pigeons, but Marina liked the idea of creating a way station for the birds. In the Hula Valley in Israel each year, corn was spread out for the thousands of migratory cranes that stopped there to rest on their journey to Africa. It was not done purely out of kindness; the birds could decimate the surrounding fields, so the corn was spread to protect the farmers' crops. Still, it felt like a kind of welcoming.

After she and Jacob had bought the brownstone, they ripped out the whole rear wall and replaced it with steel-framed French doors, so that the view of the garden was elegantly segmented, the kitchen airy and bright. The old painted floorboards they had uncovered under several layers of linoleum proved beyond saving, so they were torn up and replaced with a pale grey travertine. Under the morning sun the floor took on the hue of an old shell, something pure and ancient, with its tiny rippling veins and stony swirls. It embarrassed Marina sometimes, the pleasure this house gave her. The delicate spine of stairs threading through the floors, the intricate cornices, the black-and-white-tiled entrance hall; there was nothing infelicitous, nothing that was not beautiful. From the very beginning it felt to her a place where they could all be their best possible selves. The homes that had come before – the dark apartment where she and her mother and brother had lived for so many years on Union Street in Crown Heights; the crowded dormitories of her college years in California; the tiny studio over a Caribbean grocery store in Los Angeles; even the Park Avenue apartment – all seemed transient and inadequate now, places she had to pass through to come here.

She made a pot of mint tea and looked around the room. There was the vase full of pale-pink peonies that Rose had brought her the day before, the gleaming oak kitchen table that a carpenter friend had made for them. There were the rows of handmade ceramic plates lined up on the shelves, the crumpled newspaper that Jacob had left folded open to the unfinished crossword, the flyer on the refrigerator announcing a lecture on Yehuda Amichai at the 92nd Street Y. This was her home, her light-filled kitchen. All of these things belonged to her. Standing there with the teapot in her hands she was filled with a weird sense of terror. Everything they had created, all this reassuring domesticity, could vanish in an instant, could prove to have been provisional. An illusion of happiness. She could be cast out from this place, everything she had loved shimmering behind her in the distance. Marina put her hand to her chest, resting her fingers against the sudden quick skipping of her heart.

This was foolishness, pure foolishness. She knew it was something to do with her mother, this inability to trust happiness

43

when it came, to feel always the impossibility of its permanence. Nothing would disappear, nothing would evaporate. They were safe, all of them. This house would stand, she and her husband would go on loving each other. Ben would come back to them. They would go to Fire Island next month. This book she was writing would turn out well, better than she imagined. Marina picked up the teacup from the counter and walked upstairs to her desk.

Jacob arrived home late in the afternoon. Even after all the years of living together, something in her still lifted when she heard the click of the front door opening and his voice calling out to her. Her husband, home from work, his shirt a little wrinkled, the top button undone. He kissed her on the lips and presented a loaf of bread to her from behind his back with a flourish.

'The last loaf of marble rye. Wrestled from the hordes at Zabar's.'

'Ah, a true warrior. Thank you, darling.'

'I'm going to put the kettle on. Shall I make a pot?'

'Yes, I'll be right down.'

Marina stood in the doorway for a moment and watched Jacob absorbed in the rituals of homecoming: taking off his jacket, emptying his pockets. His leather satchel bulged with the files of the patients he had seen that day. Later that evening he would read through the notes he had made, underlining, summarising. Such a mind for detail, such a care in her husband for his patients; and yet he also had the knack of distance, the line that had to be drawn. A holy circle around his own self. In his office in Chelsea the shelves were crammed with long rows of his patients' files, battered manila folders full of scrawled notes and observations. Marina thought of those rows of files as the spreading body of memory itself. Lives shadowed by loss and longing, by betrayal and loneliness, and by ordinary humiliations. Sometimes she felt an irrational jealousy towards Jacob's patients. It was ridiculous, she knew, and she would never admit it to him. There were several patients he had known for much longer than he had known her. Some had been in therapy with him for twenty years. Every week they brought their lives to him to be deciphered, offering themselves up to his wise listening, his carefully dispensed counsel.

Back in those first days in California, Jacob had made notes about her in the same way that he jotted down certain observations during a session with a patient. He admitted this to her later and she was delighted at the chronicling of remembered phrases, things she had said that had struck him, expressions she used. A poem about swallows by Nemerov that she quoted. A story about her West Indian landlord, who played the clarinet and had named his small daughters Swing and Sway. She remembered laughing with him about it during one of their first meetings. He read his scribbles again and again after they parted, Jacob told her, as if they might reveal something vital about the nature of their relationship. She had found this reassuring, the realisation that he too was an obsessive archivist, a noticer and preserver of things.

They were oddly formal, their first encounters in California: Jacob regarding her from behind his desk as if she were one of his patients come to spread her life out before him. He was a visiting professor, she was a graduate student in the final throes of her doctoral work on the Romani. Marina had written to him after the public lecture he had given on psychotherapy and grief, asking if he would meet with her. She would like to interview him, she wrote, about his work on fairy tales and psychoanalysis

45

for a paper she was writing on the improvised storytelling of the Romani. She slipped the letter under the door of his office late one afternoon. The audacity of it had amazed her; it was not in her nature to be so bold. All week she waited in a kind of nervous suspension for his reply. Five days after she delivered her letter, a folded note appeared in her pigeonhole in the departmental office. He would be happy to meet with her to assist with her project, Jacob wrote in the unruly, looping handwriting that was now so familiar to her. She had manufactured the research paper as an excuse to meet with Jacob; she could think of no other way to get close to him, but later on she did write it after all.

Jacob was almost forty when she walked into his borrowed office at Berkeley. She saw the curiosity on his face as he watched her walk across the room, the grace of his movement as he stood up to shake her hand. What did she know about him then? Marina researched him obsessively after that first lecture, hurriedly read his two books, looking for fragments of biography, as well as all the articles she could find. She sat in the library for hours, a stack of journals in front of her, the Californian light streaming in through the window and illuminating her tiny study carrel. In an interview Jacob had said that the stories of his ancestors in Poland struck him so deeply because they sounded like fairy tales themselves. A family hidden in a forest; a great-uncle who walked barefoot a hundred miles to save his only pair of shoes; a cousin who travelled halfway around the world, only to meet and marry a girl from his own village; a prescient rabbi who had spirited his grandfather to safety in America.

And then there was his childhood in Israel. It was not included in any of the official biographies on his book jackets, but she had found an early essay about childhood and community in which he said that his American-born parents had made Aliyah in 1948, that he was born on a kibbutz in the Jezreel Valley in the north of the country the following year, but that his parents returned to New York when he was four years old. It seemed portentous to Marina that they were both born in Israel. That they were bound together in some way by this biographical coincidence.

That first day, although she was supposed to be interviewing him, Marina found herself telling Jacob about the fairy tales that had surrounded her as a child. The old collection of Grimms' tales that Dov had found at the Brooklyn Library the year they came to New York, the only stories that her mother could ever be persuaded to read to them. Bones that sing tales of hidden deaths; children who set out into the world to discover what fear is; stolen babies; brothers transformed into deer. Their mother's own history, in those childhood nights under the tilting spread of light from the lamp, was wayward and mysterious to them, but in the stories Marina and Dov sensed something slipping out of her. It was the only time she would let them come near her, sitting between them on the old sofa by the window, the heavy book balanced on her knees. The nearness of her, the rise and fall of her jutting collarbone as she read, the curtain drawn against the sleeve of ice at the window – all of these things would burn in Marina in the years after Gizela left. A mother reading to her children. Surely she had loved them. Surely.

It was the small tales that had haunted Marina the most. A handful of words spinning out a kind of confused despair, a bewilderment at the way the world was. She told Jacob about the tale of the obstinate child – in German *das eigensinnige kind*, which means literally 'the child with its own mind'. No me͏ story if the child was a girl or a boy, no name, no reassͱ of detail. All the reader was told was that the child would not do what its mother wanted and, because of that, God had no goodwill towards it and let it become sick and die. When the child was buried, it kept pushing its little arm up through the earth until finally its mother came and knocked the arm down with a stick. After that it was peaceful under the earth for the first time.

'My mother told us that the story was a warning to naughty children. I think she was hoping we would see it as a parable about obedience. But to me it always felt like a glimpse into the horror of things. There was something about it that terrified me: the anonymous, unloved little child under the earth, its hand pushing up through the damp soil. And then there was the ruthlessness of the mother. And the malevolence of God, too, I suppose. All pretty bleak. But it was the story I asked for over and over.'

Jacob was watching her closely as she spoke, his head slightly bent, his cup of coffee untouched in front of him. He looked bemused, and suddenly Marina was embarrassed at having said so much. The words had come out at the wrong angle, making the story seem odd, perhaps casting her as strange and dark. A perverse child, haunted by loss. Of course he would be analysing her, judging her, thinking her damaged and peculiar. This was supposed to be an interview, not a therapy session.

'I suppose it's a silly story really,' she said, looking down at her hands.

'Not at all,' he replied. 'I think there are stories like that because we have always been haunted by the unmanageable. By things that are vast and dangerous. We don't know how to approach them, so we tell stories around the edge of them. It's one of the oldest impulses in the world.'

She looked up at him then. He had allocated an hour for their meeting. An hour for them to take the first steps into each other's lives. Even now, years later, she still felt the strange shadow of what might never have happened if she had not slipped her letter under Jacob's door, if he had not responded so graciously to a stranger's request. It would rise up unnervingly at times. A sudden pang; the knowledge she might never have had this.

That evening she and Jacob walked over to 116th Street to buy tamales for dinner. The temperature had dipped slightly and there was a breeze coming off the river, a balminess to the evening. The streets seemed so much more forgiving under the blue summer twilight. The sidewalk stores along Second Avenue were humming. A flock of starlings rose up above the Capri Bakery, scattering and re-forming in a kind of ballet. On every corner people were selling things. Mexican women with thermoses of cold *agua de horchata*, tamales and plump *gorditas*. A Dominican man with neat rows of sugared churros lined up on his wooden cart. A young boy carrying a box of candy bars slung around his neck. Further along 116th Street the El Paso taco truck leaned in against the curb, a long line of people trailing down the sidewalk waiting to be served. People stood in doorways or in clusters outside the bodegas. It was like a vast, makeshift market.

'It's such a comfort to me, you know,' said Marina, gesturing to the street in front of them. 'All of this. The city. All this life.'

'I know.' Jacob smiled at her and took her hand as they crossed the road.

They always bought tamales from the young woman on the corner of Second Avenue. Marina was ashamed of her terrible Spanish, her fumbling attempts at conversation. The Mexican woman smiled patiently at her, counting the change into her hand and folding extra napkins and plastic forks into the bag. '*Gracias, buenas tardes. Equalmente.*' Such a lilt to the language, a quiet graciousness to these women. She wondered what their lives were like.

She and Jacob walked home through Mount Morris Park, passing through the arc of trees and the beds of wild roses that lined the southern side of the park. There was an animated game of basketball taking place on the court, tall boys leaping around like young colts, with their thin legs and flailing arms. Ben used to come here sometimes to play, joining in with the neighbour-hood boys in that gracious, easy way of his.

'Have you seen Ben today?' Jacob asked, as if he had read her thoughts. 'How is he?' When he spoke about Ben these days, Jacob's voice took on a hushed, strained tone.

'Okay, I suppose. I don't know. He worked this morning, went up to his room when he got home. I haven't seen him since.'

Actually, she had seen Ben. When she had taken her sandwich out to the garden at lunchtime she had looked up and seen him standing on the fire escape outside his bedroom on the fourth floor, staring at the building opposite theirs. For a terrified moment Marina wondered if he was going to jump. She walked out further into the garden, standing in the small rectangle of grass in the centre and waving up at him, trying for a casualness she did not feel. He must not see their fear, they must not hover over him; it would only drive him further away. Already he must find their confused watchfulness suffocating. Ben peered down at her from the fire escape and raised his hand in a sort of salute before climbing back through the window and pulling it closed after him. Of course he had not been going to jump. He was standing in the sun for a moment, that was all. She did not tell Jacob this.

'Well, he's working. I suppose that's something.'

'Yes,' she said. 'It gets him out of the house, at least.'

Jacob had insisted on the job. He could not countenance Ben's strange idleness, his slow drifting around the house, the hours he spent in his room. If Ben wasn't going to study or do something else constructive then he could look for work and pay rent, Jacob told him. To their surprise, Ben had promptly found a part-time job at the Fine Fare supermarket on Lenox Avenue. It was not exactly a victory, but it was something. He got up and went to work every day. Once, Marina had stopped by to pick up some milk and glimpsed him through a doorway, sitting on an upturned crate with two young Mexican men, chatting animatedly in Spanish. She turned away before he could see her. The closed door of his secret life.

Later that night she and Jacob read in bed, their books propped up on their knees. She loved these moments of shared concentration, each of them immersed in their own reading, sometimes offering each other a few lines, a beautiful sentence. Jacob turned his page down and closed his eyes while she read him a quote from the book of essays by an Australian writer she was reading. It was about mothers, about the intense love that flows from mother to child not being returned in the same way.

'But I'm not sure that's always true,' she said. 'Dov and I loved our mother in a way that she could never love us. Everything that happened came from that love.'

'Hmmm,' Jacob said softly, and she could almost feel his quiet thinking, his deep concentration. It must be cultivated from his work, from all those hours of listening, this ability to absorb a thought without immediately needing to respond. 'I think it's often that way with damaged mothers,' he said at last. 'They inspire that kind of imbalance. The child has to do the greater share of the loving.'

He closed his book and put it on the bedside table. 'Tell me something,' he said, reaching his arm out for her. This was another one of their rituals, the slow unspooling of their thoughts late at night in bed. Marina found herself hoarding things for these moments before sleep, her head against Jacob's shoulder, his hand in her hair. They had always brought each other these gifts: lines from books they had read; phrases overheard on the train or in line at the post office; a red leaf fallen from a tree in the park. It was a private currency, this careful noticing of the world, these whispered recountings late at night. If Jacob were gone, who would she narrate her days to? Who else would want to know the shape of her mind? She moved closer to him, the length of their bodies pressed against each other, his thigh sturdy and warm against hers.

Marina thought of the little boy she had seen on the street; his small luminous face, that tiny bare foot.

'I met a child this morning. A little African boy,' she said. 'Well, not really met. He had a tantrum on the street and I went to check that he was okay.'

'Where was the mother?' Jacob's voice was already drowsy, his eyes closed as he listened to her.

'That's the strange thing. She just turned and walked away. I wasn't even sure at first if she was the mother, she seemed so disconnected from him.'

'What did you do?'

'I couldn't just leave him. I took him over to her. He had such an unusual look on his face. Weirdly self-possessed. It made me think of Ben – how adult he seemed even when he was very small. The same gravity. The mother didn't acknowledge me. But

I thought about them all day. About what sort of life they might have together. What happens between them. I was thinking about how much we don't attend to here in the city, how life bumps against us and slips past every day, unnoticed. I guess it's probably linked to all those new lectures I wrote this semester on urban loneliness. The student feedback was good, by the way. They just sent me the surveys. They want to run the course again next year. I was thinking that I could get you in to do a guest lecture on psychiatric conceptions of loneliness. They seem to be much more relaxed about all the interdisciplinary stuff now that the feedback has been positive.'

Jacob's breathing slowed as he slipped into sleep, a tiny quivering at the edge of his eyelid. Sleep always came swiftly to him. Marina reached across him to turn off the light and he took her hand and clasped it above his heart. He had begun to hold her this way early on in their relationship, in those first Californian days, when what was between them had a slightly illicit, provisional feel. A decade later there was still this gesture, this unspoiled core that sustained them through any arguments, through small resentments and divergences. Her hand against his heart.

Narrowsburg, Upstate New York
December, 1997

The old nun could hear the tamped-down gonging of the evening angelus bell. A smell of cooking in the air, something warm and bland. Somewhere a bishop had written that the bell must peal as the shades of night are falling. She had always liked the poetic turn of phrase. Behind the doors of the tiny convent bedrooms, or downstairs where the sisters gathered, there would be a whirr of prayers. When the bell tolled the faithful must fall to their knees and recite the 'Ave Maria'. She buttoned up her cardigan and glanced out of the window at the fading midwinter light and the skeletons of trees lining the path. In spring there would be blackberries there, the old wild tangle of green. There was no groundsman at the convent now, no money for help. She would have to kneel there in the dirt herself, weeding and thinning, black-nailed and sweating. There was no want of work for her, no want at all.

How odd it was to be here in Narrowsburg; the damp and silence of the old convent, the creak of it at night, the mornings as bitter as those of her Irish childhood. She could feel the cold in her bones, winter as a dull ache in the joints. Pain in every socket, the rubbing of bone on bone. She had never felt it before she came here, this slide into old age, this growing brittleness of her usual sturdy self.

Vera's order had come to America from Ireland more than a century ago – their first mission to the new world. Back then there was only a small band of twenty nuns scattered among the poor of the cities, their habit and veil guaranteeing them safety. A mission of mercy. All those unclaimed souls and lost children, all the wickedness of America. 'Show me the poor,' their found-ress had said. 'Show me the poor and I will run to them.'

No running left in them now. The old nun could hardly imagine those early sisters fresh from Dublin, dragging their trunks ashore on the New York dock, the sea still moving in them. Renting rooms in a boarding house in Brooklyn, ministering to the poor Irish and handing out prayer cards and rosary beads to the men lined up to enter the muck and gloom of the new subway tunnel they were building under the harbour. Praying for Europe during the Great War, struggling along with everyone else through the Depression. Soup kitchens and food pantries, meals for shut-ins and vagabonds, prayer meetings and vigils for the sick. The slow spread of the sisters; a house in the South Bronx, then one in Harlem. A small convent and then another.

Peak and decline. It would all end here, upstate in the Catskills, their last bastion. The old retreat centre two hours north of New York converted hastily into a makeshift nursing home. Vera could never think of these as real mountains. She had grown up in the green shadow of the Derryveagh Mountains, by the edge of a wide lough. Just a sliver of her life spent there under the Atlantic sky. She had not been to Donegal for more than forty years, but here in Narrowsburg it came back to her in odd snatches: the sea cliffs, the dripping fields, a pair of brent geese coasting above the lake, the wind coming up and bringing a sea-smell with it. How she had missed the place in those early American years.

By the time she had joined the order the poor were not so pliable or reverent anymore. The ones who believed had their own storefront churches and charismatic preachers. There was gunfire in the street, a sister was threatened with a knife, another had her veil ripped off by a sneering gang of boys. Cars were torched, windows smashed, walls streaked with spray paint. A nun from another order was attacked when two men broke into her house through a roof shaft that had been left unlocked. They carved forty crosses over her body with a kitchen knife, sordid stigmata. Forty crosses. Hard to imagine. The nun had never recovered. She left the order and went back to her family in France. The word was that the local Italian mafia had ordered the men killed when they heard what had happened. Avenging angels, they must have felt themselves. Not too long after that a man with a drugged glaze to his eyes pushed Vera up against a wall in the stairwell of the Wagner housing projects, his hand at her throat. She had been sure he was going to murder her, had started whispering a Hail Mary. 'Go home, sister.' He spat it at her, and she felt the sharp snap of the gold chain with the cross around her neck. She was twenty-two years old.

There was a ripple to the air in Harlem then, something fire-blown and desperate, all hard edges. She felt that people wanted a hiss of anger, a turning of her back, a stumble from her to prove that the sisters in their brownstone were not so far above them, after all. Such complex deciphering was required. Their spiky accents and street lingo and tinny music. The projects. The rage. The grief. The missions in Mexico and South America were more straightforward. The sad smiles and dark eyes of the faithful lined up with their babies tied to their backs. '*Madre*', they called the sisters, ducking their heads to kiss the nuns' hands. They loved the nuns, those faithful women; did not snicker or spit or rage against them.

Still, she had never wanted to leave Harlem. Not for South America or India or back to Ireland, or anywhere else. Certainly not Narrowsburg. She did not like it here. The shabby country-side, the unravelling townships with trailers gathered at their fringes, clapboard farmhouses cut off from the river by new roads. There was a heavy weight over it, a lost prosperity. Harlem was where she belonged, was where she had done her work. It was the place she wanted to die.

'The Lord will gather you in.' Vera liked the ring of the words. That was the work left to her now, to gather in the old, the dying nuns. Close up the houses and the half-empty convents in Philadelphia, in Worcester, in Dobbs Ferry. Move out the last few sisters, sell off the properties, sign her name on a hundred documents. A sad business: the moving trucks, the cleaners, the brown-suited broker with his leery grin. 'Say a prayer for me, Sister.'

Every decision was a betrayal. Which house to sell first. Where they would live. How much help they could afford. What services to stop. What they could bring with them to Narrowsburg. They blamed her, the other nuns. Of course they blamed her – she was the instrument of their dispossession. Each of them was ready with one grievance or another. The tears over leaving behind an old flowered armchair, or a brass bedframe. Sixty years of prayers by the side of that bed, one sister had sobbed, the gush and heave of her crying making Vera want to walk out of the room.

Nothing holy could be discarded. The crucifixes and icons, the plaster statues of Mary, the endless rosary beads and the bottles of water from Lourdes were packed away in cardboard boxes in the basement. All the trappings of faith, none of its serenity left to her. No immense design anymore. When Vera packed up her own home, the brownstone across from the park in Harlem, she left the wooden crucifixes fastened to the walls. She had come to that house as a postulant nearly half a century before. Nineteen years old and the first time she had left Donegal. Eight brothers and sisters lined up on the sagging porch to say goodbye, the little boys running after the car, her mother crying into her apron. A waste, they had all said. In another time, another family, it might have been a fine thing, an honour. A child for the Church. But not for the Dohertys. Vera was the family beauty. They did not want her wasted on God. She could have made a good marriage, could have helped them that way. But she had been full of the fire of faith, the bright sure certainty of it. All the nuns had. So many lifetimes of good works. The Bronx, Harlem, El Salvador, Brazil, the Mexican border. How far they had roamed.

What were they now? The hollowed-out core, the weary faithful huddled in their armchairs around a gas heater. Twenty-four frail old women, all of them flaxy grey and watery. Threadbare skin and bruised veins, a powderiness to their cheeks, a looseness to their bodies. Sometimes she slipped in behind the other sisters during compline, the night prayers. They wore their nightdresses, bending creakily down on the old wooden kneelers, rosary beads twisted through their fingers. Limbs shifting and failing, wheel-chairs and walking frames lined up at the back of the room, a soft, drifting scent to their bodies. Vera could have picked up her guitar and accompanied them in the hymns, but she let their voices rise and quaver on their own. She was too tired. Sixty-seven, and the youngest of them by nearly two decades. She wondered sometimes where she had hidden herself, what had happened to the kind, faithful fire of her.

The Lord grant us a quiet night and a perfect end. Twenty-four deaths for her to preside over. Hands to hold, bed linen to change, pills to administer, consoling words to murmur to faraway rela-tives. 'Gone to God.' Space for them all in the small convent cemetery on the side of the hill.

Some nights she sat for hours going over the accounts, the ledgers reaching back through the decades. Their empty coffers. How could they have believed that they could pay for the upkeep of all those half-empty old houses for so long? The heating, the roof repairs, the rewiring. The Lord did not provide. *Deus abscon-ditis.* She had studied it once at a theology seminar in Rome.

The grizzled old retriever, Lily, stretched out under the desk, resting her muzzle on Vera's foot. The dog had belonged to the sisters in Philadelphia, had slunk in off the streets five years earlier and they had no heart to turn her out. Vera had not wanted to bring her to Narrowsburg when they sold the Phila-delphia convent. There was no money to care for an animal and she did not want to be responsible for one more living thing. She had told Sister Grace to give the dog away or take it to an animal shelter. What a ruckus that had caused. They had all banded against Vera, even the ones who had no love for animals. Someone had slipped a quote from St Francis under her door: 'If you have men who will exclude any of God's creatures from the shelter of compassion and pity, you will have men who will deal likewise with their fellow men.' Pointed, that, Vera thought.

Sometimes she felt that they were not her sisters, these old women, but her children. Let the dog come, she said in the end, let the damn thing come. Grace was dead now, a heart attack at the end of the summer, and the dog had taken to following Vera from room to room, her toenails clicking softly on the floorboards as she padded along the halls. A shelter of compassion and pity. It sounded like a lovely thing. She wished that someone would make one for her.

Outside it had started to snow, the shiver of it clouding the maple trees. Once, the first snow of winter had felt like a benediction to her, the silence, the ceaseless soft energy. Snowmen in Mount Morris Park, the flushed, shiny faces of the neighbourhood children, the bright membrane of white over the streets. Here, snow was another hazard to overcome. Ice on the path, the sidewalk to dig out, a hard sting on her cheeks when she went to check the mailbox. But still there was something of the miracle to it.

Christmas night. The world hushed and holy again. Back in Harlem she would have earned a virtuous rest by now. Mass at dawn, the morning spent visiting the needy faithful, bestowing blessings, chocolates for the children. Climbing endless flights of stairs, bouncing a baby on her knee, slices of fruitcake and foil-wrapped tamales slipped into her bag. Then the Christmas lunch at the brownstone, the doors open to all who cared to come. Christmas carols in Spanish, the little Yemeni girls from the bodega in their velvet dresses, the noisy goodwill of the day. It all seemed so far away now. A life unimaginably distant from this one.

Another gong sounded downstairs. Meals, prayers, everything marked by bells, the day folded into discrete squares. There had been no time for all of that in Harlem. Just a quick prayer before daybreak when she was dressing and the slow turn of her thoughts in bed at night after the day's work. Vera could not remember the last time she had been down on her knees, except at mass, before she came here. She waited to hear the opening and closing of doors, the slow shuffle along the corridors, the hum of voices.

There was a quiet tap at her door. Sister Joseph stood there with a tray tilting sideways in her hands: leftovers from their modest Christmas lunch. Joseph was wearing a habit and veil. The only one left who still wore the old things. The rest of them went about in plain clothes now: straight skirts and polyester blouses, cardigans, nurses' shoes. It was harder for the older ones, all the changes that had come over the years. Twenty years her senior and Joseph's face was tentative, almost a cringe. Were they really scared of her?

'I thought you'd be wanting your supper up here, Sister,' Joseph said hastily, placing the tray on the table and backing out of the room. 'I know how busy you are.'

She should eat with them. She should pick up the tray and walk downstairs and sit at the table with them. She should lead the prayers and put her hand over theirs and enquire about their chilblains, their aches, their poor sleep. It had been the state of their souls that had preoccupied them all once; now it was the body and its failings. No plenary indulgence to absolve them from that.

'Thank you, Joseph. I'll come downstairs for a cup of tea with you all later.'

'You're in our prayers, Sister.' A tremble in her voice. Deferent, afraid. Just before the move to Narrowsburg, Joseph had copied out a verse from Kings in her quavering old copperplate and posted it to her. 'I will do what you have asked. I will give you a wise and discerning heart.'

Vera wanted to grasp the old woman's hand. Her job was to console them. To bring a simplicity to things. They were her flock now. She should go down and let them make her a cup of tea. In ten minutes. In ten minutes she would go down to them.

She stared out of the window, the hum of the grace before meals drifting up from downstairs. The snow was coming more heavily now, the wet flakes dissolving when they hit the glass. Joseph had put a square of the dark chocolate Vera loved beside the plate. In spring there would be a flower, in fall a red maple leaf.

She had to be stern with them, turn her back on their confused sorrow. All that raging and crying and praying when she had cast them out of their homes, broken their little clusters of community and deposited them all up here, away from the world. Betrayed them. Perhaps she had done the wrong thing. But there had been no choice. Better that she turned them out than let the banks do it.

How many years would it be before they were all gone? Hard to imagine the long exile that might stretch out before her; a strange kind of suspension. There would be no return to Harlem. The house there had been sold to a family. Jewish, the broker had told her.

She stood up and slipped her feet back into her shoes. From the window she could see a figure turning off the road, pausing by the green letterbox, then walking slowly up the path towards the house, leaving wet footprints in the newly fallen snow. Vera stepped closer to the window. A single jet stream cut through the cold sky. Surprise moved through her. It was the African girl from Harlem, the one Cecile was always trying to befriend. What was her name? Something unlikely. Constance, that was it. What on earth was she doing here? The girl drew closer to the house and paused, looked up at the window where Vera stood. She wore a woollen hat pulled down low over her face. Just one canvas bag hung from her shoulder. No sign of her child.

Harlem, New York
July, 1997

Nearly a month passed before Marina saw the African girl and her little boy again. She and Jacob went to Fire Island, catching the train up to Long Island and then the tiny ferry from Sayville across the sound. A journey between islands, a slate-roofed cottage on a narrow slip of a sandbar out in the Atlantic. They came every summer. It had become part of the fabric of their year, this escape from the unreasonable heat of the city, these suspended weeks so predictable in their routines that it was sometimes difficult for Marina to separate one July from the others. The familiar traditions held a kind of enchantment: the chugging ferry ride, the trip to the general store for provisions, opening up the house to let the ocean air in. They always spent the mornings on the beach, walking up to the far curve of the bay, collecting clams and shells, lying under the old canvas umbrella that they carried down from the house. In the afternoons they rode their bikes along the wooden boardwalks or into the town, sometimes stopping for coffee or ice cream. In the evenings there were games of Scrabble and cards, hours sitting out on the deck with blankets on their laps, watching the stars and talking, the crash and heave of the ocean close to them. In the darkness the sounds seemed to magnify – the wild screech of an owl, the rattle of the windows in a sudden squall of wind.

Every summer Ben strode around the small white house with the green shutters, which they always rented, inspecting for any changes, irked that a painting had been taken down, the old couch under the window replaced. Their first summer on the island, when he was ten years old, he proposed solemnly to them that they should leave New York and come to live here in the cottage. Marina remembered his cross face when they laughed, the flash of his thin legs as he ran off to the beach. Such a little boy he had looked, down there at the edge of the water, leaning over to peer at something in the sand.

It was on the same stretch of beach, several summers later, that Ben suddenly seemed to her to have become a man. It happened all at once, an unexpected metamorphosis. Seventeen years old, striding out of the surf and shaking the water out of his hair, wrapping a striped towel around his waist. It struck her that there was hardly anything of the child about him anymore. How odd that it had crept up on her unawares like that; she saw him every day and yet suddenly there he was, this tall, graceful man.

It was strange not to have Ben there with them that summer. Marina knew that the time would come when he would be drawn away by other things: travel, work, a woman. But this was far harder than she had imagined. That he would simply refuse to come with them. Every time she walked past his bedroom, with its single bed and small window looking over the garden, a flutter of unease moved through her. What was he doing now? Was he still going to work? Was he eating?

The evening before they had left the city, Jacob had stopped him as he slipped out of the kitchen, his hand on his son's shoulder. 'Come with us,' he said. Marina could see how hard Jacob was trying not to make it sound like a plea, to keep a lightness in his voice. Ben ducked from his father's reach and walked towards the door. 'I have work.'

'Surely you can get out of it. Come to the island, and then you can go back to school in the fall. Come on, Ben, you need to snap out of this.'

A long silence. At the kitchen sink, her back turned to them, Marina realised she was holding her breath.

'I'd rather stay here,' Ben said quietly and left the room, the stairs creaking as he walked up to the top floor.

When she and Jacob set out for the station the next morning, Ben was already gone. She had heard the clatter of the door as he left the house before dawn for an early shift at the supermarket. It felt like a cruelty, what he was doing, but she knew it was not. He had just stepped back to where nobody could reach him.

One afternoon when Jacob headed out to cycle to the far end of the island, Marina walked into Ben's room and sat down on the bed. The nightlight he had used as a child was on the bedside table. Illuminated, it cast a scattering of stars across the ceiling. She remembered Ben's frustration that the constellations were not marked correctly, that the projection of stars did not accurately reflect the night sky. For a long stretch of his childhood he had wanted to be an astronomer. On many of the clear summer nights here on the island, he would sit on the deck for hours watching the stars through the telescope they had bought him for his twelfth birthday. Several mornings they had found him asleep out there, wrapped in a blanket, his laminated star charts spread around him. He had tried to explain the Harvard Spectral Classification system to her once. 'Many stars are classified by the circumstances surrounding their deaths,' Ben said. She had written that line down in her journal, thinking it strangely poetic. So often, listening to Ben's intensely relayed facts, she was reminded of her brother, of Dov's own sweet earnestness. She thought of her brother's silk star-map tucked away in a chest, the buttons he had painstakingly sewn to mark the constellations.

It had always been there in Ben, this desire for things to be done properly, this serious questing for knowledge. A few days before they left for Fire Island Marina had stopped by the super-market and found him stacking the shelves. He had calculated the arrangement of bottles of seltzer water precisely, he told her, so that he knew exactly how many would fit on each shelf. A slip of excitement in his voice as he spoke of vectors and angles, his old love for mathematics still there. It was just a glimmer of hope, but a quiet sort of relief flooded through her as she walked home. There was still something he cared about. He would come good, she was sure of it.

Marina lay down on Ben's bed. The pillow smelled of old lavender. Their second summer here she had brought the old volume of *Grimms' Fairy Tales* and it had become a tradi-tion for her and Jacob to sit on Ben's narrow bed and take it in turns to read him a story. It would strike her every evening they read together how very strange it was to have this reconstituted tableau. Dov and her mother gone, but this man and child here with her, the same old book held up to a circle of light, the sea wind buffeting the shutters as they read to each other, an easy banter between them.

Ben's favourite story was the one about a bright shepherd boy who thought of clever answers to a king's riddles. He asked for the story again and again, even though he knew it by heart. So many of the stories were like this, Marina thought; about children who had to rely on their own resources. Clever, imperilled boys and girls, who had to outsmart those who would do them harm and secure their own survival. 'Where are the parents in these stories?' Ben asked her once. 'When the shepherd boy gets adopted by the king because he's so smart, what happens to his own parents? Didn't they want to keep him?' She could see his younger face vividly, the high forehead, the clear brown eyes. Even then, the presence of something unknowable in him. 'I don't know,' she told him. 'I don't know where the parents are.'

Sitting on Ben's bed, she wished that time could wind itself backward, to all the other summers. To the forts made of logs and the fireflies caught in jars and the walks into the holly forest to search for deer. All of it – the cottage, the summer, Fire Island itself – seemed somehow tarnished now that Ben had turned his back on it. His distance from them was like an ambush. There was something so complete and alarming about the way he had stepped out of his own life. 'I have no idea,' he said candidly, inflexibly, when they asked him what he was planning to do, whether he would return to his studies. There was such a singularity in his refusal of the future.

Through the window she saw Jacob cycling home along the sea road, his hair whipped back from his face by a squall that had blown in from the Atlantic. Soon he would be walking up the front steps, looking for a cup of coffee, a piece of the ginger cake she had made that morning. He stopped to pat the neighbour's cat, a tentativeness in his knee as he bent down, an old tennis injury.

When she had first met Jacob she wanted to hear the catalogue of every wound, everything that had marked his body before she had known him. The tiny scar at his temple, the faded brand of a dog bite to his calf, which had needed seven stitches, the appendicitis that had struck him when he was sixteen.

But it was the things that hadn't left marks on the body that had caused the greatest damage. The death of his father, Max, when Jacob was in his final year of medical school, the terrible sound of his mother weeping behind her closed bedroom door at night. 'Oh,' his father said when the heart attack had seized him at the dinner table. Then, 'I'm sorry.' Decorous to the last.

And there was the more complicated grief of his first marriage. Marina could only imagine it was his father's death that had propelled Jacob into that early, misguided entanglement; that he fastened on to Leni because there was no shadow to her, no yellowing bruise of mourning. She was an escape from the grief of his parents' home, the door to his father's study tightly closed, his mother and sister quiet and sorrowful. A picnic in Central Park, a drive to the Jersey Shore, a winter coat on sale at Bergdorf Goodman: the ordinariness of Leni's desires must have been a reprieve for Jacob. It was in his power to make her happy then.

Jacob had met Leni in the first year of his psychiatry residency, the spring after his father died. She was a typist at the hospital; the only daughter of a wealthy businessman from Ossining. A spoiled girl, Rose called her, ruined by her father's indulgence. 'That girl, she wanted too much from the world,' Rose once said sadly, shaking her head. Marina thought at first that it did not seem a bad thing – to want too much from the world. Surely it was better than wanting too little. But Rose made it clear that the things Leni wanted were the wrong things. She was disheart-eningly beautiful, no one could deny that. Marina had seen the photographs of Leni as a young woman that remained in Rose's albums; her long dark hair, her startlingly blue eyes. There was a fickleness to Leni from the very beginning, Rose had told Marina, a tricky sort of restlessness. She was prone to long sulks and fits of annoyance, seeing slights where there were none, falling out with her friends for no real reason. She would turn her back on Jacob in silence for whole days if he did something to offend her. She was so young, still emerging from her childhood, still finding her feet as an adult, as a wife. Yet Rose and Leah had thought that Leni and Jacob might find a way, that the couple could remake themselves to fit each other, and they tried hard with her. All the invitations to art galleries and concerts, to Rose's WIZO fundraisers, to Leah's book club. They tried to include her in their preparations for the Jewish festivals, coaxing and tending her for Jacob's sake.

Leni cooperated in the beginning, smiling indulgently across Rose's dining table as Jacob recited the Friday night prayers, trying for the inflections he remembered in his father's voice speaking those same words through the years of his childhood. It was a sweet but faintly ridiculous novelty to Leni, all this archaic tradition and commemoration. Still, in the early days of their marriage she listened politely to Rose's careful explanations of the rituals, like a wilful but temporarily obedient child. She admired the embroi-dered challah cloth from Israel, the candlesticks that had been carried in Rose's grandmother's trunk all the way from Warsaw.

Leah appointed herself as Leni's historical guide, horrified at the glaring gaps in the girl's knowledge of Jewish history, of any history. She printed out articles for Leni, borrowed books from the library at Columbia, where Leah was in the final year of her social work degree, marking the pages she particularly wanted Leni to read with strips of coloured paper. Her conversation with Leni took on an educative flavour, which made the younger girl uneasy and petulant.

How Jacob hoped that Leni would learn to love them, that she would be a fourth in their close circle. They would have given her their hearts, his sad mother and his earnest sister, but Leni did not want them. He saw the barely perceptible rolling of her eyes when Leah would bend towards her with a confidence, the way she would pick at a flake of her nail polish while Rose was speaking to her. Catching the train home from Rose's house on Friday nights, Leni would make a game of parodying Leah. 'Did you know it was Heinrich Heine who said that since the Exodus from Egypt freedom has always been spoken with a Hebrew accent?' she would intone, her voice mocking his sister's solemn, professorial inflection. Leni was a good mimic, quick and sardonic. Leah, with her flushed face and her wild spill of curls, her rucksack weighed down with books, was easy game for Leni's sharp tongue.

A few months into their marriage, Leni and Jacob stopped going to the Shabbat dinners at Rose's house. Leni wanted to meet friends for dinner, to catch the train to parties in Brooklyn or walk to the jazz club down the street from their apartment. Jacob would sit in the corner of the noisy bar, exhausted from the week of work and study, his foot on the table leg to stop the wobble and spill of their drinks, and watch Leni flit around the room. It had caused him enormous sorrow, Marina knew, this abandonment of his mother and sister. Those Friday evenings were something hallowed in their family and his absence was a terrible betrayal – not only of Rose and Leah but somehow of the memory of his father, too.

Leni resigned from her job at Beth Israel soon after she and Jacob were married. The work was unglamorous and dull, she told him. She wanted to do something that would stimulate her more. She could apply for college, or take a photography course. She flipped through course booklets from the New School and Cooper Union, lying on her stomach on their unmade bed, her long legs flicking up behind her. Her friends had been mostly secretaries and nurses from the hospital, or girls she had gone to school with in Ossining, but soon she began to court the wives of Jacob's medical friends, arranging lunches at the Boat House in Central Park or afternoon tea at Barneys. He could see the vague shape of the life Leni was imagining for them, the moneyed glossiness of it. She complained that their apartment on East Second Street was too small, too ramshackle to entertain their friends. She railed at him over the buckling linoleum floors and the swollen window frames, the disconcerting shudder of the pipes at night through the old tenement building. Often her rage over the apartment was so unreasonable that Jacob felt there must be something else behind it, some other way he had failed her.

In the second year of their marriage, though they could barely afford it on his resident's salary, Leni convinced Jacob to buy a summer share in a house on Long Beach. He had refused for a long time but succumbed to her one afternoon late in the spring, dipping into the savings fund he had started to buy an apartment. He remembered her sheer crackling joy that day, the press of her slim arms around his neck and her lips against his. 'Do I tell you enough how much I love you?' she whispered in his ear. The truth was that Leni rarely told Jacob she loved him. Her feeling for him was something confounding and slightly mysterious; he could never entirely get a handle on it. 'Ditto,' she would murmur distractedly when he professed his love to her. 'Ditto, darling.'

Once, when Jacob and Marina were walking around the reservoir in Central Park, he told her that during his first marriage, when he had stumbled home from an overnight shift, sometimes instead of falling into bed immediately, he would catch the train to the park with Leni and watch her running around the reservoir. He would sit on a bench beside the bridle path, frayed with exhaustion, and stare after her as she made her way around the track. He was so tired that the world would waver a little, and he would focus on Leni's tanned legs, the pale-green silk of her running shorts, the slap of her braid between her slim shoulder blades. Leni seemed her most serious and concentrated self when she was running, her gaze fixed on some point in the distance, her mouth slightly open, her gait graceful and constant, like an elegant racehorse.

Under the terms of their summer share Leni and Jacob were entitled to three weekends a month at the house in Long Beach; an upstairs bedroom in a sprawling shingled cottage by the shore. The lease was shared with five other couples and the place had the riotous feel of a summer colony. The crunch of tyres on the gravel driveway as people arrived and departed, the blare of a record, bursts of laughter and doors slamming, endless games of tennis, the clatter of feet up and down the stairs. Jacob found it overwhelming: the noise and the late nights, the clamour of voices and music on the deck below their bedroom window, the kitchen full of empty champagne bottles every morning. Often he would stay behind when the household repaired to the beach in the mornings, lying on the sofa with a book in the sudden silence of the empty house.

A few weeks into the summer, his roster at the hospital changed and he had to work Saturday and Sunday evening shifts. There was no reason for Leni to miss the weekends on Long Beach just because he could no longer go with her. He would watch her pack, tying a silk scarf carefully in her hair, the glossy mass of it falling down her back, sliding the diamond earrings her father had given her on their wedding day into her small, perfect earlobes. Someone's car would pull up on the street outside their apartment, the sharp blast of the horn startling him, and she would be gone.

The tiny apartment seemed filled with the most cavernous loneliness on those weekends. A dread would take hold of Jacob as he walked slowly home from the hospital at dawn, stepping out into the blue hush of Union Square. The only people there at that hour were stallholders setting up for the farmers' market and the vagrants who had spent the night in the park. Sometimes he would stop and buy a cup of hot apple cider and a bread roll, and linger on one of the benches, reluctant despite his exhaustion to return to the empty apartment. Walking back through the East Village he would see the last of the late-night revellers stumbling out of bars, weaving towards the subway station. Everyone seemed impossibly young. The city, his home for his entire life save those early years in Israel, suddenly felt desolate and pallid. As if it were not his home at all, but some other, unloved place he had to endure.

He started going to Shabbat dinners at his mother's house again. Rose and Leah tended to him, cooking his favourite dishes and packing little parcels of leftovers for him. Nothing was said about Leni's absence. It was almost possible to pretend sometimes during that summer, Leah told Marina once, that Leni did not exist. That another, more expansive future still awaited her brother; an accomplished, enduring love.

⌐

The following winter, Ben was born. Jacob was a father. Leni had given him that. In spite of everything that happened afterwards, Jacob told Marina, he could not for one minute imagine a life in which Ben did not exist. He would race home from his shift at the hospital, almost jogging down Broadway to see his son. The separation from the baby in those long hours of his working day was something he felt viscerally, he said, a tightness in the chest, a persistent, panicky pain.

Ben's birth made everything clear for Jacob. The boy was a little flare to lead them on. He would give weight and shape to their lives, which had previously seemed somehow unguided and insubstantial. He hoped Leni would feel the same; that mother-hood would coax her into becoming a more acceptable person. Her love for the child might transform her. Such redemptions were possible.

They worried all through Leni's pregnancy, Rose and Leah told Marina, that the baby wasn't Jacob's, but the moment they saw Ben they knew. Even as a newborn, he looked exactly like his father; it was like holding Jacob in her arms again, Rose said.

When Ben was two months old, Leni left him with Jacob to go skiing in Aspen with some of the wives from the Long Beach summer house. The baby wasn't breastfed, and he would be perfectly happy with Jacob, she argued. It was only five nights, hardly an epic separation. Ben wouldn't even notice she was gone. Jacob didn't have the heart to fight with her. He took leave from the hospital and stayed home with the baby. Ben screamed so violently that Jacob was terrified he would do some damage to himself. Jacob walked around the dark apartment for hours with the baby in his arms, rocking, patting, soothing, staring down at his son's tiny face, contorted with rage. Every night felt endless. In the mornings he fell asleep on the couch, the baby resting against him, his tiny chest rising and falling as he drifted into sleep at last. Sometimes he would wake to find Ben staring up at him, almost studying him, something knowing in his eyes.

Jacob had once heard another doctor at the hospital speak about the irrational jealousy he experienced with the arrival of his first child. The intimate world he had lived in with his wife was taken over by the baby's enormous needs, his friend told him, and he felt cast out. His love for the child was never in question, but he missed his wife. She and the baby were bound together in an exclusive, fleshly union and he could only stare in from the outside. For Jacob it was the opposite. He and Ben were closeted together in an intimate cocoon; it was Leni who was the outsider. When he saw the cab pulling up outside the building on the sixth day and Leni stepping out on to the sidewalk, it seemed that she did not belong to them at all.

And yet Jacob did not doubt that Leni loved Ben. 'Sweet pea', she called him, bending down into the crib to tickle his stomach or stroke his hair. It was the same name, Jacob realised, that her own mother sometimes used for her. Leni had never been adequately parented. She was trying the best she could, but the model that she was attempting to replicate was flawed. She had no sensible women friends who could guide her. He suggested that perhaps Rose could come and spend time with her and the baby when he was at work. Leni was furiously affronted. 'I don't want your mother here, interfering,' she yelled at him. 'He's my child.' Her refusal was so vehement, her rage so uncalled for. Jacob began to wonder if the child's birth had unbalanced her.

When Ben was two years old Leni announced that she was starting a new job. One of the doctors who had been part of the Long Beach summer share, a surgeon named Michael Hadley, had offered her a position as a receptionist at his consulting rooms in Gramercy Park. Jacob was surprised that Leni wanted to return to secretarial work. She had complained often about how dull she had found the administrative work at the hospital. She was going even crazier being stuck at home all day, she told Jacob. She wanted to be in the world again, and day care would be good for Ben; she had found a centre just around the corner from them. There was nothing Jacob could say – everything had already been arranged by the time she told him.

Six months later Leni was gone. This part of the story Marina knew well. The letter on the kitchen table, propped up next to the fruit bowl; the apartment empty of everything that belonged to Leni. Nothing but some strands of her long hair left curled into Jacob's brush, an empty perfume bottle on the bathroom shelf. She had left for London. Michael had a fellowship there and she was going with him. She would be in touch about seeing Ben; perhaps she would come back and visit at Christmas time. Jacob had no idea how long Leni's affair with Michael had been going on; whether it stretched all the way back to that summer on Long Beach or if it had only begun after she started working for him. It didn't bear thinking about, he said.

From the kitchen of the beach cottage, Marina watched Jacob turn down the front path and make his way up the wooden stairs to the deck. The rain had made an early dusk and there was a sudden edge of cold to the day. The glittering sunlight of the past few weeks had given way to an unseasonal grey. Jacob stamped his feet on the mat and came over to kiss her.

'I thought we could make soup tonight. It feels like the weather for it. There's that roast pumpkin left over from yesterday.'

'Yes. And champagne in the fridge.'

'Soup and champagne. Sounds like a fine combination.'

Marina slipped her hands under Jacob's shirt. There were times when a visceral ache rose up in her at the knowledge that he had suffered. There was a whole tract of his life he still could not enter with safety. It merged with her desire for him, this fierce, protective urge. She pressed her lips to his neck. The taste of his skin was different in summer, a layer of salt to it.

'It's good weather for a siesta, too,' she said, leading him into their small bedroom at the back of the house.

Later they lay in bed together. Jacob slipped his arms around her, his head resting on her shoulder. The sound of the ocean floated through the open window, a rhythmic heave and suck. Rain splashed against the boards of the deck. Marina could feel Jacob's breath on her neck, the slow unloosening of his body as he drifted into sleep. There was a magnolia in a green enamel vase on the bedside table. How strange, Marina had thought when she came across the small tree, that such a blowsy, wintery flower should grow here in the sand dunes. The bloom looked like an enormous soft butterfly.

Several weeks passed before Jacob told Rose and Leah that Leni had left. He disguised her absence, taking leave from work and spending the days at home with Ben. He would take the little boy to Tompkins Square Park in the afternoons, the two of them sitting on the benches by the dog run. Ben was almost inconsolable during those weeks. He adored his mother with a love that was ardent and hopeless in its enormity. He was transported by the sight of her, lovesick and quivering in her presence, anxious when she was away from him. In the days after she left, Ben asked for her again and again. The longer Leni was gone the more he wanted to see her, waking up in the night sobbing, trailing around the apartment, peering into every room as if she might suddenly materialise. There was nothing Jacob could do to comfort him. No word came from her. She did not call or write.

After a month Jacob found out the details of the hospital in London where Michael was working and telephoned him there. Would Michael ask Leni to call and speak to her son, Jacob said. If she called the apartment, he would put Ben straight on the line. It took a great deal of will for Jacob to keep his voice steady. Michael said that he would pass the message on to Leni, that they had been very busy and he was sure she would call as soon as she could. He sounded mild and agreeable, as if they were discussing a minor business arrangement. There was a long pause, and then a burst of background noise on Michael's end of the line; he was terribly sorry, he would have to be off – they were paging him. Never a dull moment here, Michael said before hanging up.

Jacob was devastated in the weeks after Leni's disappearance, not so much for his own sake but for Ben's. Jacob had become accustomed to her absences; it was easier sometimes when she was not there. But this was different. It was one thing for Leni to leave him, but to spurn her son's guileless, trembling love was unforgiveable. She had always been an insufficient mother but no lapse, no error she had made while she stayed with them could ever compare to the enormous breach her departure had created in Ben's small existence. Gone, she would loom too large in her son's imagining and he would not be able to right himself in the world. If she only had agreed to remain with them, her failings would be ordinary ones and her power to wreak devastation would be diminished. But she left, and did not come back for three years. Marina knew that Jacob believed that Ben's current grief was the same old sorrow, a seam of pain running through these years all along. Ben had seemed unscathed and yet he was not. Like some dormant tropical disease, his grief over his mother's betrayal had flared up again.

The weather never recovered during their last week on Fire Island. Drifts of rain streamed over the bay and soon the place felt water-logged, the sea and the sky coming together in a grey haze. The little cottage was chilly and dark, a spreading damp in the walls, draughts flowing in under the doors. Marina found an old fisher-man's sweater stowed away in one of the cupboards and took to wearing it. She liked the way the wool still held the smell of the sea. They stayed indoors, listening to the radio or reading, a hush of rain all around them. It was almost cool enough for a fire. Packing up the house on the last day, Marina wondered suddenly if they would ever come back.

Back in the city, Marina began to work again on the book, writing through the heat of the mornings, the window lifted up a crack to let in the sounds of the street. Some days the whole city seemed to waver under the humidity. There had been a flare-up of violence in the neighbourhood while they were away, as if the heat had finally driven people into unreason: a shooting in East Harlem, where a child had been caught in the crossfire, and a large-scale drug bust at the Wagner housing projects. The news was full of pictures of sullen-looking young men being pushed into police cars.

Many of their friends thought she and Jacob were crazy when they bought the house in Harlem. People were moving to the uncharted parts of Brooklyn, out to Clinton Hill and Fort Greene, or even north to Washington Heights and Inwood, where there were suddenly farmers' markets and organic cafés on every corner, but Harlem still held an air of danger and dissolution. It didn't seem to be redeemable in the way of those other neighbourhoods. The vacant lots between the buildings were full of remnants of an old wilderness; vines growing over hillocks of garbage, weeds spilling out of the rusted bodies of abandoned cars. Once, Marina thought she spied a thin brown fox disappearing down a storm pipe. Probably just a stray cat, Jacob said, but she preferred the idea of a fox, the revenant wildness of it.

In the afternoons she walked to Central Park and looped around the Harlem Meer, sometimes venturing further south. Some days she walked the whole length of the park, turning back when she saw the horses and carts lined up outside the Plaza Hotel. It always surprised her to come to the end of the park and find the city there waiting; the glary bustle of midtown and the throngs of summer tourists. In Harlem she could forget about the press of the city itself, its clamour and clutter, its raucous aliveness.

The long afternoon walks had become part of the fabric of her study of the Hasidim. After a morning at her desk, reading the transcripts of the interviews she had conducted, taking notes and writing, the walks through the park felt like a meditative continuation of her work. She was wrestling with the book, had not yet settled on the right way to approach the subject. It would be so much easier to write a panoramic history of Hasidic Judaism in America, but she wanted a more intimate and interesting story. How she hated the idea that it was even possible to pin down an entire people, to unravel their complexity on the pages of a book.

It had always seemed strange to Marina that her book on the Romani had been so lavishly praised as a sweeping cultural history of the Gypsies, when to her it was full of sweet hesitance and mystery. The Romani were a people who had tried, as best they could, to live outside history, to elude the kind of chronicling that an anthropologist might attempt. Their very survival depended on secrecy, on silences and disguise; they were not going to offer themselves up to an outsider. Or if they were willing to speak to her, it was only an abridged kind of telling. For every word of the Romani language she had learned there was another – a secret synonym – that she would never know. Even the words she knew carried nuances she could never be sure of, could be twisted to mean something else entirely. She had decided very early on in that project that she would not write the book as an anthropologist or a historian but in another way, at once more intimate and more distant. She wanted the story she was telling to be as much about its gaps and silences as what was on the page. How much of any life could ever really be known?

It was the same with the Hasidim. Most of those she had interviewed so far had been scrupulously polite, if sometimes suspicious of her motives. They tried to answer her questions, provided her with the information she requested, but there was a distance to everything she learned. She had not yet discovered an opening and she was not sure how to find one.

'The Satmarers don't see you,' a young woman named Frieda told her. 'They don't even register your presence. You are completely outside their world. They are not like the Lubavitchers. They have no interest in trying to bring you back to the Torah, getting you to do mitzvot. It doesn't matter to them if you are observant or not. What you do doesn't matter to them at all, because no one outside their world exists for them.'

Frieda had chosen to leave the Satmarer sect, and Marina thought that perhaps this could be a way into the book, this notion of the outcast, the one who risks everything to leave. Because the young woman had lost her family, her community, her six-year-old son. She lived in a tiny studio apartment in Queens, barely making enough money at her job in a café to survive. She had no skills when she left the community, Frieda explained to her. Her schooling had ended at seventeen, when she was married. She hadn't even spoken English fluently – Yiddish was still the language of the Satmarers. There was another man, too, a Skverer Hasid, who had recently left that sect. He had agreed to meet with Marina the following week. But was this notion of the exile from the faith the right beginning? Would it position the book too firmly outside the movement, cast her on the side of the defector?

It was part of the work of the book, this feeling through, this settling on the way into the story. In her heart she recognised the near-impossibility of the kind of work she was drawn to, the danger of deforming missteps, of complete failure. It was part of what drew her to it – the delicate balancing act required, the fact that success was far from guaranteed. Nothing could ever be unravelled to its core. But surely it was like this for any creative project. If she were writing a novel, she would feel the same way. A professor in graduate school had told her once that her particular talents might be better suited to fiction. His remark was not intended to be kind. She was too drawn to the irrelevant, the professor had said, to culs-de-sac and false paths, to ever be a decent historian.

Walking home from the park one afternoon, Marina paused outside the corner bodega to read the flyers and handwritten signs plastered over its walls. Her back ached from the bend of her writing that morning and there was a damp patch of sweat between her shoulder blades. She stepped inside the bodega for a bottle of water. These little stores seemed to contain the whole world. She wondered how so many of them could possibly survive.

The African girl was standing at the counter. The boy was tied to her back with a yellow wrap that knotted above her breasts. His head lolled to the side, eyes half-closed, his skin shining. Marina remembered the sharp set of the girl's shoulders as she had stood on the sidewalk several weeks earlier, the impassive way she had watched the child screaming, the clasp of her fingers around his tiny arm.

The Yemeni shopkeeper was waving a plastic card at the girl. Marina knew this man, had seen him bent over the counter helping his curly-haired daughters with their homework, a pencil tucked behind his ear. He was usually mild-mannered, gentle with his little girls. Once, he had asked Marina to help him write a letter to the Immigration Department, a sponsorship application for a sister from Yemen. Marina had taken the letter home and typed it up for him, correcting his stilted English and reordering his paragraphs. That was several months ago, she realised, and she had never asked him what had happened, whether his sister was given a visa.

'Finished,' the shopkeeper said loudly to the African girl. 'Food stamps finished. No money left.' He pointed to the spread of groceries on the counter. A tin of baby formula, apples, a carton of eggs, a bottle of milk, a box of teabags. 'No money. No food,' he said emphatically.

The girl stared at him blankly. Her hair was braided in neat rows, beads of sweat dotting her forehead. The shopkeeper put the card down on the counter and tapped on it. 'No more food stamps.' He raised his voice. 'Go on, you go now.' His hand pointed to the door but the girl did not move. Her lips broke open slightly but she said nothing, staring down at her feet. The little boy's eyes were open now, alert and watchful.

Marina felt a terrible pulse of pity for the girl. She looked so young and bewildered, so resolutely encased in whatever sorrow she was carrying. Marina stepped up to the counter and took out her purse. 'I'll pay for her groceries. How much is it?'

The shopkeeper gave her a tight, embarrassed smile as he swiped Marina's credit card through the machine. 'They come in here all the time. Food stamp cards get rejected, spent it all in the first week. Got no idea how to budget, need food for their children. I can't be a charity. It's tough. It's tough for everyone. Me too. I have children too.'

The African girl stood silently beside Marina as the shop-keeper packed the groceries into plastic bags and placed them on the other side of the till. Thirty-seven dollars, the groceries cost.

They walked out of the shop and turned together in the same direction. The girl stood in the middle of the sidewalk as if she had nowhere to go, the little boy leaning around her shoulder and staring at Marina.

'He's happier today,' she said, not sure if the girl understood English. 'No more crying.' She had no idea if the girl remembered her, if she had even really registered Marina that day on the sidewalk.

A plastic bag blew up against the girl's legs and she kicked it away half-heartedly. She looked exhausted, a slight glassiness to her huge eyes.

'Would you like me to help carry your shopping home?'

The girl said nothing, but she did not walk away or resist when Marina reached out to take the bags from her hands.

Marina followed a half-step behind for several blocks, the little boy twisting his head back to stare at her. A tight surge of dread as she turned in at the gate of the housing projects on Madison Avenue. Murder cities, they called them. The sign near the entrance had been scorched and spray-painted over, and litter piled up against the edges of the towers. Inside, the walls of the foyer were covered with garish swirls of graffiti, the mailbox doors hanging open on broken hinges. Marina felt a faint shame in her fear. The projects scattered throughout the neighbourhood were places on the fringes of her world. A backdrop to all those boys being hustled into police cars, a block to quicken your step on. The towers were named after senators and men of state. 'A wonderful community', some of the entrance signs said.

Marina walked towards the lift but the girl motioned to the stairwell on the left side of the entrance foyer. 'Broken,' she said softly. It was the first word Marina had heard her speak. So perhaps she did know English. The soles of the girl's plastic shoes slapped against her heels as she trudged up the stairs. Marina followed her, the bags of groceries carving sweaty welts into her palms. The place felt subterranean to her; subway tiles and dimly lit halls, tinned laughter blaring from behind a door, a child crying somewhere. The stale smell of cooking lingered in the stairwell.

When they reached the sixth floor, the girl turned into the corridor and opened a door halfway down. Marina stepped inside after her, a musty waft of heat engulfing her as she stared around the tiny apartment. Cracked linoleum, a flimsy card table pushed against the window, an enormous torn couch taking up most of the room. Through a door she could see a single bed. She thought suddenly of her own house. The high ceilings and French doors, the rows of bookshelves, all the unused rooms. Jacob's wealth. Had she let herself move too far into the soft, glassy draw of it? When she was a child, heat and hot water had not been constant

86

things. One pair of shoes, a patched coat in winter, bent into the shape of some other child's shoulders. But it had been a euphoric kind of poverty on the kibbutz, a badge of honour, a stripping back to bare necessities. Nothing like these towers and their dull, institutional horror had existed in her childhood. And yet these housing projects had risen, too, from someone's utopian vision. Safe spaces in the sky for the poor, all stacked up on top of each other, slums cleared, creaky tenements razed.

The African girl unknotted the sling and let the little boy slide on to the sofa. She kept her head down as she took the shopping bags from Marina and set them on the small table, then stood against the kitchen counter, her arms folded across her chest. It felt like twilight in the apartment, the two windows covered with dark fabric. There were no lights on and Marina wondered for a moment whether the electricity was connected.

She stood there, feeling foolish. She could turn around and walk away right now, but she wanted to offer something to the girl; what it was she was not entirely certain. She sat down on the couch next to the child, who stared sleepily up at her, fighting to keep his eyes open. Across the room the girl reached over and pulled the curtain straight. The apartment was like a stifling bunker. Hard to imagine that they were six floors above the baking sidewalk.

'It's very hot here,' Marina tried slowly. The girl stared down at her feet. Everything around her, Marina thought, seemed provisional. The room, her few possessions, the sleepy child.

Marina could hear shouting from somewhere above them and then what sounded like the snarl of a dog. A door slammed loudly and someone yelled out. Beside her on the couch the little boy sighed as he dozed, a tremble in his chest. His forehead was creased into tiny lines, his thumb in his mouth.

'How long have you been in New York?' Marina asked.

The girl walked to the bedroom and came back with a piece of folded paper. It was an immigration document, passport-sized photos of the girl and the child pinned to it, she staring blankly ahead, his face crumpled into tears. Constance and Gabriel Nsengimana. Marina scanned the birthdates. Constance's was 1977. The same year as Ben. Twenty years old, then. And the little boy was not yet three. A stamp on the top of the page showed the date of entry into the USA as the previous September.

The birthplace for both of them was marked as Rwanda. The name of the country contained all its horror. Three years already since the genocide there, all those people left marooned in terror for those long months of slaughter. Marina remembered the sickening images on television. The rows of bloodied bodies; mutilated, macheted, hogtied. The men castrated. A woman whose four limbs had been cut from her. Each report was more horrifying than the last. She had read the newspaper in those days with a rising sense of terror. What had been the reason for it? Was there ever a reason?

The bodies of the dead, she remembered reading, had been tossed into a river, travelling hundreds of miles downstream to Lake Victoria. Thousands of bodies, the shores of the lake awash with them. A fisherman had found a cluster of babies tied up in a canvas sack; another had found three children joined by a single pointed stick thrust through their stomachs. The Ugandans had tried to bury the bodies, she remembered. They had dug shallow graves and held prayer services. But soon there had been too many.

Marina thought of the pictures that had accompanied the stories. A bleached skull glistening in the rushes. A withered wreath of red and white flowers that someone had placed on top of one of the hastily dug mass graves. A tall nun with a rosary twisted around her wrist covering her eyes and crying.

Constance was squatting on the floor against the kitchen cupboards, staring fixedly in front of her. What had she seen in those months? What had happened to her family? Marina handed the piece of paper back to her, feeling suddenly ashamed. Did Constance think that she needed to prove her legitimacy with a legal document? That thirty-seven dollars' worth of groceries had bought Marina some path into her life?

Outside it started to rain, the sudden roar of it like a surge of traffic. A cracking summer thunderstorm. The child stirred at the noise. Constance rose slowly to her feet and walked to the window, lifting the curtain to look out. The view of the sky was mostly blocked by the next tower and the girl let the cloth drop and stood there silently, her shoulders hunched.

She looked so out of place by the window, transplanted from whatever town or village had been burned away beneath her to this apartment six floors above Harlem, the plaster crumbling down the wall beside her. There was no landscape Marina could picture Constance against. Everything receded behind her like a stage set; the tableau of the tiny apartment, the brown towers of the projects, the streets of the city. She would never know what memories of home flashed up for the girl, what curve of land or stretch of river she held in her dreams.

Before Marina left, she wrote out her address and phone number in careful print on the back of the receipt for the groceries. Constance stood in the doorway and watched her walk away down the dim corridor, the child's wail starting up behind her. As she hurried towards the stairwell Marina heard the catch of the door closing and the clink of the chain being drawn. She could still hear the little boy's screams from several floors down.

It was late afternoon by the time she got home. The rain had stopped as suddenly as it had begun, but there was a heavy, bruised feeling to the afternoon. A leaden cast to the sky, the promise of another storm. She pushed open the wrought-iron door under the stairs and stepped into the coolness of the house. There was a perpetual grey semi-light in this room just below the street level; they always kept a lamp lit on the table in the tiny downstairs vestibule. The nuns who had lived here before them had a pendulous glass lantern permanently burning in the downstairs window to show that this was a place of sanctuary, the doors of the church always open. It was heartening to Marina, the warm glow of the lamp, the inherited sanctity of the place. It was up to them to maintain it, she thought.

Jacob was already home, his briefcase and a pile of newspapers on the hall table, a clattering noise and the smell of something cooking in the kitchen. He always finished work early on Fridays. The eve of the Sabbath. They never missed the Friday night dinners at Rose's house. Sometimes it felt like the week coalesced around these Shabbat meals; the walk across the top of Central Park and south to the Upper West Side, the five of them gathered around Rose's dining table, the predictable order of the evening.

Jacob was boiling oranges in a pot on the stove for a cake – his Aunt Esther's recipe. She had been a woman with a litany of desserts and, childless, had bequeathed her zealously guarded recipe book to Jacob, her favourite nephew. Almost every Friday since Esther had died two years before, he had baked one of her

90

cakes to take to Rose's house for Shabbat, carefully deciphering Esther's handwritten recipes. It was a kind of mourner's Kaddish, they joked.

Marina sat at the kitchen table, watching Jacob mix the batter for the cake, a smear of flour on his shirt.

'Do you remember the Rwandan genocide?' she asked him.

He looked up at her, wooden spoon in his hand. 'God, where did that come from? It's not something that you forget.'

'But can you remember the details? Was there a war going on?'

'There's always some sort of war going on in Africa, isn't there? Why are you asking?'

'I met that African girl again today. With the little boy. They're from Rwanda.'

'What African girl?' Jacob asked.

'The one I saw on the street before we left for Fire Island. I told you about them. Her name is Constance. And the child is Gabriel.'

'Where did you see them?'

'Just at the bodega.' She did not tell Jacob that she had visited Constance's apartment. He worried about her, she knew, ranging around the streets like she did. They still didn't know the neighbourhood, he often reminded her, didn't know which blocks they should avoid, which corners were the dangerous ones. Jacob didn't even like walking past the projects; to set foot inside them would seem a rash and risky act.

Marina watched as he poured the batter into a cake tin and placed it in the oven. They should know, she thought, exactly what had happened in Rwanda three years before. A handful of details, a collection of images – it was not enough. Not to know, to choose wilful ignorance, was a kind of dishonouring.

Narrowsburg
June, 1999

Constance sits back on her knees in the dirt of the small graveyard with her hands folded in her skirt. She has a habit of coming up here in the afternoons when most of her work is finished and the nuns are resting, or on Sundays, when no work is supposed to be done. At first she just came to keep the weeds down, cutting back the hogweed and crabgrass and sorrel. The wildflowers she let stay, but the yellow of them against the old gravestones made her think about how weary and moss-covered they were. The names of the dead nuns were all covered in a spreading pale green. So one day she carried up a bucket of soapy water and a scouring brush and scrubbed all the stones clean, her fingers turning red and sore with the effort of it. Now she comes to clean the gravestones every few weeks.

The spring before, she planted some pale roses and now they are spreading over some of the graves. She has planted other things, too. There is a hardware store in the town where they sell seeds in packets with pictures of the flowers on the front. She was afraid at first of going to the town. Her face, she thought, might be in the papers. Someone might come to take her away; what she had done surely deserved punishing, and in this country there were rules for everything. But she kept her head down and the people in that small town barely looked at her. Even so, she prefers to stay close to the convent. A garden, a river, a graveyard. It is enough.

One of the seed packets she chose had a bright orange blaze of colour. The flower is called Devil's Paintbrush. Constance thought the nuns might not want it, not with that kind of name. But Sister Vera laughed and said God wouldn't concern himself about a silly name someone had given a pretty plant. They made a garden too, she and Sister Vera, a big green square beside the kitchen. Neat rows of lettuces and cabbage, runner beans, tomatoes staked with old stockings. Most of what they eat comes from that garden now. The things from home cannot grow in this country. Bananas, yams, manioc. Better not to have them.

In the north corner of the graveyard, under a spreading tree, are the new stones with the names of the dead nuns written on them in gold letters. Three new graves since winter. Kathleen. Mercy. Elizabeth. To see those gravestones with the nuns' names on them is an odd thing. The names seem something separate from her memory of the nuns themselves. Kathleen's hair was fine and soft as a baby's. Mercy kept old lace handkerchiefs tucked into the sleeves of her cardigan. Elizabeth sang with a voice that quavered on the high notes. This kind of knowing will fade away one day. All that will be left of them is the names carved in stone.

There is another new stone, with the child's name on it. The nuns made it. A small angel perches on the stone, its wings spread as if it were about to fly away. The stone itself has a kind of black fleck in it and it is so full of shine Constance can see her own face in it when she bends down next to the grave. Her hair is not braided anymore, just left as it was and cut short like the nuns'. She dresses like them too now. Straight skirts and blouses and cardigans, sometimes trousers when she is working in the garden, laced-up leather shoes, flannel nightdresses for warmth in winter. A long time ago she put away her cotton pagne. Sister Vera drove her to a shop in the town that first winter and chose things for her. 'If you're going to stay here, you'll need some proper clothes,' she said. *If you're going to stay.* Just like that. As if it was already decided.

Sometimes she can see the child's face very clearly, his eyes and the way they would stare at her. Watching her, waiting to see what she would do. Other times he seems only to be something she dreamed. So much of her life feels like that. Sometimes now it is hard to tell the things that happened and the things that did not, to sort between the daytime and night-time thoughts. Best that it can all slip into a kind of not-knowing, like that feeling of waking from a dream and wondering for a moment if it was true. She hardly knows how to arrange things in the right order anymore. Just the other night she woke with the birthing of the child in her mind. She has not thought about that for a long time. All that blood and somebody's hands pushing on her stomach, somebody else placing a damp twist of cloth between her teeth so she could bite down. A high keening she barely recognised as coming from her. An animal sound. Better that she should die in the birthing, she had thought then. Her living had already snatched away the luck from another life.

'Where is your child?' they asked her when she had come here to Narrowsburg. She knew that would be the first thing they would

94

ask. 'What have you done with him, your little boy?' 'Dead' was the only thing that she could say. She had thought about it all through the journey there, that this was how she must tell it. If she told them what had really happened, they might make her go back for him. So saying he was dead was not a lie but a kind of saving. Yes, a saving.

She had thought of a story. For the hours on the buses she thought of how she could tell it. The story was about a sickness and a hospital in the city. She had seen enough dying, knew how a face moved to a yellow dullness. She could tell them about the dying, but she was afraid they would ask her the rest of it. About doctors and papers and the grave. Then her story would give way on one side or another, like a wobbly table. In the end she didn't have to say anything. They didn't ask her questions after that first day. They knew already that she didn't like talking. The nuns said the child's name in their prayers and she thought that was all right. A prayer could do him no harm. There were no answers to prayers. No Lord's miracles to fill people with plenty. She knew this.

After a long time here in Narrowsburg, it was in her mind that she might tell Sister Cecile. She is the oldest of all of them and it has been a whole winter and a spring since she left her bed. Constance sits by her in the afternoons. There is not much else to do for her in her dying. It is not hard work like some of the others were. Sister Cecile just lies there, looking out at the tops of the trees in her square of window. She never asks for much, just to have the window open, even in the cold. The smell of the garden coming at her through the window is like the smell of Ireland, she says.

Ireland was the place they all came from. Somewhere far away and green. Always they talked about how green their country was. Narrowsburg is green too, but not like Rwanda. And not in the long wintertime when the sky is the colour of a stone and it snows and snows. She can never get used to the months of cold. No matter how long she stays in this country she does not think her body will ever be used to it.

Sister Cecile is the one who gave her that prayer card with the Angel Gabriel on it, back in the city. Constance still has it, slipped into the place between the mattress and the wood of the bedframe. 'A child needs a shelter,' Sister Cecile said back then to Constance. 'You must find a way in yourself to give that to him, as the Lord has for you.' The Lord had given her no shelter, but she wants to tell the old nun that she has done that – found shelter for the child. She wants to tell her and then have it put away, what she has done. She thinks that perhaps one day she might, and Sister Cecile will put her hand on her arm like she does sometimes when Constance sits by her and say that it was a good thing.

But then the nuns made a grave for him. She cannot tell now. That shiny gravestone with the gold letters cost a lot of money. She knows because she heard Sister Vera say that she wished she could just bury the nuns with crosses made of wood like in long-ago times. All that wasted money was one thing. What she did was another, and perhaps if they knew it, they might not want her to stay there anymore. If she told Sister Cecile that she just turned around and left the child, maybe all the kindness would go out of Cecile. Constance could be cast out from here. Better that they do not know.

Constance takes off her cardigan and spreads it on the grass. She lies down under the tree. She likes the way the light looks through the branches and the warm feel of the soil under her.

She closes her eyes for a moment, a weariness coming over her. Every morning she wakes when it is dark; sometimes there are still stars in the sky. She is the only one to hear the first bird and the cicadas in summertime. She keeps the kitchen window open while she is putting on the big pot for porridge or chopping vegetables for a soup, listening for the high hum of the insects. It is a way to say the day has started, a different way to the nuns' morning prayers. After she has scrubbed down the kitchen, light comes into the sky and the others start to wake. Then the hours are easy to fill. Nearly all the nuns have to be helped now. Out of bed, to wash and dress, a pair of glasses found, a blouse ironed, shoelaces tied up. She was shy with it at first, pulling off night-dresses, her hands on the soft withering skin, holding their arms tight as she helped them into the shower. But it has become like any other work that needs to be done. Like washing the sheets and clothes and hanging them up on the line at the side of the house, or mopping the floors, or sweeping the leaves from the path.

You must be tired, Sister Vera says to her sometimes, wanting her to rest. Constance has forgotten what tired is or is not. Better to have something to bend her back over, for her hands to do. She sits up and brushes the leaves off her skirt. Corduroy, the fabric is called. It is soft like the fur of a small animal. There is a notebook in her room where she writes down the names of things. Corduroy. Maple tree. Crab apple. Only a handful of them needed for talking, but she likes to know them. She whispers them over to herself at night sometimes when she cannot fall asleep easily, the same way she used to chant English numbers when the child was wailing.

Constance looks up at the sky through the branches. Already a shift in the light, a widening of shadows. Soon the nuns will be shuffling down to the small chapel for vespers, the evening prayers. The day is divided into times for praying. God wanted so much of people's time, Constance thinks. Sister Cecile told her that it was written in the psalms. She has found the right page for her and read the line aloud, her finger moving under each word. 'Seven times a day I have given praise to thee, for the judgements of thy justice.' Thy justice. Sister Cecile has never told her what that meant. What they should give praise for seven times a day.

Constance stretches slowly to her feet. She needs to go and see to dinner, heat the soup she made that morning and set out the bowls. There are stewed apples and vanilla ice cream for dessert, a jug of lemon cordial cooling in the fridge. She has learned all the things the nuns like. As she comes up the path that curves around the back of the house she sees Sister Vera standing in the vegetable garden. She is wearing one of Constance's aprons over her blue dress. Her hair is mostly still dark, but there is an edge of grey to it. She stands there very still, her arms folded across her chest. Many times Sister Vera misses prayers. Constance sees her from the kitchen disappearing up the path to the apple orchard and the woods beyond while the others are all in the chapel. Some days she will stay away for the whole afternoon. Once, earlier in the spring, she didn't come back until after night had fallen, after the rest of the nuns had eaten dinner and gone upstairs to sleep. Constance waited anxiously in the kitchen for Sister Vera to return. She hates the dark herself, the thickness of it up here in the mountains. Not one flicker of light. Not one consoling noise. Just when she thought she would have to take the flashlight they kept in the laundry and go out searching, Sister Vera came through the kitchen door. She didn't say anything, just lit the stove and put the kettle on. She made them both a cup of tea, stirring sugar in for Constance. They sat there in the kitchen for a long time with their tea, no talk between them. Then one of the sisters called out from upstairs. A clatter somewhere above them and another call.

'Sometimes,' Sister Vera said to her at last, 'I just need to go away for a little while. To put it all down for a moment. Just for a moment.'

She didn't have to say more about what she meant. Constance knew. Sister Vera was like the mother of all the old nuns. It had been that way sometimes for Constance with the child in the city. One day in summer, when it had been so hot that the sweat came down her forehead and into her eyes, she stopped in a small park and untied the wrap that bound him to her back. He had been squirming and kicking her and when she slapped his legs to make him stop, he only kicked harder. She staggered then, almost tripping over, and the child screamed so loudly that people stared at them. Suddenly the weight of him felt too much for her. She did not think she could take one more step, could not carry him for one moment longer. The heat had brought a kind of dizziness over her. She put the little boy down on a bench and walked away very quickly along the path out of the park. She would walk around one block, she thought. Just one block on her own, to know what it was like. To not have to carry him, to not have to take his hand to hurry him along. Nothing would happen to him in the space of just one block of walking. But she could not stop after one block. The heat that day was so thick there was a shimmer in the air, but she could not stop walking. She walked all the way to the start of the big park and stood by the water. There was a small beach on the lake there and some children were throwing rocks into the water, the grey ducks gliding away out of their reach. What would it feel like, Constance wondered, to put her feet into that water? To sit on the sand with the cool of the water at her feet.

Then a panic came over her and she turned and ran back towards the child. Fourteen blocks. She counted each one in her running. How could she have left him for that long? She ran across the avenue near the small park and a man driving a taxi yelled something angry and sounded his horn. When she came through the park gate she thought for a moment that the child had gone, that someone had taken him. But there he was, sitting very still on the bench where she had left him, not even crying. Just looking straight ahead with a strange, pinched sort of face. He didn't make a sound when she walked towards him, but she could see a tremble in his lip and when she picked him up his heart was beating very fast. She held him against her, pressed into her chest so it felt like there was no boundary between them, that his pounding heart was her own.

It must be like that for Sister Vera too, Constance thought. Setting one foot in front of another until you are far away, as if your own body wants you to be free. But Sister Vera came back. Just like she had.

Harlem
July, 1997

When Marina, Jacob and Ben walked south towards Rose's house they passed the housing projects where Constance and Gabriel lived. There was a small knot of people gathered in the courtyard, an old woman sitting on one of the benches, clutching the handle of a shopping trolley and muttering to herself. A man with a large brown dog on a leash emerged from the building. Marina wondered if it was the same dog she had heard barking when she was there. There was a ripple of something; she could understand why Jacob was so wary. In some of the projects in the Bronx there had been reports of people pitching air conditioners and television sets on to policemen patrolling the courtyards. And always the talk of gangs and drugs, of young men stabbed to death in stairwells. In the winter a makeshift shrine had appeared outside one of the towers, rows of candles lined up against the walls, a cluster of pastel soft toys, a bunch of carnations wrapped in coloured cellophane.

Marina counted up six floors and tried to remember if Constance's apartment was on the east or west side of the building.

One of those lighted windows was hers. For a fleeting moment she wanted to dash up the stairs and collect Constance and her child, take them along to Rose's house for dinner. But what could it possibly mean to Constance to be plucked out of her squalid apartment building and brought under the cloak of their benevolence for a few hours? She tried to imagine the girl at Rose's dining table, eating soup, a linen napkin across her lap, her face illuminated in the flicker of the Shabbat candles. It was impossible.

Ben walked silently beside her and Jacob, his hands in his pockets. She remembered how he used to skip ahead of them so that he could turn back on the path and face them, some new story bursting out of him, a brief backwards jog while he gesticulated. These Friday night dinners at his grandmother's house were the only thing he had not refused this last year. There was a faint dread every week that this would be the night he wouldn't join them, but so far he had always appeared downstairs before they set off. It was heartening to see him there in his clean shirt, his hair freshly washed, a waft of cologne in the room, even if there seemed to be a faint exhaustion in him, a slight tremble in his voice.

Ben loved his grandmother. Much of his youth had been spent in her company. In the months after Leni left, Rose had put aside her own obligations and devoted herself to her grandson's care. For a time, Jacob and Ben came to live with her in the apartment on the Upper West Side. The little boy's life had been tipped up and Jacob didn't want him to be left with strangers while he was at work. So they moved back to Jacob's childhood home, the same apartment in which Rose herself had grown up. Another single bed was moved into Jacob's old bedroom, and father and son shared the room for two years. It gave him enormous comfort, Jacob once told Marina, to be able to hear his son's quiet breathing at night, to watch the small curve of him under the blanket in the bed across from him. When he came home from work to find Rose in the kitchen and Ben playing with the same ancient Meccano set that had been his as a boy, Jacob felt that his life had unspooled in reverse. An odd kind of rewinding, which had brought him back here to his boyhood home, under his mother's care once more.

It was very hard for Rose, Marina knew, when Jacob and Ben eventually moved into their own apartment. That wrench, all over again, of her children leaving. She had lived alone for years before they came, but all of a sudden the silence of the newly empty apartment had seemed impossible to endure. It seemed, in its blank immensity, to be the same silence that had flooded every room in the months after her husband had died.

The neighbourhood changed swiftly as the three of them walked further south. The streets grew cleaner and more decorous. Window boxes and planters full of daisies appeared. The streetlamps glowed warmly though it was barely dusk. A woman with two pugs on tartan leashes stood beside them on Central Park West as they waited for the light to change. Ben bent down to pat the dogs and they wheezed excitedly as he stroked their heads. He loved animals. Marina could hardly remember the long catalogue of pets over the years: a pair of white mice, countless fish, a blue-winged budgerigar, a small tortoise, an injured rat he had found lying on the sidewalk and brought home wrapped in his school sweater. How he had tended all of those creatures. Perhaps he needed something to love. She thought of Constance and the tight circle of her fingers around her child's wrist. And her own mother. That closed bedroom door, her children reading quietly at the kitchen table, whispering to each other so they would not disturb her. Having something to love, Marina thought, was not always the answer.

They had performed great feats, she and Dov, to elicit their mother's love. Marina thought of all the cups of tea, the flowers placed on the lacquered tray with her breakfast, the incessant tending. Dov was only nine years old when they came to Brooklyn, but in some ways he was already like a small adult. He tried to care for his mother in the same way he had cared for Marina in their years in the Children's House. But Gizela was forever ignoring the gifts they presented her, forever unloosing their hands from hers and striding ahead of them on a path. She could not stand to be close to them for too long, and often on weekends or during the summers she would disappear from the apartment for hours on end. They did not know where she went – as far as they could tell she had no friends in the city. She had found work doing typing from home and every few days a new sheaf of pages would appear on the small desk in her bedroom. Marina and Dov never saw any evidence of these transactions and did not know who gave her the work. In the evenings they could hear the clatter of the keys, racing and halting and then speeding up again. It felt reassuring to them. Gizela was safe when she was typing, sitting at her desk in the circle of light from the fringed lamp.

Once, Marina and Dov followed her when she left the apartment. They had been eating breakfast in their pyjamas but as soon as they heard the front door of the building close, they ran to pull on their clothes and walked after their mother, hanging back a block so that she would not see them. Gizela trailed slowly along Eastern Parkway, her pale-blue coat billowing out behind her, her long hair in a plait wrapped around the crown of her head. She walked west all the way to the waterfront at Brooklyn Heights. It was early on a Sunday morning and the place was empty of people. Gizela stopped by the railing of the promenade and leaned over and looked down at the water. Then she stepped up so that her feet were on the iron girder. Marina could feel a terrified panic coursing through Dov. He reached out and took her hand, but neither of them moved towards Gizela. It felt as though they were suspended there for a long time, all of them frozen into a strange tableau. They were waiting, Marina thought, for their mother to show some awareness of their watching. To glance back with that slightly startled expression that came over her sometimes when she stepped out of her bedroom in the mornings and saw them eating their breakfast. To remember that her children were there, that they were hers.

After what felt like hours, but could only have been a few minutes, Gizela unhooked her feet from the railing, stepped back down on to the pavement and strode away. As they walked home together, Marina saw that Dov's trousers were wet. She must have been only six or seven years old, but Marina had never forgotten the tremble in her brother's fingers, the bloom of damp on the pale fabric.

In the downstairs foyer of Rose's apartment building Marina paused for a moment and glanced at her face in the warped old mirror above the hall table. She looked like her mother. This unnerving recognition happened to her more and more now. The past never lost its power, the force of it so strong at times that it threatened to sweep everything else away. She had cut her hair to just above her shoulders that summer. Long, it reminded her too much of Gizela. What was it about her own face now that called forth Gizela? After so many years of absence, her mother had become something drifting and unshaped, her piercing, unsettled beauty a kind of myth. It was the grey eyes, Marina thought, and the pale skin. She remembered staring, transfixed, at the same tracery of veins visible at Gizela's temples, the blue web-work almost like a faint tattoo.

Leah burst through the door behind them, an enormous bunch of pink roses in her arms. When she embraced Marina, the soft, faintly foetid smell of the flowers rose up between them. Her hair was piled up on top of her head and her cheeks were flushed from the heat. Leah often complained that all her parents' good looks and charm had gone to Jacob. She denigrated herself constantly, not recognising her own beauty and instead railing about her gracelessness, her unruly hair, wishing she were taller, more elegant.

'Hello, my loves,' Leah said happily. 'Would you look at these roses? Doesn't it feel like they've just been plucked from a misty English garden? Of course, they'll probably be dead in about two minutes in this heat. I shouldn't have wasted the money. Sinful, I know. But still.'

Leah reached up to kiss her brother, resting her hand on his cheek for a moment. Jacob could chafe against his sister, finding her too stern in her moral intensity, her ceaseless reforming zeal. But there was a profound goodness to Leah. It seemed the most essential thing about her. She ran a migrant advocacy centre out of the wood-panelled basement of an old brownstone in East Harlem. There was a food pantry attached to the agency and often a long, disorderly queue of people lined up along the sidewalk with their shopping carts. A few times since she had lived in Harlem Marina had walked over to help with the Saturday morning food distribution, standing in a chain of volunteers and handing out tins of food and bags of rice and beans. She liked to watch Leah during these shifts; the way she darted in and out, weaving her way between the crowds, stopping to take someone's hand, bending down to greet a baby strapped into a stroller, chatting happily in Spanish. Leah was animated, illuminated by her work. It was the place where she seemed best able to show the full extent of herself. All her flashing cleverness and competence were channelled into the people she helped, all her passion and fiery indignation. Her clients worshipped her and her staff loved her, too. They did more than she asked of them.

Leah was forever agitating for change, forming coalitions and organising marches and protests, sit-ins and bus trips to Albany to meet with senators. She spoke on the radio, her whole being enlarged by her ardour. More than once she had been arrested. Last summer Marina and Jacob had posted bail for her after she had joined a group of nuns and peace activists from the Catholic Worker House, broken into a nuclear weapons plant in Tennessee and painted biblical quotes over it. They had splashed bottles of human blood over the bunker wall and hammered off a small chunk of the uranium storage facility. Leah was held in a county jail for several days and was hit on the ankle with a police baton, which cracked the bone. The injury had saved her from more serious charges.

Jacob and Rose were appalled by Leah's behaviour. A social conscience was one thing, Rose said, but to be arrested, to cut through three fences and wilfully damage government property. To use human blood. The whole thing felt reckless and unseemly. Leah was unrepentant. It was her job, she told them, to help hack away at the ropes of oppression in this country, and sometimes drastic action was needed for the voices of justice to be heard.

She had painted a verse from Isaiah on the walls of the nuclear plant, the one about turning swords into ploughshares. At least she had used the Old Testament, Ben quipped at the time.

There were moments when Leah's single-minded zeal and her wounded ardency reminded Marina of Dov. There was his desperate obsession with Hasidism when he was sixteen, his intense devotion to the rabbi who was his teacher then. Two years later he spent a whole summer volunteering at a cemetery in Poland, cleaning damaged Jewish graves in a town where there were no longer any living Jews. But Dov was never a revolutionary like Leah; he did not have any serious interest in changing the world. His various obsessions were all part of the ceaseless, doomed project of deciphering their mother. Even the act of cleaning graves in a country they had no connection to was a kind of atonement. They had not suffered as their mother had suffered. Although the things that had happened to Gizela were concealed from them, it was not possible for Dov and Marina ever to forget this.

Standing at the foot of the stairs, Leah seemed a milder, less intense version of herself. Long, beaded earrings dangled from her ears. She looked almost bridal with her armload of pale roses. Leah had remained resolutely single since a disastrous engagement when she was in graduate school. There had not been even the hint of a romance in the years Marina had known her. If she ever had lovers, she was silent about them. Once, she said to Marina, laughing, that she had never been a party to love.

Rose had been praying all these years that Leah would come to her senses and marry a suitable man. Children, she pronounced, would subdue Leah. Marina hoped for a more devouring sort of love for her sister-in-law: an exotic Chilean political asylum seeker or a brilliant human rights lawyer. She had hoped for love for Dov once, too; one that might steady him, shift the circumference of his world a little. But no woman, in the end, had been able to compete with Gizela.

They walked up the stairs together, a kind of procession, Jacob at the front bearing his cake, Leah behind him with her flowers. Rose stood at the door waiting for them, wearing a high-necked silk blouse and the amethyst brooch that had been her grandmother's. She had bequeathed it to Marina, Rose had told her solemnly. By rights it should go to Leah, but she would have no use for it, and the thought of the brooch tucked away in a drawer made Rose terribly sad. Marina was the one who would wear it.

Rose took each of their faces between her hands, peering at them as if trying to decipher the minute changes of the last week, to sniff out any shadows cast. She lingered over Ben longest, staring at him until he ducked his head and put his arms around her to avoid her scrutiny. Rose looked tiny in his embrace.

'Come on, girls, I want you to light the candles with me,' Rose said, ushering them into the apartment and untying her apron.

Marina watched as Rose recited the prayer over the Shabbat candles, covering her eyes with her hands. There was a purity to the silence that fell around them as they watched her, a hushed reverence. Every Friday of Jacob and Leah's lives Rose had done this, week after week, year after year. Even on holidays the ritual accompanied them, the silver candlesticks wrapped carefully in a cloth and packed in a suitcase when they drove to Cape May in the summertime. On a trip to Florida, the candlesticks were left behind in the back seat of the taxi that collected them from the airport. It became a family legend – the frantic search, the honourable taxi driver, the safe return.

Marina could not imagine her own mother ever having said a prayer or lighting a candle in observance. In their house there had been no traditions, no incantations. Gizela scorned anything connected to religion. Mrs Zelman, the mother of the Hasidic family that lived downstairs from them in Crown Heights, taught Marina the prayer for lighting the candles on the eve of Shabbat. It was something every Jewish girl should know, she said. The Sabbath is like the cathedral of the Jewish people, Mrs Zelman told her. It is the temple in time, not in space. Every week all Jews enter it and are enriched. Ours is not a God who demands holy places or lavish buildings, but holiness in time, and sanctity in his chosen people. Most of what Mrs Zelman said seemed strange and confusing to Marina, but she was touched by the woman's urgency in the telling, her belief that Marina needed to know these things. She was welcomed into a sacred circle just because she was Jewish. Several years later, when Dov entered his phase of religious zeal and fervent observance, Marina understood the compulsion entirely. To be wanted, to be deemed a soul singled out for favour, these were no small things.

Mrs Zelman wrote out the prayer for Marina, transliterating the Hebrew words into English. Pressed into her hand, too, was a box of candles with a picture of the Lubavitcher Rebbe on the packet. When Mrs Zelman gave her the carefully printed document and the candles, Marina found herself crying. She must have been seven or eight years old and her tears were an immediate shame, mysterious and consuming. Mrs Zelman watched her for a moment, her head tilted to one side. She was a short, stout woman with thick, lank hair and soft, doughy features. The mother of many children, she never seemed to be harassed or exhausted like so many of the other Hasidic women around them. Often when they passed each other on the street or in the foyer of the building, Mrs Zelman would give Marina a wink, as if they were complicit in something. She seemed always to be wearing a striped apron and she herded her children around with tremendous good cheer.

In her ordinariness, Mrs Zelman loomed for many years in Marina's imagination as an elemental, luminous creature, an object of mute veneration. When Marina saw her on the street surrounded by her children, a surge of yearning so powerful it made her tremble would take hold of her. She wanted Mrs Zelman to pinch her cheek, to touch her hair, to pass her one of her endless grocery bags to carry. Even for Mrs Zelman to look up and see her was enough.

Several days after Marina had burst into tears in her kitchen, she found Mrs Zelman waiting for her in the foyer of the building one afternoon. She and Dov went to different schools then, and he came home later than she did. Mrs Zelman beckoned Marina inside her own apartment and brought her a piece of apple cake on a patterned china plate. Strangely, none of her children seemed to be at home. Would Marina like anything else? A glass of juice, perhaps? Marina was tongue-tied and awkward; Mrs Zelman's mere proximity was overwhelming. She did not know why she had been summoned for this private audience and was barely able to respond to the Hasidic woman's questions.

Mrs Zelman sat down at the table and smiled at her. 'Meir and I have talked about this. We'd like to invite you to come to the Catskills with us for the summer. There's a bungalow colony we go to every year. A lake and woods. And activities for the children. Some study, too, but we make sure there's a lot of time for fun.'

Marina was stunned. The thought of spending an entire summer in Mrs Zelman's presence, living in the same house as her, seemed like an impossible fantasy, something conjured by a sorcerer. A whole different life unfurling in front of her. The summer transfigured. A lake and woods. Sitting there at the table across from Mrs Zelman, Marina could hardly breathe.

Mrs Zelman looked hard at her as she cut another slice of apple cake. 'We know,' she said, pausing for a moment, 'that you are alone quite a bit. And that summers can be lonely times. Do you think that your mother could spare you?'

Marina was unable to speak but eventually she must have communicated that she would like to go to the Catskills because Mrs Zelman took out a writing pad and composed a letter to Gizela. She folded the letter in half, put it in an envelope and wrote Gizela's name on it. How they decided between them that a written invitation was the best way to put the suggestion to Gizela, Marina could not remember. But she walked upstairs with Mrs Zelman's letter in her hands and placed it on her mother's pillow.

Gizela gave no indication that she had read the letter. She made no reply and the invitation was never discussed. Marina did not dare ask about it. To raise the subject with Gizela, to say that she wished to spend the summer with the Zelmans, felt akin to some terrible heresy. A betrayal of the small circle of their exis-tence together. And yet how desperately she had wanted to go. Even the very word 'bungalow' took on a mystical cast. Marina whispered it to herself in bed at night. Three whole months in Mrs Zelman's company. It hovered over her, the spectre of her longing, tremulous and hopeful. While no answer was given to the invitation, its possibilities still seemed alive, however unlikely their fulfilment.

Mrs Zelman asked Marina several days later whether Gizela would allow her to come with them, and Marina was stricken. She and Dov never spoke of their mother to anyone; how could she explain that it was not possible for her to ask Gizela for an answer? That it had been almost too vertiginous a leap for her to have passed on the letter in the first place? It would have been easier for her to lie and tell Mrs Zelman that her mother had said no, that she wanted Marina with her for the summer.

Mrs Zelman was standing in the shadowy stairwell and in the shaft of morning light that fell through the old casement window her skin glowed. Strands of her hair slipped out from under the scarf she always wore. Marina could not lie to her. At last she whispered that Gizela had said nothing, that she did not know if her mother would allow her to come or not.

'You leave it with me,' Mrs Zelman said to Marina, patting her cheek briefly. 'I'll speak to her.'

When she came home from school that afternoon, Marina knew immediately that Mrs Zelman had been in the apartment. Gizela's bedroom door was closed and she did not emerge from her room that evening. There was a general sense of agitation, a feeling that their small, sealed world had been intruded upon. Marina sat down at the table and stared at the room around her. Had Gizela invited Mrs Zelman to sit down? Had she offered her a cup of tea? It was hard for Marina to even begin to imagine what might have passed between them. What Gizela might have said to her. Marina sat there for a long time, seized with terrified dismay.

Two days later she bumped into Mrs Zelman on the street. It was a Saturday and Mrs Zelman was walking to shule with her family, a cluster of the smaller children holding on to the stroller she was pushing, the older boys ahead with their father. When Mrs Zelman saw Marina, she disentangled herself and walked over to her. 'I'm so sorry, sweetheart,' she said. With that she leaned forward and took Marina's face between her hands and kissed her forehead. She pressed her lips against Marina's skin for a long moment before pulling back and hurrying after her family. As she walked home Marina lifted her fingers to her forehead where Mrs Zelman had kissed her, half-expecting to find her skin emblazoned. They were children so unused to being touched. Marina could not help feeling that Mrs Zelman's kiss was a message. She had tried, the kiss seemed to say, and now she could do no more.

Marina sometimes thought of Mrs Zelman on those Friday evenings at Rose's house, the fervent way she had whispered to her all those years before about the meaning of the Jewish Sabbath. Jacob's family was not religious in the way the Zelmans were. They observed the Jewish rituals as a kind of continuity, a long and consoling chain of tradition. The patterns they provided were a comfort, and a commemoration too, of all the other women who had lit Shabbat candles, all the other men who had bowed their heads and blessed bread and wine.

'Shabbat shalom,' Rose said, kissing Marina again as she stepped back from the candles. 'Now, come and help me with the soup. I've made the pea.'

Leah followed them into the kitchen. 'Oh, you know I'm crazy about the pea soup.'

'Well, if you're so crazy about it, you should learn how to make it so you can have it when I'm gone.'

'That's awfully morbid,' said Leah. 'You're only seventy.

Hardly about to shuffle off your mortal coil. You'll probably be making pea soup at my funeral.'

'Don't be so sure,' said Rose, her back to them as she ladled the soup out.

Marina carried the bowls to the dining table. How enchanted she had been when she first came here, how delighted by Jacob's family and by the apartment itself, with its reassuring air of permanency. There were muted Persian rugs and glass-fronted bookshelves that locked with a tiny key; the long narrow kitchen with its hand-tatted lace curtains and perpetual smell of baking; the lounge room with its faded velvet ottomans and haphazard stacks of books; the lordly ginger cat curled up on an armchair. Everything in the apartment had a story: the chain of dried rosehips on the mantelpiece that Leah and Jacob had made as children to decorate the sukkah at the Feast of Tabernacles; the goose feather that Rose's own father had used to ceremoniously dust the apartment before Pesach to make sure that not one crumb of bread was left behind; the leather-covered collection of Chekhov's plays that were rumoured to have been given to Rose by a love-sick Russian conductor.

Marina was amazed at first by the ease with which Jacob and Leah inhabited the place, their casualness about all these hallowed objects, this vast and mysterious treasure trove that was their child-hood home. Four generations of Jacob's family had lived here across nearly eight decades. A substantial accretion of American years. It seemed improbable to Marina – so much time in one place. Jacob's father, Max, would have liked a big house across the river in New Jersey or out on Long Island where his brothers and their families lived, Rose had told Marina. It was the only thing in their marriage that Rose and Max ever seriously fought over. This had been her parents' home, with its glimpses of the leaden slick of the

Hudson and the green burst of the park, and Rose could not for one moment imagine leaving it. She was afraid that she would not know how to remember her parents if she left the place where they had all lived, she confided to Marina. Her mother's walnut writing desk with her letter opener still in the top drawer, the brass hook in the hallway where her father's hat had always hung, the corner of the kitchen bench where the yahrzeit candles stood – every memory of her parents was anchored here. Marina recounted this to Jacob and he told her that it was exactly the same for him, that he could still feel his father's presence every time he stepped into the study. Sometimes, he told her, he was even convinced that he could catch a whiff of Max's pipe smoke.

There was a portrait of Max as a young man above the dressing table in Rose's bedroom. It was a drawing that Leah had made from a photograph of her father in Israel, holding a scythe aloft as he stood on the back of a tractor. The image was portentous, heroic. Max was not just a young farmer in the fields, but a valiant new kind of Jew reclaiming his land. Nationhood itself was partly an act of planting in those early days of the tiny new country. Making the desert bloom was at the heart of the Zionist project, and so Jacob's parents became farmers.

Rose and Max met during the war. They were both part of a Zionist youth group. In 1948, when the state of Israel was declared, they moved to a kibbutz in the north of the country. No one had been more surprised than their own parents. Rose was a gifted pianist, already in her third year at the Brooklyn Conservatory, Max a medical student. Promising futures stretched out before them, futures that had not been available to their own parents. They were not expected to give all that away for a place that was barely a country yet, where settlers lived in makeshift camps in the desert alongside thousands of Europe's refugees.

But Max and Rose believed that what they were doing was necessary and heroic, that they were engaged in a creative endeavour the like of which was not to be found in the whole history of mankind. Marrying quietly on Rose's twenty-first birthday, they set out for Haifa a week later. Both of their mothers wept on the docks the day they set sail, and begged them not to go. But the young couple was resolute, inflamed with idealism. They wanted to be part of the rebirth and rehabilitation of their people.

They joined a small kibbutz, working as farmers on the edge of the Jezreel Valley. Rose was offered work in the kitchen or the laundry, but she refused. She wanted the hard turn of the hoe against the dirt, the righteous pain of hunching over in a field all day. It was difficult for her to explain the passion that had driven her then, that had driven them both. And they felt a new desire for each other in their tiny one-room cottage with its too-small bed, a desire that seemed inseparable from their love for the country itself.

There was a searing heatwave during their first summer in Israel, and Rose would drench sheets in cold water and hang them beside the bed, hoping for a filtered cool when the desert winds swept in. As exhausted as they were after the day's work, they were freshly enthralled by each other's bodies. It was a completely new world they were making; they felt their bodies, their very selves, made anew too. They were so young, so stridently idealistic, so very far from everything familiar.

When they first arrived in Israel Rose and Max decided to delay having children, but in their second year on the kibbutz Rose fell pregnant. It was like the seasickness she had felt on the boat coming over. She knelt among the rows of newly planted seedlings and retched, clammy and dizzy. One of the women brought her ginger tea in an enamel mug and she lowered her face over the pungent steam.

Rose felt sure, from the beginning, that the child would be a boy. In the dining hall, the men clapped Max on the back. A pregnancy was a shared celebration. Under the strict socialist philosophy that governed them, children belonged not to their parents but to the kibbutz, to the new nation and its future. They were raised communally in the Children's House, living in dormitories under the care of a nurse. The truck that brought the new mothers home from the small army hospital where they gave birth delivered them straight to the steps of the Children's House to hand their babies over. Mothers did not sing their children lullabies, or wash their clothes, or clean their faces, or rock them to sleep. These kinds of intimacies were discouraged – for the sake of the children and the country. It was believed that the ties of the nuclear family would divert energy away from the communal project, distract people from their larger work.

During the long months of her pregnancy, Rose thought she could do what was required of her: she could come home from hospital and hand her baby over to the nurses in the Children's House. She could allow the kibbutz members to vote on the child's name, could content herself with the single hour a day that children were allowed to spend with their parents.

On the kibbutz they were surrounded by stories from the Torah and, walking in the dry hills that rose from the newly irrigated fields, Rose found herself thinking about Abraham, who had been willing to sacrifice his own son to God. She thought about the parents who had sent their children away to safety during the war, had put them on trains or placed them in the arms of rescuers, knowing that they were unlikely to ever see them again. They must all do what was asked of them. Her child would not be killed, would not be lost to her. He would grow strong and proud among his kibbutz brothers and sisters. He would have a hundred mothers to care for him.

But when Jacob was born she knew none of this was possible. She lay in the narrow camp bed in the hospital holding her baby against her breast. Every part of him seemed miraculous: the tiny questing mouth, the curling hands, the curve of his nose. He had her father's chin, Max's long fingers. He was their singular creation, hers and Max's. She did not want him to be a communal child, did not want others to hold him or care for him. She did not even want to pass him to the nurse so that she could rest. Something had happened to her during the long hours of labour, and in those first moments when they placed the baby in her arms. Rose wondered how the other women could do it. How could any mother give her child away, even if it was only a partial relinquishing? It seemed so cruel, this forced separation. The socialist philosophy, appealing in theory, had a deep coldness curled in its strict heart. Holding her baby in the crook of her arm, his small mouth searching for her breast in the darkness, Rose was afraid.

Her mind was already made up when Max came to visit her and the baby early the next morning. They would leave the kibbutz. There was nothing Max could say; he knew that there was no swaying her. Rose did not even want to go back to retrieve her belongings – their departure would need to be swift. She was terrified she would not be allowed to leave, that they would somehow take her baby from her and force her to stay. She did not want to see anyone from the kibbutz, did not want them to try to talk her out of her desertion.

She felt queasy on the bus that took them away. In her arms, the baby stared up at her with a strange, knowing look. She could not help feeling that it was a kind of rescue, that she had spirited her child away to safety.

They lived for a time in a small apartment in Tel Aviv. It was a surreal place, a new city without its own past, yet mired in history. Forty years earlier there had been only sand dunes where the new white city now stood, with its squat Bauhaus apartment blocks, its straight roads and wide boulevards. From the window of their apartment they could see all the way south to the port of Jaffa, where Jonah had set sail, where King Solomon had shipped the cedars of Lebanon that were used to build the first Temple. To the north the city slipped away and became an Arab village. Everyone seemed to have come from a mysterious elsewhere. The air was searing, the summer evenings long and uncomfortably hot. It had been there on the kibbutz too, this scorching heat, but in the city it was unbearable, the glare of the sun too dazzling against the white walls of the new buildings. When they walked along Rothschild Boulevard with Jacob in his pram, the streets seemed illuminated by a harsh radiance. Rose loved the high, clear sky of the north but in Tel Aviv it felt as if there was too much light.

The streets of the new city were full of the Jews of Europe, those who had slipped in before the war, and those who had come after. They were a sombre, bewildered presence, their faces marked with a terrible, stunned despair. The facts of the war were still slowly filtering through then, the full catalogue of horror not yet known. Rose remembered the first time she had seen a tattooed number on the arm of a German man at the market, the sudden chill that had moved through her.

There were too many refugees and not enough apartments, not enough jobs. They had to write and ask Rose's parents to send them money until Max found work in one of the seaside cafés, washing dishes and clearing tables. The café sold Viennese tortes, cherry strudels and cheesecake. Sometimes Max would bring home leftovers and they would eat cake for dinner, sitting out on their tiny box-like verandah and watching the sun slip down over the water, the night hot and still. Rose's days at home with the baby seemed to stretch endlessly, a strange haze of feeding and rocking and sleeping. Time contracted and expanded in odd ways. She would look at her watch, sure that it must be time for Max to come home from work, to find that only an hour had passed.

It was not the life they wanted. They had come to Israel to farm the land, to create a new world, to be part of a grand project. On the kibbutz they had felt heroic, their lives full of conviction and purpose. In Tel Aviv they were poor immigrants, scrabbling to survive, stumbling over a new language. They could hardly manage to pay the rent on their two-room apartment. Every time Rose opened a letter from her mother with money slipped between the pages, she felt deeply ashamed. They were not here to be supported by others as if they were irresponsible children who had run out of money on a holiday abroad.

In every letter, her mother implored her to come home, to give up this foolishness and return to New York. In one letter she sent a clipping about a concert at Carnegie Hall. Rachmaninoff's Piano Concerto in C Minor. It was the piece that Rose had played for her end-of-year recital at the Brooklyn Conservatory the month before she had left New York. She pinned the advertisement to the wall of their tiny kitchenette. She found herself staring at it often, standing in the kitchen with the baby held against her shoulder. There was a photograph of the Russian pianist who would be performing, her long dark hair curling perfectly between her shoulders, her fingers poised above the keys. Rose stretched out her own fingers. How many hours she had spent practising the Rachmaninoff, how intimately she had known the piece. It had once belonged to her and now she seemed permanently excluded from it. She could barely imagine sitting at a piano.

Rose and Max began to research other places they could live. They had heard about a different kind of collective settlement called a *meshek shitufi*. It was like a kibbutz in many ways, but the nuclear family was preserved. Farming was collective but children lived with their parents. There was a place near Tiberias that needed new members, a small farming settlement established by German refugees several years before.

Jacob was a year old when they moved to the *meshek*. Less than a year later Leah was born in a tiny hospital in the nearby town. It had been a miscalculation, the second child. Of course they had wanted more children, but later, when they were more settled, when Jacob was older. Leah was born four weeks early, squalling and red, her eyes yellow with jaundice. She was sickly from the beginning, refusing to take the breast, alarmingly small and thin. It was her own fault that she could not sustain this child, Rose was convinced. She was always hungry herself. Food was scarce and there were strict rations in those days. One hundred grams of meat per adult per month. For weeks when several of their crops failed there were only eggplants to eat.

In their second year at the *meshek*, four men were attacked by Arabs. They had been on overnight guard duty, clustered around a small fire at the north perimeter of the settlement. Rose had never seen so much blood, flesh ripped open, the soaked red cotton of the men's shirts, the wounds that would not stop bleeding despite their frantic swabbing, their hastily made tourniquets. There was no doctor on the *meshek*, and in the hours they had to wait for help from the next town, two of the wounded men died. One of them, a young Polish man who had fought with the partisans during the war, died with his head resting on

Rose's knees, a whimper coming from him that sounded like a small child, like one of her own children crying. The young man was wearing a woollen scarf that Rose had knitted for him the previous winter. He had been overwhelmed when she had presented it to him; Rose had been a little embarrassed by the immensity of his bewildered pleasure. He had looked so thin and cold, his clothes so inadequate for the winter, that she had used some of the wool her mother had sent her to knit sweaters for the children to make the scarf for him. The young man had marvelled over it as if it were a miracle, and tears had filled his eyes when he tried it on in the dining hall. No one had been kind to him for a very long time, Rose realised. She knew little about his life, but someone had told her that his parents and sister had been killed at the beginning of the war, when he was only twelve years old. He must be the same age as she was, Rose calculated as the man lay there with his head in her lap, his cries suddenly exhausted. He let out another soft moan and his head rolled sideways.

After the bodies were taken away, Rose removed her blood-soaked dress and buried it in a corner of a field. She could not stop thinking of the sound the man had made as he died. It could have been Max.

Things were not the same after the attack. They were such a small band of settlers, so woefully unequipped, so close to the border. There was a fear among them that had not been there before. Rose was unable to look out across the land without seeing the possibility of danger. She could feel herself becoming fretful and anxious, a panic in her every time Max was rostered on for guard duty.

That winter a disease took hold among the chickens, wiping out the entire flock. Four of their best milk cows were stolen one night. There were arguments among the leaders: some wanted to change the structure of the *meshek*, to move from collective farming to individual allotments. Three families left – two for South Africa, another for Tel Aviv. Towards the end of the winter, both the children came down with the flu, Leah's illness turning into a chest infection and then a terrifying fever. Rose had never heard a child scream so much. She and Max took it in turns sitting up with Leah at night, sponging her with a wet cloth, rocking her writhing body. The *meshek*'s only truck was broken down and there was no way to get to town to the hospital.

Early one morning, Max came home from guard duty to find Rose sitting at the kitchen table in her nightdress. She was bent over, with her head resting on the table, her eyes glazed with exhaustion. Jacob and Leah were curled up on the floor asleep at her feet, the stiff wool blanket from the bed draped over them. Rose raised her head and looked at him. It was not yet light outside. 'It's time to go home,' she said.

Rose spoke sometimes about the humiliation of their return to New York. Her mother had wept to see her leave home, she told Marina, but Rose wept every day of their passage back. On the ship, she willed the journey to pass more slowly, wishing they could be suspended at sea forever. The press of waves, the tilting horizon through the small window of their cabin; she wanted to stay cocooned in her bunk.

When they docked in New York it seemed impossible to believe that they had really left Israel. If she refused to disembark from the ship, Rose thought desperately, she could reverse it all and will them back. Their failure, she knew, would cast a shade over every part of their lives, would taint whatever future they tried to create.

They had stepped out of their American lives, never planning to return to them. When they came back it was too late to pick up where they had left off – those paths were closed to them now. A return to medical school was impossible for Max with a family to support. A friend of Rose's father gave him a job selling advertising. Max hated the work, the slickness and pushiness that was required, the ceaseless persuasion needed to make a sale. He was a quiet man, reticent and gentle. It was entirely the wrong career for him, Rose told Marina, but it was the only one that had presented itself. Still, Max was diligent and determined and he wrung a living out of it. There was no other choice. He created a false self, a screen he pulled down every morning when he stepped on to the train for Manhattan, his leather briefcase in his hand. It pained Jacob as a young man, Marina knew, to realise how much his father dreaded his work.

Rose and Max rented a tiny apartment on the top floor of an old clapboard house in Queens. It was all they could afford. The streets were lined with squat row houses and peeling ironwork fences, weeds growing up through the cracked concrete of driveways. It was an enclave of decrepit suburbia, utterly disconnected from the city.

Marina had taken the train out to Queens with Rose a few years before to see if the house was still there. The neighbourhood had reminded her of a seaside town in winter. There was a cluster of palm trees on the corner of the street; they were stunted and short, like trees growing beside a freeway. Those trees had felt like a small mockery to her, Rose told Marina. A daily reminder of what they had lost. When she walked Jacob to school each day she would circle around an extra block so she could avoid the palms.

'I know it's silly,' she said to Marina as they sat together on the train home after they had gone to look at the house. 'I didn't have a claim on a word as grand as exile. America was my own country, after all. To everyone else I'd simply been away for a spell and come home again. A kind of extended holiday. But exile was the only word I could think of to describe the way I felt. I thought so much about my grandmother in those days, how often she'd cried about missing Poland. It became a joke among us as children – how sentimental she was about even the direst Polish dish. When she talked about Poland, it was like she was describing a mythical realm. Not a real country at all. We didn't really have any way to understand what she had lost. When I came back from Israel I wished I'd been kinder to her. But I was envious, too. It's irrational, but her loss felt more legitimate than mine. She'd fled persecution; we had just chosen to leave. We'd left our lives in New York, and if there was a banishing from Israel we'd brought it on ourselves. I had undone what my parents wanted most for me: to know what it's like to be born in a place and to stay there. To not have to leave.'

Eventually Rose and Max remade their lives in New York. One of Rose's former piano teachers found a part-time job for her in the music library at Queens College. A neighbour watched Leah while Rose shelved books and sorted sheet music in the dim stacks of the library. Piano notes floated down from the practice rooms on the second floor. Rose was only a few years older than the students. How she must have envied them. Marina had asked her once if it had not been too painful to work at a music college, to spend every day so close to her own forsaken future. It did not do to think like that, Rose told her. She had work, she had her children, her husband. That was enough.

Rose had tried to preserve some of their Israeli life in New York. They would speak Hebrew around the dinner table every night, she decreed. They must not lose the language of their country; the children should be fluent so that they could return one day. But after a few months in New York, Jacob and Leah wanted to speak only English. They were American children now, not Sabras as their parents had planned. Ungrateful *American* children. It was an insult that Rose used when she was angry with them, a twist to the word in her mouth. Eventually their Hebrew slipped away, resurrected haltingly, temporarily, when Jacob was studying for his bar mitzvah.

In their last weeks in Israel, Rose had tried to regard the country in a way that would help her to remember it for Jacob and Leah. She had no camera so she tried to hold every detail, every scent and taste in her mind. The cast of the light over the valley in the late afternoons, the particular green of the olive leaves in the summer, the curves of the Judean hills, the almost unbearable sweetness of a ripe fig. She had always seen Israel in this heightened way, Rose had told Marina. After centuries of banishment and longing, Israel had become a kind of myth. Before they had moved there it had seemed a country half-dreamed. They could hardly believe that the land itself was a physical place. The first thing she had done when she reached Israel, Rose said, was to find a patch of dirt and put her hands down in it. Once she had returned to her American life, Rose realised that her own stories of their years in Israel felt like fairy tales to her children, too. Soon her nostalgia for the particular kind of halva she had loved from the market in Tiberias, or for an Israeli date, so different from the wizened, imported ones available in New York, would become the subject of loving eye-rolling. Her children would learn about Israel as she had – at Hebrew School on Sundays. They would know the country from the Torah, from books and from stories. They would not remember it.

Rose and Max returned only once, for two weeks' holiday the year before Max died. It was still their country in the way that it was every diaspora Jew's country, but it no longer belonged to them. Staying in their hotel on Hayarkon Street in Tel Aviv, they were tourists now, walking along the promenade and marvelling at all the changes, joining a day trip to Masada with a group of Americans. Everything felt like a false echo of their old life there. Back in the hotel room at night, Rose turned to the wall and wept. She could not help it. She had thought that this trip back would be full of happiness, a joyful homecoming. But being in Israel again only felt like a cruel taunt. They had planned to visit the *meshek*, but Rose could not bear to go. How could she sit there and drink tea with all their old friends who had stayed behind? Who were living on in their primitive houses and farming their country and fighting for it; who were bringing up their children as proud Israelis, letting them go to war, letting them die defending their land. 'How can I sit with those people and talk to them about our safe American lives, our spoiled American children?' Rose had asked Max. 'How can I?'

Nearly half a century later, Rose presided over her American Shabbat table, her grey head bowed and her eyes closed as Jacob recited the prayers. Her fingers rested lightly on the back of the chair, liver-spotted and bent now, a swelling around her joints. There was a cragginess to her features, something haggard but dignified. And still in her face the shadow of her old beauty.

Marina watched the familiar tableau: Leah talking intently to Ben, their heads bent together, Jacob cutting the plaited loaf of challah into thick slices. How hungry she had always been for her husband's memories, his history. Apart from the years in Israel, the life of his family had continued in a predictable unfurling. When Jacob was seven years old, Rose's mother died and the family moved into the apartment to live with her father. Jacob and Leah grew up in their mother's family home, their childhood resembling Rose's. They sailed wooden boats in the Central Park pond just as Rose and her brothers had done as children. In wintertime they rode their bicycles to the Museum of Natural History, or walked with Max to the library to choose books. The children adored everything about their father: the solid heft of him, his wool caps and sweet pipe-smoke smell, his abiding calm. Max never lost his delighted sense of wonder about the world, Jacob told her, his intense interest in everything that crossed his path. He was capable of spending hours playing with his children, never tiring of their games and stories. When he came home from work, Leah and Jacob curled in against him on the sofa, a cradle for each of them under his arms. How Marina would have loved such a father for herself. Sometimes there was a swift flicker of jealousy when she thought of Jacob's child-hood, and then a quickening of shame. How could she begrudge any child such a safe, cocooning love? It was what she would want for her own child, if she had ever had one.

Her own father, Yoav, hovered outside her memories. She had only one photograph of him, and sometimes when she looked at it his face startled her. He was so unknowable, so mysterious to her. If Gizela could seem like someone dreamed, someone fantastical, she had no grasp on her father at all. He had left so little trace in the world. Dov, four years older than Marina, remembered their father teaching him how to make a fire on the kibbutz. 'A Hirsch fire,' he had said proudly as he showed his son how to build a careful pyramid of kindling, how to coax the flames into life. She and Dov had clung as children to this memory of their father and the reference to his own family, to a lineage of Hirsch men and women who no longer existed. Her father was killed the summer after the fire-lighting lessons, when she was four years old. Apart from Marina and Dov, he was the only Hirsch. The only one to have come out of Russia after the war, arriving in Israel at the age of twenty-one.

The picture she had of him was a black-and-white photograph from the archives of the kibbutz where she was born. There were several kibbutzniks in the picture, wearing shorts and smiling. Some of them held farming tools; one woman clutched a chicken in her arms. They were so young. Orphans and survivors, most of them, fresh from the war. How could they be smiling, Marina always wondered. How could any of them be smiling? In the photograph they looked like teenagers at a summer camp. She did not remember this cheerfulness from her childhood.

Her father was standing at the edge of the group, his arm resting over the shoulder of the man next to him. He was smiling, too, and squinting slightly in the bright desert light. No matter how many times Marina scrutinised his features, she could see nothing of herself or Dov in his face. No familiar lineaments, no shadow of recognition. Sometimes she wondered if her father might have been like Jacob's father. A sturdy, sensible grace to him, a listening air. He could have shepherded the four of them. Dov might not have died. Her mother might not have been lost to her.

Marina glanced out of the window at the glimmer of trees in Central Park. A run of green against the still-light sky. Often

in summer she longed for an earlier darkness, a blotting out
of the city. The table had been cleared and Rose and Ben had
brought out the Scrabble board. She could hear the whistle of the
kettle from the kitchen, the clink of cups as Leah prepared the
lacquered tea tray. There was always tea after the meal, even in
summer. It was part of the tradition of those Friday nights.

There was no photograph of her mother in the kibbutz archives.
Gizela had lived in Israel for more than a decade but had somehow
avoided photographic chronicling. Her mother was given to slipping
away, to removing herself. Marina could never understand how she
had endured for so long living in close quarters with others, how
she had been able to bear a communal life. Sitting at Rose's table,
watching the candles melting down and looking around her at the
crowded bookshelves, the blue velvet love seat with the camel-hair
rug folded over its back, the framed family portraits, the violets in
their pots on the windowsill, Marina wondered if there had been a
room like this locked away in the core of her mother's memory. An
apartment in Prague, the sound of church bells and the rap of shoes
on a cobbled street drifting up through a window. An old piano,
a walnut writing desk, a silver-plated menorah. The same Hebrew
words, a woman's pale hand cupped around a flickering candle,
a plaited rope of challah. A lost world. When she was growing
up there was barely a discernible trace of her mother's history, no
memory that veered deeper into the past than her arrival in Israel
in 1951 at the age of eighteen. Whatever she and Dov knew about
their mother's life had come to them as a barely drawn portrait, a
truncated outline: six years in Prague, seven years in Suffolk, five
years in New York, the years in Israel and then back to New York,
a widow with two young children.

When they were children, the word Prague became a talisman
for Marina and Dov, a secret charm that might hold the key to

Gizela. Because there were only shreds of their mother's personal history available, they became obsessed with the city itself. The leaden Vltava River, streets full of narrow doorways, stone buildings that seemed to contain a darkness, a swirling winter mist over it all, the Bohemian mountains disappearing into an ashen sky. Street names they could hardly pronounce, bottles of cherries, yew trees in a green square of park. The two of them were sure that the buried colours and sounds of their mother's childhood must still be alive in her, but not once could they evoke any hint of recognition. For several weeks they regaled Gizela with names and recipes and stories they had dredged up from books in the school library. Czech words, the names of railway stations and public squares, pictures of the Palace Gardens and the squat-pillared bridge, memorised phrases. She and Dov offered all these things up to Gizela, watching her face for some small flicker of recognition. A shame burnt in Marina when she thought back to it: how could they not have known how painful this prodding must have been for their mother? The world of her childhood, and everything it contained, had been razed in her absence, and the life she had lived since was not the one intended for her. Another country, another language – everything had been forcibly transposed.

Gizela never responded to their offerings, only turned away from Marina and Dov in the same way she always did when she wished to close a door between them. They were walking together through Central Park one morning at the end of summer, on their way to an errand in Midtown, when a squirrel ran up a tree beside them. 'Veverka', Marina remembered announcing, her eyes on her mother's face, a pleased triumph in her recall of the Czech word for squirrel from one of the children's dictionaries she had been studying. Gizela stopped walking, turned and stood in front of Marina, seizing her upper arms with both hands, her fingers pressing painfully into her skin. 'Enough.' She hissed it fiercely, her face very close to Marina's.

Many years later, at university in California, Marina had listened to another student speak about his preoccupation with the Ukrainian city of his mother's birth. A city that no longer existed, except in memory. Razed to the ground during the war and rebuilt by the Soviets under a new name. A swallowed history, a place that lived in shifting fragments. A city that belonged now to another nation, whose cemeteries were covered in new roads with Russian names. The only photograph of his mother in her hometown, the young man told Marina, was a portrait taken in a photographer's studio, a watercolour print of a Mediterranean terrace rising up behind her solemn face. Another kind of elsewhere.

His story had made Marina think of that day in the park with Gizela so many years before. The flash of something in her mother's eyes, the tight pinch of her grip, Marina's wince of shame. All these dismantled memories. A city erased, a child-hood erased. The Romani name for it was the right one, she thought: the Great Devouring.

Sitting at Rose's dining table, the distant hum of Broadway beneath them, Marina knew that she had been handed another history. Her own portrait, taken on the day of their wedding, sat there among the cluster of pictures Rose kept on the bureau. The elderly rabbi who had arranged passage for the family to America nearly a century earlier; a formal portrait of Max as a child in Poland; Rose as a girl in braids; Jacob in his bar mitzvah suit; Leah in her graduation gown; Ben as a little boy with his arms around his father's neck – she had been graciously invited to step into all of this.

She looked up and saw that Jacob was watching her. He might have read her thoughts. He came over and kissed her on the cheek, his arm around her shoulder. It was hard for her to imagine a time when he was not essential to her. This was the world's only comfort – someone folding you under their wing.

Harlem
August, 1997

At the beginning of the summer a pair of child's shoes appeared, strung up high on the telephone wire outside the brownstone. They dangled there, framed perfectly in the bedroom window like a kind of sentinel. If Marina woke in the night the first thing she saw was the shoes, lit up in the orange glow of the streetlight. She noticed other hanging shoes in the neighbourhood. One day she asked the Italian woman behind the counter of the bodega on Lenox Avenue what the shoes meant. She feared that they were a haphazard memorial, markers of a violent death; a stray bullet, a murdered child. She had lived in Harlem for several months and still felt it like a strange country around her; she was not yet used to the noise, the smell of garbage rising up in the humidity, the faces staring out of doorways. She knew that there were codes and cues she had not even begun to understand, that she lived on the edge of others' history.

The shoes marked a place where children lived, the woman told her. A warning for gangs and dealers to stay away. A symbol of protection for the whole block. Marina was pleased by this; she liked the idea of the neighbourhood shadowed by these modest sentinels. Later, much later, she began to think that the small shoes were a portent, as well.

Jacob worked less in the summers. Many of his patients went away and there was always a slowing, a loosening of their routines. Sometimes he had a whole morning free during the week, and he and Marina walked together through the park to one of the museums. Jacob loved the Met – the cavernous galleries, the cool, hallowed glory of it. He could spend hours there, wandering from room to room, his hands clasped behind his back. Today Marina watched him standing reverentially before a painting. In the early days of their courtship they had visited a gallery in Los Angeles together to see a Jackson Pollock retrospective. She had been charmed then by Jacob's almost prayerful contemplation, the studious way he moved through the gallery. She remembered staring at him instead of the paintings, the way his hair curled against the collar of his shirt, the generous curve of his lips, the blue ink spot on his breast pocket. She was hoarding all these details for later recollection, she realised; a bulwark against his future absence from her life. There had been no talk of permanency between them in those early days in California. She had always known that when the semester finished he would be returning to New York, to a life whose shape was entirely unknown to her. Perhaps there was even a woman back on the other coast, though she did not think so – he seemed so essentially solitary. It felt to her such wild good fortune that they had fallen into this enlivening passion, this temporary companionship. She did not dare to expect more.

When she returned to her apartment after the day in the Californian museum with Jacob, she contemplated her bookshelves made of planks, the single iron-framed bed inherited from the last tenant, the chipped teacups lined up on the kitchen bench. All of it spartan and bleak. There were no pictures on the walls, no framed photographs. Only a pile of books on her small writing table, an ancient armchair where she sat to read in the evenings, a bare bulb illuminating the room. It was not a home at all. She stood in the middle of the apartment staring around her for a long time. It occurred to her that what she had thought of as an elegant sufficiency, a valiant sort of austerity, was actually closer to deprivation. It was not until the unexpected arrival of Jacob in her life that she realised how lonely she had been.

Sometimes she thought of that Los Angeles apartment, of the years she had spent there studying and writing, the alarming swiftness with which her whole Californian existence was dismantled when she moved back to New York to live with Jacob. Six boxes it had come to in the end, mostly books. She wondered if it was something she had inherited from her mother, this skill for stepping out of one world and into another. The flint of recklessness, the uneasy thrill of it, a swerving of a life from one course on to another. Though so little of what Gizela had done had been her own choice.

Marina stood beside Jacob, who was peering closely at a Cézanne still life. The painting was all order and containment, a balanced elegance to it. Jacob loved this painting, not so much for the lavish talent on display as for the fierce attention it revealed. Marina slipped her hand into Jacob's. Even now, all these years later, there was still an erotic charge between them, an overwhelming bodily tenderness. She loved to stand close to him, to feel their bodies in proximity.

He turned to her. 'They teach you how to love the world, still lifes. The lovely, perishable things of the world.'

'Those apples look like you could eat them,' Marina said.

'Apparently Cézanne was obsessed with getting the colour exactly right. I read somewhere that he used something like twenty different shades of red on one apple.'

Marina rested her head on Jacob's shoulder. Still there was this tendency in her to see these moments as future memories she must hoard carefully. To not believe in the continuity of things.

After Jacob left to catch the train downtown to his practice Marina walked home slowly through the park, planning the afternoon's work. More and more she found herself writing about Frieda, the young woman who had left the Satmarer sect. Was she trying to understand what makes people stay, she wondered, or what propels them to leave? She thought this notion of defection might be a way to begin. But was it the right approach? She could, she thought, write about Rose and Max, about their departure from Israel, the idea of self-imposed exile. She could write about Gizela. But then it would be a different book, one that strayed dangerously into autobiography. The reason she had chosen to write about the Romani for her first book was because it was a subject so wildly removed from her own experience. After everything that had happened with Gizela and Dov, it was a wide field, a foreign place. But everything is autobiographical in the end, Jacob would say. We never escape ourselves.

As she approached her own block, the streets grew quieter. Everyone had retreated indoors to escape the sweltering afternoon. Harlem seemed to her to have its own weather, cruelly severe and much more extreme than the rest of the city. She felt an overwhelming urge to go into her bedroom and lie down underneath the fan.

Walking towards the brownstone she saw the Rwandan girl and her child sitting on the front steps. Constance was bent over with her head resting on her knees, her hands clasped around her shins. The little boy, Gabriel, lay on his back on the step below her, his feet drumming against the iron railing. He stared at Marina as she stood at the bottom of the steps and something in his expression made her think of Ben, the way that even as a small boy he would lean in closely and try to read her, like a pensive animal following a scent. A certain coaxing of clues.

'Hello there,' she said softly.

Constance lifted her head slowly and stared up at Marina, her thin face flushed, a bleariness in her eyes as if she had just been sleeping. She stood up. Standing to attention, Marina thought, a cringe and a fear in her beneath that dark glare. How long had they been sitting there waiting for her?

'Would you like to come inside? I can make some tea.'

In the kitchen the high whistle of the kettle startled the little boy and he came to stand beside Marina at the bench. His head reached to the middle of her thigh. He watched her intently as she filled the teapot. It was far too hot for tea but she didn't know what else to offer the girl. She drank tea, Marina knew – there had been that box of tea bags in the bodega. She found a packet of ginger biscuits in the pantry and handed one to the little boy. He took it warily and retreated to the corner of the kitchen, staring at it. There was something so unusual, so elemental about him. A disconcerting gravity. Marina set out the Limoges teacups and poured milk into a small jug. It felt faintly ridiculous, this manufacturing of an impromptu tea party. Constance ignored the plate of biscuits, but she heaped sugar into her tea, clinking her spoon against the edge of the cup as she stirred. She was beautiful, Marina thought suddenly, with that lustrous skin, those sharp cheekbones. The little boy came tentatively over to the table and Marina put a cushion on one of the chairs and lifted him up. His face was just visible above the edge of the table. He carefully held the glass of cold water she poured for him, tipping his whole head back to drink.

Constance sat across the table from her, a hunch to her shoulders, her eyes down. She made no effort to respond to Marina's faltering attempts at conversation. Eventually a strenuous silence settled between them. Gabriel sat gravely at the head of the table, staring at her. He was still holding the biscuit in his hand. Marina was not quite sure what she was supposed to do. She looked around her guiltily. The house must seem impossibly, wickedly grand to the girl. But Constance seemed to show no awareness of her surroundings; there was no flicker of interest, no gaze around the room. It was as if the world had lost the ability to make any impression on her.

Finally she reached into the canvas bag on her lap and pulled out a letter. She slid it across the table towards Marina. So there was a reason for her sudden arrival. 'No understand,' she said in a low voice.

It was a notice from the Department of Social Services, addressed to Ms Constance Nsengimana. Her Public Assistance benefits and Food Stamps were being discontinued because she had failed to report to a recertification appointment at the Public Assistance office two weeks earlier. She had been advised in writing of the appointment. Now her case had been closed and she would need to reapply if she wished to continue receiving benefits. Marina read the letter over again.

Constance was staring expectantly at her, still clutching her bag. Marina folded up the letter and put it back in the envelope. She needed Leah. Leah would know the rules, the loopholes, the phone calls to be made. This was her domain: righteous indignation and advocacy. But Leah was in Guatemala. She had finally been forced to use some of her annual leave and had gone to a yoga retreat in Antigua.

Constance stared into her lap as Marina tried to explain.

'Did you get another letter? Before?'

The girl looked bewildered. 'Which letter?' she asked softly.

'From the same place.' Marina tapped the envelope on the table and Constance stared at it. 'About an appointment. A few weeks ago, maybe?' It was beginning to feel like an interrogation. She had no idea how much English Constance understood. Or if she could read. If she couldn't understand this letter, how could she have understood one about an appointment? She tried again. 'There's a problem. No more money.'

Constance stared at her, saying nothing. The same feeling came over Marina that she sometimes had before a group of students. It was a kind of internal floundering, an inability to summon up the professorial, authoritative self she needed. But with her students at least she had the refuge of the subject at hand, her careful lecture notes, her professional authority.

'No money,' Constance repeated slowly, as if she were testing out the words. Then she sighed and put her head down on the table. Marina looked at the small swirl of her ear, the pattern of the braids curving neatly back around her skull. Who braided her hair, she wondered suddenly. She knew nothing of this girl's life, the economies of the household she ran there in the projects, if she could even call it a household. What any of it, this whole existence in New York, meant to her.

As if he somehow sensed his mother's defeat, Gabriel began to cry. His arms flailed around and he knocked the water glass off the table, sending the pieces shattering across the floor. Before Marina could get to her feet, Constance reached out and slapped the child on the cheek. It was a hard slap; the crack of it seemed to fill the room. The little boy was quiet for a moment, shocked into silence before he started wailing again. Tears streamed down his face, and his mouth opened wide as he cried. Constance said something to him in her own language – a low, harsh hiss of words – and the little boy only screamed louder. He was a picture of abject misery, his whole body quivering, his face streaked with tears, lips trembling. Marina wanted to go to him, to pick him up and hold him, to wipe his face. But she was wary of undermining his mother's authority. If she comforted the little boy it would be seen as a criticism of Constance's discipline, however unwarranted, however cruel it had seemed. She couldn't insert herself between them like that.

'It's all right. It's all right, just an accident,' Marina said softly, fetching the dustpan and broom and bending to sweep up the pieces of glass. The little boy looked down at her as she crouched on the floor, and she reached out and patted him on the leg. He was wearing the same blue plastic sandals as that first day on the street several weeks earlier. The buckle was still broken and the soles were worn almost bare. The child needed proper shoes, something in leather, sturdy, fitted in a children's store. Like the shoes Ben used to wear.

As she got to her feet she heard herself explaining to Constance that she would help her. They would go to the Public Assistance office together tomorrow and sort it all out. Everything would be fixed and she would help her with money for food and rent until it was. Did she understand?

⤳

After they had gone Marina sat down at the table and took a sip of cold tea. She stared at Constance's empty cup, at the plate of ginger biscuits. It was hard to imagine they had really been here at her table, the girl and her child. When she had told Constance she would help her, there had been only a barely perceptible nod. It was the same look, Marina realised, as when she had paid for the groceries two weeks before. The girl would acquiesce to her, would allow Marina her benevolence, but she would not thank her for it.

That summer they all spoke of Constance as the Rwandan girl, rather than referring to her by her name. It was as if the country, and what had happened there three years before, was a shadow over her, exacting sorrow and also a kind of fear. There was something sharp and glittering in her eyes that unnerved those who were near her. None of them, Marina realised, knew how to approach her.

The day after Constance came to the house she, Marina and Gabriel sat for three hours on plastic chairs in a crowded waiting room at the Public Assistance office on 125th Street. They lined up at the front desk and the woman behind the counter stared at Marina. 'What are you, her social worker?' she asked. 'Yes,' Marina answered almost immediately, 'that's right.' As soon as she said it she felt a new authority. She would pretend she was someone like Leah. A valiant defender. Someone who knew how to navigate the system. It would be a similar kind of impersonation as her professorial self. 'I'm here to speak with someone about a problem with her case. It was closed in error,' she said. Standing beside her, with the little boy tied to her back, Constance was silent. The woman handed Marina a slip of paper with a number on it and directed them to the third floor. 'It's going to be a long wait to see someone if you've got no appointment,' she said, watching them as they made their way to the elevators.

From the third-floor window a view of the city unfolded drearily to the south, chimneys and iron fire escapes garlanding the buildings. Starlings rose up against the brown towers of the projects. What was it that García Lorca had said about dawn in New York groaning on fire escapes? Something about spikenards of anguish. A hurricane of pigeons. It was one of the poems she and Jacob used to read to each other. She must look it up again.

The waiting room was hot and dense, the ceiling fans broken. A young woman sitting across from them pulled a red and white box of Crown fried chicken out of her bag and started feeding the child beside her. Gabriel stood next to Marina's chair, staring at her, his finger in the corner of his mouth. At first he stayed just beyond her reach, ignoring any attempts she made to talk to him. He turned his face away from her when she looked at him. Could he be autistic? Wasn't avoidance of eye contact one of the signs? But no, Marina thought, looking over at Constance, who sat staring fixedly ahead of her, there were other reasons the little boy was like this. And she had been that way as a child, too. Never knowing where to look, what to say. So often she had felt herself to be almost invisible, to be barely existent in the world. It had startled her as a child when someone spoke her name; as if she had not expected it to be known by others. Perhaps all unsheltered children felt like this.

After a while the little boy reached out and touched the shell button of her dress, his small finger pressing against her. Constance leaned forward and swatted his hand away, pushing him hard enough that he took a few faltering steps backwards and sat down on the floor, a surprised look on his face. Then he began to cry. It was the same furious sorrow as when he had wailed in her kitchen the day before. Constance ignored him, folding her arms across her chest and turning her head away. The cries turned into angry screams, and he lay back on the floor and kicked his legs. 'Shut that kid up,' a man yelled from the other side of the room. Marina bent down and picked Gabriel up from the floor. She could not remember the last time she had held a child in her arms. He was hot and damp, the shudder of his crying still moving through his body, which was surprisingly light, but taut and strong. At first he stiffened in her arms and she thought she would have to put him down again, but then he surrendered. He let himself be held.

It struck her how unknown this child was, how unprotected. Apart from his mother and now Marina, did anyone know his name, or his birthday? He shifted in Marina's arms, leaning back tentatively at first and then succumbing, moving to make an easier place for himself against her. He stopped crying and his breathing slowed gradually. He smelt of soap.

They sat there together among rows of others in the sourness of the room, the hard cry of a woman turning away from one of the counters making them all start. Gabriel's head pressed heavily against her breast as he fell asleep, a faint tremor under one of his eyes. Looking around, she wondered how the others in the room must regard her. A white woman. A social worker. A do-gooder. It was an uneasy thing, this proximity to real need, this guilty knowledge of her higher place on the food chain. When she had dressed that morning she had tried on several outfits in front of the mirror. None seemed right. Even the simplest of her dresses felt too showy, too expensive. Eventually she had settled on a pale-blue linen dress, ballet flats. She hesitated over jewellery, wearing just her wedding ring in the end. She could not shake the uneasy feeling that she was putting on a costume for a role in a play. Leah would know what to do, would know how to coax Constance out of herself. She would know how to speak to her, how to resolve this business with Public Assistance.

When Marina was brushing her hair that morning, Jacob came in to kiss her goodbye. Marina had not told him about Constance's visit to the house the day before. She had been on the verge of bringing it up several times during the evening but had found herself hesitating. If she told Jacob about the strange afternoon tea, she would also have to tell him about the reason for Constance's visit. He would think that she had been rash to involve herself, would tell her it was not her responsibility to sort out the girl's financial affairs. It had always been there in Jacob, this ability to preserve a sensible distance from the sorrows of the world, to keep sight of the line between compassion and overstepping. Not everything could be salvaged, he had told her once. She would tell him about Constance after they had been to the Public Assistance office together, Marina decided. Over dinner, a bottle of wine between them. By then the task would be accomplished and she would hopefully have a successful mission to report on. She would turn it into a story for him, a kind of anthropological foray to relate. Yes, it was best not to alarm him unnecessarily.

When she had walked into the projects to collect Constance that morning, Marina had felt a small surge of dread and then a creeping shame at her fear. How sheltered her life had become. A few people were gathered in the foyer and they fell silent as she walked through the entrance door. A cool, watchful appraisal. There was a low whistle from one of the men and a loud burst of laughter, something ugly in it. She felt her heart thumping. The fluorescent light was flickering as if any moment it might sputter out. The lobby was stale-smelling and squalid, piles of trash and cigarette butts clustered in small eddies in the corners. The knot of men parted to let her pass and she hurried up the stairwell.

Constance opened the door immediately, as if she had been waiting for Marina's knock. Had she been standing there by the door, Marina wondered. There was no sign of the little boy and for a moment Marina thought that perhaps Constance had left him with a neighbour or a friend, but then he came out of the bedroom, standing warily in the doorway. She watched while Constance hoisted him on to her back, tying the cotton fabric firmly above her breasts. It was only nine in the morning and the girl already looked exhausted, something vacant and detached in her expression.

At last their number was called by a weary-looking young man with thick glasses, and they were ushered down a drab grey corridor and into a small cubicle. Gabriel was awake now and he sat very still on the chair between them, staring around. There was a damp patch of sweat on Marina's dress where he had been pressed against her. On the pin-up board behind the desk Marina noticed a typed Bible verse. 'Cast your cares on the Lord and he will sustain you; he will never let the righteous be shaken.' It made her feel hopeful, the sight of the laminated scripture with its background of a gaudy sunset, as if the man would somehow be required to be kind to them because of his faith. Mercy would be demanded of him. He looked like a young monk, Marina thought, as he sat there typing rapidly at his computer. There was a red apple and a small container of juice sitting in the corner of his desk, like a child's packed lunch. She thought of

Cézanne's red apple in the painting she and Jacob had seen the day before. She looked up at the Bible verse again. Were they the righteous ones?

Eventually the case worker turned to face them. An avalanche of language, terms Marina had never heard before, acronyms she could not understand. Outside, the wail of a siren rose up through the tiny window. Marina felt as if she was advocating in a language she could barely speak. She wanted to defend Constance, but she felt too tentative, too unsure of all the arcane mechanisms involved. Again, a panic-stricken sense of not knowing the right thing to say came over her. Constance herself sat there staring fixedly at her feet; she seemed not to be listening. It was as if she had removed herself entirely so none of this could touch her.

'If you don't reopen her case,' Marina said at last, 'this woman and her child will not be able to eat. They can't wait four to six weeks for a new application to be processed. Is there anything that can be done?'

The young man took off his glasses and rubbed his eyes. He picked up a green form from a tray on his desk and put his glasses back on, then sighed as if he had decided it was easier to succumb to her. To show mercy.

'It's irregular, but we'll do the recertification now. Extenuating circumstances. They can process it in twenty-four hours.'

An hour later, as they were getting up to leave, Marina thought of something else.

'If she gets a letter for another recertification, she won't be able to understand it. That's why she didn't come to the last appointment.'

'You can be her authorised representative.' The young man pulled out another form and started to fill it in before Marina could say anything. 'Copies of all correspondence will be sent to your nominated address and you can act on her behalf. Just fill in your details here and she can sign and authorise it.'

Marina hesitated. Did she really want to take on this responsibility for the girl, the intimacy of this involvement in her life? Perhaps it could just be for now. She would talk to Leah when she returned from Guatemala, see if there was some sort of service available to help. Surely people could not be left as profoundly adrift as the girl and her child seemed to be. Marina watched as Constance slowly wrote the letters of her first name at the bottom of the form. She leaned over the desk, making the shapes she had clearly memorised and then staring at the result as if it were something both miraculous and suspicious.

It was mid-afternoon by the time they emerged from the building. The sky was so grey that it seemed as though an earlier dusk had settled over the streets, a disconcerting, humid twilight. A hot wind whipped the pages of a newspaper past them as they walked down 125th Street. Nearly a century before, this had been the Harlem of the jazz era. The Renaissance. Musicians, gamblers, poets, prostitutes. Girls who came up from Carolina in pressed cotton dresses. Gangsters, tricksters, fortune tellers and preachers. The Apollo Theater, Minton's Playhouse, the Cotton Club, the Savoy Ballroom. Even the names sounded magical. Now the street was full of decrepit shopfronts, Caribbean restaurants and dollar stores. In the shadows of the elevated train lines, young men spread out blankets and sold CDs, shoes and handbags. They passed several shops advertising African hair braiding, improbably glossy wigs lined up in their windows. Did Constance come here to have her hair done, Marina wondered, looking over at the girl's dark head with its neat rows of braids.

When they reached the Starbucks on the corner of the boulevard Marina paused. 'Would you like to have some lunch? Gabriel must be hungry.' Constance said nothing but she stopped walking and stared at the café. Silence, Marina thought, must mean assent. In the café she ordered iced chocolates for all of them, cheese and salad sandwiches in plastic containers, three slices of banana bread. Gabriel stared at his drink as if it were something wondrous, poking his finger tentatively into the cream. Marina broke his sandwich into small pieces, spreading them out on a napkin for him. Constance ate slowly, making no effort to help Gabriel with his food. She had a capacity to absent herself so completely that even her child seemed invisible to her.

Halfway through the odd, improvised lunch, Marina looked up and saw Ben standing in the queue at the counter. He was with a young woman with black, heavy hair. She had a narrow face, something of the *mater dolorosa* about her. The girl was talking and Ben was staring at her with undisguised ardour. Marina could see why – she was incandescent. Shining hair falling almost to her waist, those huge eyes. She looked Spanish, or South American. Where did she come from, this luminous beauty? Wearing a sleeveless white dress that fell below her knees, she looked like she had stepped out of a Gabriel García Márquez novel, the beloved only daughter of a wealthy coffee-*finca* owner. Marina chided herself immediately for such a cliché; she was probably a graduate student at NYU. She watched the girl and Ben as they ordered their drinks. He was solicitous, attentive, touching her arm gently. His eyes were alight in a way she had not seen for a long time. There was something more pliable, looser about him. He placed his hand lightly on the small of the girl's back as they turned away from the counter, cups of iced tea in their hands. Marina wondered if they were already lovers. She had come home one day earlier that week to find two teacups in the sink. It had seemed a hopeful sign to her then – that someone had visited Ben, that they had made tea together. Now she tried to picture this girl at the kitchen table drinking tea, or sitting on the edge of Ben's single bed, bending down to unfasten her sandals.

A line came to her: 'Your body can fill my life, just as your laughter can drive away the dark wall of sadness.' It was from a poem by José Valente that Jacob had sent her, just after he had left California to return to his life in New York and she had slipped, disconsolate, back into her meagre existence. She had felt marooned, stricken, able only to lie in bed staring up at the cracked ceiling with its spreading water stains. Her pillow still held Jacob's scent from the day he left, the persistence of it increasing her desolation. He had stopped by her apartment unexpectedly on the way to the airport, the cab waiting in the street outside. When he left she stood in the window, wrapped in her Japanese robe, watching as the car slipped off into the pale dawn light, resolutely bearing Jacob away from her. She wondered then if she would ever see him again.

Two weeks later a letter arrived in her pigeonhole at the university. A twin, she remembered thinking, to the one she had slipped under his office door only three months earlier. The Valente poem, typed out on a sheet of paper. On the reverse side, in Jacob's unruly handwriting, two lines. 'I don't want to be away from you anymore. Come to New York.'

Ben stopped when he saw Marina sitting at the table by the door. She watched him take in her lunch companions with a slightly surprised look, the girl behind him. Her face was solemn and composed, a certain ruefulness there even as she smiled when Ben introduced them. Please don't let her be melancholy too,

151

Marina thought. Let her be joyful. Let her make him laugh. She was wearing a gold chain with a small cross attached to it. 'My friend, Alma,' Ben said. Nothing more. Marina echoed his words, introducing Constance as her friend too, though it felt like the wrong word entirely. Constance did not even lift her head to acknowledge Ben and Alma. *My stepson.* Marina wondered if Constance had any idea what the word meant. Did such a term even exist in the place she came from?

'All right,' Ben said. 'We're off. I'll see you later on.'

He held the café door open for Alma. Marina watched them step around a dustbin that had been tipped over on its side. Alma's white dress seemed like a hopeful sort of flag against the grey of the street. Of course Ben was in love with her; how could he not be?

Later that night Marina stood at the bedroom window, watching the last of the light fade from the sky. Nine in the evening and still there was no pure darkness. The whole day had felt faintly penumbral but now that the real dusk had fallen the weather was kinder, a breeze from the river coming through the open window. Above the street she could see the shoes suspended from the wire. Aloft and swaying gently in the wind, they seemed an entreaty. She recalled Gabriel's face as she had held him against her that morning. What were he and Constance doing now? Did they sleep together? She had only seen a single bed in the apartment.

Ben had returned home early in the evening and, for the first time in months, come downstairs for dinner. Jacob was out at a late meeting, so it was just the two of them. Marina made an omelette, opened a bottle of good wine. How many evenings had they spent together like this over the years, eating dinner or sitting with their books or watching a film? When she had returned to New York to live with Jacob, Ben was only ten years old. Jacob was still running the Child and Adolescent Psychiatry Department at Bellevue Hospital, working long hours. She remembered the frequent calls from the emergency room late at night, the unsettling jangle of the telephone and Jacob's murmured responses, the long spaces of listening. Usually those calls ended with Jacob slipping quietly into his clothes, fumbling in the darkness for his shirt, the click of the apartment door closing behind him as he left for the hospital. Sometimes he would come home before dawn for a few more hours of sleep; more often he would work on through the day. Marina watched him battle his tiredness at the dinner table on those evenings, trying for her sake, and for Ben's if he was with them, to appear animated, interested. It moved her deeply, knowing the enormous effort it must be costing him. She and Ben always knew when he was exhausted, conspired to finish dinner quickly, smiling at each other as Jacob laid his head against the back of the armchair and closed his eyes.

From very early on, it seemed to Marina, she and Ben had been knitted together by their love for Jacob, and by an equally powerful need to protect him. More recently, she wondered whether it was this long habit that prevented Ben from expressing the real depth of his current grief. Whether his need to shelter his father had created this sad gulf between them. And that perhaps, too, it was why he chose to speak to her, and not Jacob, about Alma.

Ben stood beside her at the kitchen bench as she whisked the eggs, the glass in his hand lurching as he spoke. 'Tell me about her,' Marina had said quietly as she poured them both wine. The doors to the garden were open, the early darkness casting the kitchen into dimness. Alma was the sister of Juan, a friend Ben had made working at the grocery store. They had come, Alma and Juan, from El Salvador the year before, crossing Guatemala and Mexico, through the desert. Their father had been killed several years earlier during the civil war; an older brother had been murdered after the conflict's end. Ben's description of the country that Alma and Juan had escaped was a litany of horror. Savage murders, kidnappings, rival gangs, relentless violence. And then there was the terrible journey through the desert, the border crossing. 'I know there are things she will never tell me,' Ben said. Like any lover, he wanted to rescue her. It's what we all want, Marina thought. To rescue or to be rescued.

Staring into his glass of wine after he had told her Alma's story, Ben looked grave, so sweetly earnest. At times when Marina looked at him she couldn't help imagining the bewildered face of the small boy who had wept savagely for his mother all those years ago. For so long she had believed that Ben was the very likeness of his father, but these past few months she could see traces of Leni in him. Something about the set of the mouth, the faint sloe shape to his eyes. Perhaps it was just her imagining.

She had encountered Leni only a handful of times in the decade of her marriage to Jacob, all of their meetings fraught and awkward. For the first few years Marina had lived with Jacob, Leni was a ghostly presence, revealed to her only in fragments. Whispered tales from Leah while they were washing the dishes together on Friday evenings, the odd photograph that Rose would flip quickly past in the album, Jacob's own shaky recounting. There was Leni's signature in Ben's homework diary, the name tags she sewed into the collars of his school shirts, the sandwiches Marina found uneaten at the bottom of his school bag. She would hold the grease-paper-wrapped package in her hands knowing that across the city, standing in her own kitchen that morning, Leni had made these sandwiches; had cut off the crusts and folded the bread into the neat twists of paper for her son. She and Leni held so much shared knowledge between them: the precise consistency that Ben liked his boiled eggs, his hatred of tomatoes, his insistence on flannel sheets – all these small domestic details. It was an odd thing to share a child like this, to shuttle him back and forth between their homes and yet never to speak of him together.

Following her return from London, Leni became an efficient mother. She did the things that were required of her, managing Ben's life briskly and competently. Tennis games, elaborate birthday parties, carefully planned holidays – she could not be faulted for her commitment to her son. And yet she could never redeem herself for those lost three years. Nothing that came after could stand against her decision to leave.

Leni had held a mysterious fascination for Marina in the early days of her marriage to Jacob. In the photographs of her in Rose's albums she was impenetrably beautiful. It was a cold kind of beauty, Marina had always thought, one that allowed no one close to it. Jacob looked back on that part of his life with a sorrowful bafflement. Sometimes he would refer to Ben as 'our son', meaning his and Marina's. She was touched by his generosity the first time he said it; his desire to share the joy of Ben fully with her. It was a tempting fantasy to slip into, an easy leap, but it made Marina feel uneasy too, this wistful revision of the past. Leni could never be excised from their lives like that.

Ben rarely spoke of his mother when he was with them. He knew that his life with Leni and Michael had a terrible power to wound his father. He had learned this very early on. It grieved Jacob, the idea that his son had to navigate this sort of complexity, had to hold within himself an awareness of his father's vulnerability. Jacob would have stayed with Leni, Marina believed. If she had not left him, he would have stayed. Out of hope, out of loyalty. But mostly because of his love for Ben, his desire for him not to be harmed.

Alma wanted to study medicine, Ben told Marina, offering up this aspiration hopefully, proudly, as if it might redeem everything else.

'She's incredibly clever. She taught herself English from magazines and books. She'd be a brilliant doctor.'

'But she's here illegally?'

As soon as the words were out of her mouth, Marina regretted them. How many times had Leah railed that human beings were not illegal, that it shouldn't be illegal to seek refuge? *Undocumented*. It was the word she should have used. Marina remembered the official immigration document that Constance had presented to her when she first asked her where she had come from, the solemn way that the girl had produced it. The legitimacy that had been conferred on one of these young women, but not the other.

Ben did not answer her question, as if he knew it was unworthy of her.

There was a storm that night. It seemed to last for hours, the bedroom windows rattling in the gale. Marina lay awake beside Jacob, who slept on, oblivious to the roar and shudder of the skies. She had not told him about the strange day with Constance and Gabriel, or about meeting Alma. He had come home late, pale and tired, and she had not wanted to alarm him. Now it felt as if all these things were secrets kept from him. She thought of Alma's white dress, of Ben's hand on the small of her back. And Gabriel. Marina recalled the little boy's look of timid surprise when she had picked him up from the floor, the weight of his head against her shoulder. *Gabriel.* She whispered it quietly, testing out the sound. An angel's name. It was a name she might have chosen for her own child.

Narrowsburg
January, 2000

The study was full of the steady, shadowless light of deep winter. On the crab apple tree outside the window Vera noticed a solitary red apple clinging to the bare, snow-brushed branches. Extraordinary, such tenacity. Snow had been falling against the house all week, sealing them in. She had never understood the enclosed orders, locked away from the world behind the convent walls. All that contemplation and no action. There were nuns like that in her childhood, lovely and drifting in the old garb. Veils and rosary beads, the quiet hum of prayers. The nuns of her school-days seemed to live under a great gauze of silence, everything about them hushed and quiet. The sweep of a hem along polished boards, softly falling footsteps, the gentle click of doors closing.

Vera had been on a silent retreat once, many years before, at a centre in the Arizona desert. It was after a trip to South America, travelling on crowded buses out to tiny villages to visit the scattered sisters. It had exhausted her: the long, hot hours of travel, the damp decaying smell of the jungle always near. The tropics made her long for winter, for the mist of her breath in the mornings when she set out for work. In Bolivia she had contracted malaria and spent three weeks lying in a tiny bedroom, the walls shifting and spinning around her, a yellowed mosquito net tied to the bedposts, the smell of mildew on the pillow. Lord above, she had been sure she would die there in that little netted cage.

When she had arrived at the retreat centre in the desert she was exhausted: shaky and weak, every part of her spent. The desert retreat had been an instruction not a choice. All Vera had wanted after South America was to come straight back to Harlem, to her own bed and her work. But they had decreed that she needed more rest. That the body might be better but the soul needed repose, too; something from Rilke about all things needing their just emphasis, about action not being the only way to save the poor, sullied world. Prayer just as powerful a force. Vera knew that the hierarchy of her order thought her maverick and too independent. There was only so far she could refuse them.

So a month's retreat was arranged. In the taxi from Phoenix Airport Vera had stared out of the window at the widening desert, the swathes of golden grass and the occasional swell of an orange mesa. She would think of it as a kind of limbo, she decided, a necessary waiting space before she could return to Harlem.

The retreat centre was a cluster of adobe buildings in a dusty corral. When she arrived a thin young woman took the suitcase from her hands and led Vera to her bedroom. A narrow bed with a white coverlet, a cluster of yellow flowers in a glass on the bedside table, the high afternoon sun falling through the window. There was such care in the preparation of this room: the cotton blanket folded at the end of the bed, the pitcher of iced water left out for her on the tiny desk, those yellow flowers. Someone had picked them for her. Vera lay back on the bed, pulled the blanket over her shoulders and closed her eyes.

She slept until late the next morning, waking only when the young woman, a Maryknoll novice, made her sit up in bed and drink some soup. Gradually Vera felt herself slipping into the silence of the place, the pure, clean quiet of it. And there was the relief of being tended to, as if she were a sick child. At first, every sound seemed magnified, with no rhythm of voices behind it. The flicker of an electric fan, the clang of a pot somewhere within the house, a chair scraping on the floor: everything felt more urgent and alive. At night the sounds seemed to double – the tap of the blind against the window, the rasp of the desert wind in the grasses, footsteps in the hall. But she succumbed to it after a while, as they said she would. The silence, the slow, pared-down rhythms of the day. Prayers, meals, more prayers, early nights, the pure darkness of the desert. One week and then two passed, and she began to think that, yes, perhaps she could exist in this space forever. Not tucked away from life but at the very core of it, somehow. She imagined not returning to Harlem at all, but staying there in the desert.

Her brother had been sent to the desert once by his order. A punishment. An exile. They had known about the drinking by then, though doubt was his greater crime. The drink was a weakness of the flesh; the lack of faith a failing of the soul. Far harder to remedy than a fondness for a little tipple. Lord knows it was common enough among the priests. No great sin, as long as it was kept out of sight.

Colum had written letters to her from Arizona, a handful of red sand in one of the envelopes. Perhaps he had sat bent over the small desk in this very room. Her little brother. Only seven years old when she had left home. A deep blow for him. Their mother was already exhausted by the time he was born. Worn to the bone, she said, and indeed her face was so thin that her flesh seemed only a kind of fine draping over her skeleton. Her skin might well have worn away if she had had to scrub another floor. Her poor mother. Defeated by all those children and a drunken husband. Colum was another child it was not in her power to prevent. She had taken to bed for months after he was born. Vera had been terrified that she would die, that the burden of her mother would fall to her. Their mother could not even feed Colum, only weeping silently when they tried to fasten his mouth to her breast. It was Vera who had rocked the new baby and made his bottles, and held his hand as he learned to walk. Vera who had taken him to school and taught him to tie his laces, and read to him at night. And then she had left him.

She had not seen him again until she had visited Ireland nine years later. Her mother was dead by then and her little brother had grown into a tall, quiet young man, his head always in a book. Poor Colum. Perhaps doubt was sown deep in both of them. They had their father's bad blood, after all. It was something their mother would say to them in anger.

By the third week in Arizona Vera started to take walks out into the desert. Not far from the main road, she was not that foolhardy. Just small circles away from the retreat centre – north to the crumbling bus shelter, south to the sign that marked the beginning of the Navajo Nation. She asked to borrow the centre's old station wagon so she could drive to the Painted Desert. Something about it reminded her of the sea. The vast quiet of it, the high sky and the strange rocks rising up from the dust. By her fourth week she was driving into the railroad town of Winslow every day, hungry for the world again. There were Ukrainian sisters in the town who worked with Navajo women; a domestic violence shelter with its own thrift shop and soup kitchen; a Jehovah's Witness Hall. The world was where she had always wanted to be – not down on her knees praying.

Something about the snow made Vera think of that time in the desert so many years ago. The safe, sealed-in space of it before she had stepped back into the world. In Narrowsburg she was trying for the same relinquishing, had prayed for some turning in her soul, an enlargening grace that would help her in her work here. Lord, grant me patience. It was something her own mother had said, eyes raised to the heavens, hands joined earnestly at her chest, when there was mischief with the younger children – a glass broken or a wild squabble.

It surprised Vera how often childhood came drifting back to her here. Perhaps it was because so many of the nuns had slipped into the swirls and eddies of their own pasts. A childhood farm, a lost brother, a yearning for a toffee apple. All these slippages of the mind, the brittleness of memory. Vera was terrified that she would succumb to it, too, in time: the drift into unreason, the childlike confusion. Would she recognise it at once, Vera wondered, or would the failing be a slow glide, a barely perceptible relinquishing? It was harder, she had come to realise after these years in Narrowsburg, for the sisters who knew that their minds had begun to give way. Better that her body failed first, that a heart attack felled her swiftly. A merciful exit.

Seven deaths since they had come here, three sisters gone just this winter. The week before, they had buried Sister Cecile, rain falling slant-wise at them as the coffin was lowered into the sodden ground. It had been just her and Constance and the priest by the graveside, holding their umbrellas. Afterwards, she found the girl bent over the sink in the laundry scrubbing her hands. It was Rwandan custom, Constance had told her when Vera railed at her about wasting water, to wash your hands after burying the dead. For the last weeks of Cecile's life, Constance had slept in her room, curling up on a mat on the floor beside the old woman's bed. Vera watched the girl standing silently by the sink, her hands still under the tap. Perhaps there would be some unstitching in her now. A loosening brought on by grief. Spare me any more of the sorrows of others, Vera had thought to herself and then immediately recoiled from the uncharitable turn of her thoughts these days. What kind of Christian was she?

The other nuns stayed indoors during the funeral, clustered around the heater, crocheting blankets for poor babies. It gave them something to do, though the money for the wool was another stretch in Vera's budget. The boiler had stopped working the day Cecile died. The wretched clacking and ticking of it had driven Vera mad all winter, until suddenly it fell silent and the nuns were plunged into frigid cold. The convent was too big to heat. What they needed was a wood-burning stove, an old Aga, perhaps. But then there would be wood to chop and lug in from the shed, kindling to forage for. More work for her and Constance. Still, a fire would be a comfort.

Sometimes it felt to Vera that with every passing month they all slid further back into older times, cut off from the world up here in the mountains. They rarely went into town anymore. There was a doctor who came to the house, a guiltily lapsed Catholic who felt sorry for the decrepit band of old nuns in their straitened circumstances. The supermarket delivered to them once a week, and they grew a great deal of what they needed now that the garden was so established. In the warmer months it flourished, and she and Constance would spend hours out there on their knees among the rows of vegetables, weeding and tending. The girl was not afraid of work, Vera could certainly say that for her.

She could see Constance now, making her way down the front path, swathed in her coat and scarf, a plastic container in her hands. Even bulked up in her winter gear the girl looked like a beanpole. Far too skinny. Faithful old Lily ambled after her, picking up her feet on the treacherous path. A blue jay flitted past the barberry bushes, and the girl and dog both turned to watch its path. Those bushes would have to be cut back in the spring. Their nearest neighbour, an old farmer down the end of the road, had told her that the barberries were a magnet for deer tick. He shook his head sorrowfully as he gazed out at the wild tangle of bushes, his face full of pity for the foolish old nuns. All summer they had checked their arms for burrowing creatures. Instead of divine revelation, the knowledge that came to her now was about practical things, Vera thought. Ticks and planting and mending. Perhaps it was a better way to love God. Tilling the soil. Reaping and sowing.

She watched Constance spreading a sticky paste over the branches of the trees with a small paintbrush. The dog stayed close to her. The paste that Constance was applying so care-fully was some concoction she had made to feed the birds. She wanted to help them, the girl had said when Vera told her that this kind of feeding was an interference with the natural world. The branches seemed stark against the white of the sky. Her work done, Constance stood very still on the snow-covered grass by the trees. Waiting for birds to come, Vera supposed. She remembered a winter in the city, perhaps three or four years ago, when she had come home to the brownstone to find Constance standing on the sidewalk with Cecile and one of the other sisters, her hand outstretched to the falling snow, alarmed confusion on her face.

'It's Constance's first snow,' Cecile had said excitedly. 'I showed her a snowdome at the beginning of winter but now she can see the real thing.' Constance and the child stood there on the sidewalk in stunned bewilderment, the snow spiralling in the wind, the fall of it becoming slowly heavier. The little boy looked stricken, the expression on his face not wonder at all; closer to terror. How odd, Vera had thought, that something that might have been a novel delight should cause this incipient fear. What had happened to them?

Cecile had been sure that she would eventually reach the girl back in those days. She had tried so hard. Constance's name was always on the prayer list they kept pinned to the refrigerator in the Harlem kitchen. And the child's name, too.

Vera wondered sometimes if she had done the right thing in allowing Constance to stay with them in Narrowsburg. Should she have turned her back into the world? But the truth of it was that they could not survive here now without her help. Cecile and the others had fretted about Constance when they had left the city. The girl seemed so unmoored. She knew no one, had refused resolutely to engage with any service that could have helped her. Taciturn, Vera had thought back then, though that was hardly fair. God alone knew what she had been through in Rwanda.

Cecile had written to Constance every week in the first months after they had moved here. Vera would watch the old nun walking slowly down the path to the letterbox, flicking up the little plastic flag for the postman. Perhaps there would be someone who could read the letters to her, Cecile had said, and even if there was not, at least the girl would feel them as a kindness. She would know she was in somebody's thoughts. Cecile had pressed flowers to send to Constance, sketched the curve of the mountains, folded scarlet leaves between the pages. Sometimes she copied out psalms. There was never any reply.

Watching Constance from the window, Vera wondered what had become of those letters. Had they been a comfort to the girl, or merely baffling – another thing about the world that Constance failed to understand? Had anyone read them to her? When Vera had commented on Constance's expensive new winter coat and boots, the girl said that a friend had bought them for her. Hard to imagine what kind of friend the girl could have had to lay out so much money. Had this person read Cecile's words to Constance? Whatever the answer, the letters had brought Constance here to Narrowsburg after her child died. When she arrived three winters ago she was clutching one of the envelopes, the address of the convent clearly written in Cecile's looping hand.

Harlem
August, 1997

In summer the heat and the absence of routine made the days feel long and untethered; the hours seemed to unspool in a different way. Her weeks during semester were so structured and predictable, Marina realised, her hours neatly catalogued. There was never any time to be idle.

She lay in bed watching the spill of sunlight on the floorboards. So much brightness early in the day. And yet in winter she complained about the insufficiency of the light, the shortness of the days. The blare of a car horn sounded outside the window, then two voices shouting. Their old apartment on Park Avenue had been immensely quiet, insulated from the noise of the street below. She far preferred the brownstone, which felt somehow properly located.

Marina reached for the book on the nightstand. Rilke. She had not been able to sleep the night before and had slipped out of bed to find the volume she wanted from the study. Standing in front of the bookshelves she had heard footsteps and the low murmur of voices from the floor above. She had listened for the softer tones of a woman's voice, wondering if Alma was upstairs with Ben. As far as she knew, the girl had not spent the night there before. Marina was still unsure if Alma and Ben were lovers. Ben was clearly enchanted but she had noticed a sweet shyness between the two of them, as if they had not yet given each other the permission needed for greater intimacy. And there was that gold cross around Alma's neck.

Dawn was already close, and the study felt hushed and penumbral, the street outside strangely quiet, the only sound the muted overlap of voices from above. Marina sat in Jacob's armchair with her feet tucked up beneath her, the book open in her lap. She always reached for poetry when she was sleepless, as if words released from the bend of narrative might lull her back into restfulness. It was what she was always looking for in her own work, too: the compression and lilt of poetry.

Marina Tsvetaeva had once said that an entire age could be forgiven just because Rilke had lived in it. How many times has she read the letters between Tsvetaeva and Rilke? That brief flare of correspondence, with its ravenous passion, its almost unseemly adoration. Tsvetaeva still writing after Rilke's death. Her long elegy to him, composed in the cold hush of a French winter; impossible, it seemed to her, that the world no longer contained her beloved poet. Who would not want a love like that? Writing their letters between the wars, the two could not have known how swiftly the future would devour them. Rilke dying of leukaemia in Switzerland, Tsvetaeva hanging herself in Russia in the middle of the war.

When she was a child it had made Marina uneasy to know that the poet she had been named for had died like this. By her own hand. There was something archaic about the ring of the words. Someone had said them about Dov when he died – she couldn't remember who; it seemed so long ago. Certainly not her mother. Marina couldn't help thinking of her brother's hands when the news of his death came. His long fingers stretching out to catch hers as they skated in loops around the Lasker Rink the winter before he died. The shadow pattern of leaves in the park, the slippery crust of the path, the smell of wet wool.

In all the photographs she possessed of her brother he looked like one of the pale-faced Hasidic boys who swarmed the Brooklyn streets around them. There was a thinness to his face and a fearsome hunger. Something fervent and unanswered. At times she wished Dov had left a letter for her. In those first days after his death she had been convinced he must have written something, that among his possessions she would find an envelope addressed to her. The lost letter took on a kind of mythic possibility. It might contain a startling insight, something unknown to her. It might tell her what she should do. Blank with sorrow, she imagined the letter tossed into the rubbish, left to mould in a dusty corner. But there was no need for Dov to write to her, she realised in the end. She knew all his grief. A letter setting it out would not have been a comfort but a kind of haunting. What could he possibly have said that she did not already know?

She had felt the loss of him like a phantom limb, a wail rising up in her at night that she tried frantically to contain. The night after the funeral, she had slipped out of the apartment and walked to the Botanic Garden. At the Steinhardt Conservatory she looked in through the glass panes of the tropical pavilion. Through the cold glass she saw the rich green riot of ferns, the odd tropical plants and the purple orchids. She and Dov had loved the constant humid hush of the place, the complete eradication of the outside world. She must withstand this, she remembered thinking. That night she sat for a long time under the bare trees near the Japanese garden, Dov's grey scarf wrapped around her throat. It had not felt impossible, then, that she might see her brother walking towards her over the red bridge. That they might turn and walk back towards home together.

Dov was twenty-two years old when he died. He had been named David for the king. God's chosen one. It had been voted on by all the kibbutz members. No one was named out of sentimentality, or to commemorate a lost relative. They were all given Israeli names; names that did not contain any shadow of a European past. Even Dov's nickname had been given to him by a nursery worker, not by their mother. Strange, then, that her father had been so insistent on her own name. Such an inadequate and unreliable collection of stories existed about him. Sometimes Marina thought that Gizela had deliberately withheld information from them out of a kind of cruelty. She did not know why Yoav had loved the Russian poet, which poem had been his favourite. He never spoke of it, Gizela had always claimed, except to insist that their daughter be named for Tsvetaeva. It had caused an enormous fuss on the kibbutz, but Yoav was insistent about the name and in the end they allowed him to have his way. Marina had always suspected that the name was linked to some other, more private commemoration. His mother, or a sister. A lover, perhaps. Someone before Gizela.

Once in a while Marina took out the photograph of her father, the one that the kibbutz museum had sent her. For a time she had kept it in a wooden frame on her desk, but it felt false to her. It made her think of a man she had known in California, someone she had not spoken to for a long time. He had no family

170

heirlooms, no hallowed objects, so he trawled yard sales and second-hand shops collecting sets of silver cake forks, cut crystal vases, brass candlesticks. He attached an invented story to each object: a tablecloth that had been embroidered by a great-aunt, a wicker rocker that his grandmother had loved. The stories grew more and more detailed, the objects he collected more personal. A worn spectacle case, a hand-tatted lace collar, a walking cane with a carved handle. He dreamed up names of lost relatives to match the intricately monogrammed initials on old pieces of linen. This man had seen his inventions as a kind of rescue. He had saved all of these lost objects from oblivion, woven them back into history, and in doing so created a history for himself. It had made Marina feel deeply uncomfortable. It seemed to her like a plundering, not a restoration. She could not help thinking of the original, vanished owners, the true names of the long-dead women who had carefully stitched their initials on pillowcases and napkins.

When she looked at the photograph of her father on her desk she had thought of the Californian man's house, his desire to fashion a substantial past for himself. The black-and-white image of her father in its handsome walnut frame could have been plucked from an estate sale. He was completely unknown to her, someone she held no claim on. She possessed no memory of his face or the sound of his voice. She could not remember ever being carried in his arms. It was possible, Marina knew, that he had never held her.

From the very beginning, Dov had hated the Children's House. He wanted only to be with his parents. The story of his obstinate misery was told to Marina and him many times by Gizela. It was clear it had bewildered her – Dov's tearful defiance, his stubborn

171

clinging, the strange inwardness that she had seen very early in him. He had not known any other way, had been raised from the beginning away from his parents, with all the other children. But he only wanted his mother. Three weeks old, colicky and despairing, he cried all night, stiff and furious in the arms of the nurses. As soon as he could walk he began his night-time wanderings. Slipping silently from his bed in the dormitory and putting on his sandals in the darkness, he would make his way across the grounds of the kibbutz, past the newly built dining hall and laundry rooms to the building on the edge of the fields where the married couples lived. Dov knew which room belonged to his parents, and he would open the unlocked door and curl up on the floor beside their bed. Gizela told them that one night she had stepped out of bed and straight on to the small heap of her sleeping son. Each time Dov came, Yoav would have to gather him up and carry him back to the Children's House. But the next night he would try again. Eventually she and Yoav were moved to another building on the far side of the kibbutz, too far for the little boy to walk.

Couldn't an exception have been made? Marina had asked her mother once. If it was so distressing for Dov, couldn't permission have been granted for him to sleep with his parents? It was not the way of the kibbutz, Gizela told her. He could not stay with them. It was done for the sake of the children and the country. They were Sabras and they needed to be strong. None of this clinginess and fear. Even as a child, it had sounded like propaganda to Marina. A rehearsed socialist narrative. It was hard for her to imagine such a pragmatic coldness. But everyone on the kibbutz had come out of Europe. They had all been wrenched from the known world, where mothers tended their children and ordinary domestic intimacies were possible. Perhaps their ability to love their children in the old ways had been scoured out of them, along with everything else.

Marina thought of Constance and Gabriel. She had seen them several times since the visit to the Public Assistance office. The girl was harsh on the child, quickly moved to impatience and anger with him. She would grip him roughly by the arm, slap him across the legs, flick his cheek in annoyance when he complained. At other times, she would ignore him with a stubborn persistence. It reminded her of Gizela, this ability to withdraw. Apart from Constance's bursts of anger at him, there was not one hint that she had made room for her child inside herself, not a flicker of affection or concern. She looked away while a doctor drew blood from his arm, absently set him down on a chair or the floor when he tried to climb into her lap, pushed his hand away if he reached for the food on her plate. There was not even any tenderness in the way she tied him to her back – she would reach behind her to slap his bare leg if he wriggled.

Marina knew nothing about Constance's life before, but she had read about the squalor of those refugee camps, the fight for food, for water, for safety. Surely there must have been a fierce love, some primal protective instinct, to have kept a baby alive all those months there? To have brought him with her to America. But whatever fight had been in her then, whatever might have sharpened her devotion to the child in Rwanda, seemed to have sunk away, like the rest of her, into irretrievable depths.

If Constance had retreated into a terrible blankness, the little boy seemed to have a surfeit of feeling. He would submerge himself in fits of the kind of pure rage and desolation she had witnessed that first day she had come across the two of them on

173

the sidewalk. There was a misery in him that was profoundly distressing to Marina. Anger, too. One day, at the 96th Street subway station, it had taken both her and Constance to hold him down, to drag him flailing and screaming on to the train and hold him fast on the seat. Marina had watched Constance's small hands clamped around the child's ankles, her face impassive. When Gabriel finally quietened, his head buried in Marina's lap, a gasp threaded through his sobs, Constance took her hands away, stood up and went to sit on the bench opposite them. She leaned her head back against the window and closed her eyes.

Gabriel never laughed or spoke. Marina had not heard one word pass his lips, just as she rarely heard his mother speak to him, in her own language or in any other. Constance barely said anything at all, mumbling a response to a nurse or an official when it was required, or letting Marina answer for her, staring down at her feet, or out the window, or simply closing her eyes. At first, Marina tried to fill the silence between them, telling Constance about the failed cake she had made the day before, the cat that appeared in her garden crying for milk. But the narration of the small contours of her own daily life faltered in the face of Constance's silence, the hard stare the girl sometimes turned on her. Marina often felt inept when she was with Constance and yet there was the sense that with every hour they spent together they were binding themselves to each other in an unspoken but irreversible pact.

Something about Constance reminded Marina of an injured thrush that Ben had found on the dunes one summer on Fire Island and brought home wrapped in his beach towel. The silent fury of the wounded creature, its stubborn huddle in the corner of the cardboard box. They barely knew how to care for the bird, despairing at its refusal to eat or drink anything that they placed before it. Marina remembered Ben's bewildered sorrow. The starving bird's eventual miserable succumbing to their proffered crusts of bread did not seem like any kind of victory.

Constance took the money that Marina slipped into her hand without ever meeting her eyes, a nod of her head instead of any words of thanks. It felt uneasily like a transaction to Marina, as if she were trying to buy her way into the girl's life. Still, she had seen the figures on the letters from the Public Assistance office – barely enough money for anyone to survive on. Marina was stunned at the paltriness of Constance's monthly budget. It was no wonder she had not been able to pay for her groceries all those weeks ago. How did she live?

But was living even the right word for Constance? She seemed to coast along the daily paths of her existence with a glazed sheen to her eyes, a numbed sort of antipathy. She kept herself and the child clean and fed, scrubbed the floors of her apartment with bleach, washed clothes in the kitchen sink, mixed bottles of formula, shopped at the Pathmark grocery store on 125th Street or at the bodega, brought her letters to Marina to decipher. The rest of her life, its pitch and roll, the real shape of it, was a mystery. Sometimes Marina wanted to put her hand over Constance's, or place her fingers against her cheek, but she always hesitated. What could her touch possibly mean against such a history?

Downstairs in the kitchen Jacob had folded the paper expertly, as if he were on a train and had only a small space in which to read. He was absorbed, reaching absent-mindedly for his cup of coffee. There was an open jar of marmalade on the table, made for him by a patient, the label carefully hand-printed. He was always bringing these small, tender offerings home. A box of chocolates, a loaf of rye bread, a punnet of raspberries. Technically he should not accept gifts, but he reasoned that it would embarrass his patients if they were refused. Marina stood in the doorway watching Jacob spread marmalade on to his toast. In those first cautious days in California she had longed for this – the drift of newspapers over a kitchen table, a pot of coffee cooling on the counter; these daily intimacies.

She poured herself a cup of coffee, kissed Jacob on the cheek. He caught hold of her hand. 'You were up most of the night,' he said. Her sleeplessness troubled him in the same way that Ben's sadness did. It was his fear of a deforming shadow, something not steady in her mind. Something that love could not touch. Jacob wanted the people in his care to be well and untroubled, for their griefs to be resolvable ones.

Marina sat down at the table. The wood gleamed in the sunlight. Jacob looked tired himself. He rubbed his eyes, finished his cup of coffee. 'I've been reading about some birds down in Utah,' he said. 'A whole flock of grebes heading south to Mexico crash-landed in a Walmart parking lot. Thousands of them, it says. It took days for them to clear away all the bodies. There were storm clouds that made the concrete look like a flat stretch of water. So the birds landed to rest, but ended up slamming into the pavement.'

Marina leaned over his shoulder to read the story. 'There is no precise count of the dead,' it said, 'although officials estimated that it exceeded fifteen hundred.'

'I'm sorry. It's a sad story. All those birds plunging blithely to their deaths,' said Jacob, spreading out his hands. 'How are birds supposed to know about things like parking lots?'

She slipped her arms around him and bent down to rest her face against his shoulder for a moment. Sometimes the texture of his thinking seemed so familiar to her that she felt he might be another, better version of herself.

Later that morning she stood at the corner of the park waiting for Constance and Gabriel. It was nearly September and she was longing for the weather to change, the haze of heat to recede. There was always such a sense of relief when the fall set in, with its cold spatters of rain and the promise of snow.

A cluster of pigeons descended upon an abandoned sandwich on the sidewalk with a startling flap of wings. Constance and the child appeared around the corner. Gabriel looked very small. As soon as he saw Marina, he broke free of his mother's grip and ran towards her. He dived at her, his arms wrapped around her legs.

If one part of the little boy was rage and fury, the other was reeling hunger, a deprivation Marina could sometimes feel humming in him when she held him. She was surprised at how quickly he had succumbed to her affection, how greedily he had begun to seek her out after his initial wariness. Now he whimpered and scrabbled against her as if he were trying to climb up her body, an urgency to his need. She had heard Jacob speak once about the kind of foraging practised by orphans, or by the children of neglectful or abusive parents. Not for food or shelter, but for affection. For some scrap of sustaining emotion, some recognition. Small kindnesses they could make use of to right themselves in the world. She had done it herself, she realised. A nurse in the Children's House, a kind teacher in Brooklyn, Mrs Zelman.

Marina bent down and picked up the little boy, kissing his hot cheek as he pressed his face into her shoulder. Constance slowly approached them. There was never any greeting from her except a shy ducking of her head that Marina had come to

177

realise was the girl's way of saying hello. How precarious this all was, Marina thought as she shifted Gabriel in her arms. For the past few weeks Constance had brought her letters and notices, and she had accompanied her to appointments and clinic visits, tried to decipher things for her. Today was a visit to the doctor. Constance needed her help, and yet every hour she spent with the girl felt to Marina as though it might be the last one. She might tie her child to her back and glide out of Marina's life as abruptly as she had stepped into it.

They walked together towards the subway, Gabriel still in Marina's arms. She bent down to put him on his feet but he fought her, kicking his legs and crying out frantically, so she gave in and carried him on her hip. Constance ignored them, trailing a few steps behind. Jacob thought that all of this, her entanglement with the girl and the child, was ill-advised. It was a dangerously encumbering role that she was playing, he had told her. With Constance, but especially with the little boy.

Gabriel twisted his legs tightly around her waist as they walked. How swiftly the smell of him had become familiar to her; his clean, soapy warmth. She knew that Jacob was right to be concerned. The risk of harm. She should not let the child become attached to her. He was not hers. But every time she saw him her caution vanished. Gabriel would only feel it as a cruelty if she were to try now to put distance between them, she reasoned. Another baffling rejection. Better that he knew the feeling of love, even if it turned out only to be fleeting.

In the waiting room at the hospital a nurse gave Gabriel a picture book. He held it tentatively in his hands. It struck Marina that the child might never have seen a book. Constance would not read to him. Gabriel slipped down from his chair and came to stand by Marina, leaning against her legs and resting his arm on her thigh. She opened the book and started to read the story, pointing to the words as she spoke them. Gabriel stared up at her, open-mouthed. So much about the world seemed to bemuse him.

The only child Marina had ever read to was Ben. Always with him there had been the sense that he was somewhere ahead of her. That he understood more of the story than she did. Not necessarily the words, but something at its core. She and Ben still shared books, passing novels between them. It was another sign of hope, Marina felt, that he had never abandoned his love of reading.

The doctor called them in at last. He was a mild Indian man, a lilt to his voice. He came from Madurai in the south, he had told Marina at their last visit. A town of temples. 'We have too many gods and too many people in India,' he said to her. He had a gentle way with Gabriel; there was never anything brusque or businesslike about him. 'Hello again, little man,' he said, extending his hand formally to the boy, who looked at him in surprise. The doctor did not wear a wedding ring and Marina wondered fleetingly if she could find a way to introduce him to Leah. She laughed about it with Rose, this incessant matchmaking of theirs. 'When did I turn into a bossy Jewish matchmaker?' she had asked Rose as they washed the dishes together the week before.

'When you have found love, you want everyone else to have it, too,' Rose said. 'Happiness makes us generous. When I first met Max I was unbearable. I just about drove my brothers mad with my romantic conniving. They refused to go out in public with me in case I tried to set them up with some unsuspecting girl.'

'I actually thought for a moment about propositioning that doctor for Leah,' Marina said. 'He would have thought I was crazy.'

'Who knows? He might have said yes. He's probably lonely.'

'Well, why don't you come along to the next appointment and we'll do a joint pitch. We can take him a photo.'

'Sssh. She'll kill us,' Rose laughed.

She and Rose had both turned to watch Leah, bent over the Scrabble board in the dining room with Jacob and Ben. Jacob played with maddening slowness, agonising over his letters, and the other two were huddled in conversation. Marina wondered if Ben was telling Leah about Alma. Perhaps he was asking her advice about the girl's immigration status. Leah had her arm draped lightly over Ben's shoulders, her head close to his.

'The thing about having children,' Rose said, 'is that you learn it is possible to feel someone else's pain more deeply than your own. It's the cliché of motherhood, I know. But it's true.'

Constance sat silently while the Indian doctor listened to her chest. She and Gabriel both had tuberculosis. The doctor had smiled at Marina's horrified face when she had learned this on their first visit. It was much commoner than you would think, he had told her. Even here in New York. Not just a nineteenth-century disease, after all. Many of those who came from refugee camps had it, especially the children. There were very good new drugs now. It was not something to kill you anymore. And not easily contagious; it was not a risk for her.

Constance and Gabriel were nearly at the end of their long

course of medication. 'Just a few more weeks,' the doctor said to Constance, 'and you'll be good as new.'

They walked home along the edge of the park, Gabriel holding Marina's hand, singing as he walked. When she had first heard him singing, she thought it must be a Rwandan song; that it had come to him from Constance, or from a time before their life in New York. But the words were made up, Constance told her when she asked about the song. They were not words at all. It was no song she knew.

The little boy's world was so small. For so long it had contained only Constance. No one sang to him or read to him. He had never been to a library, a swimming pool, a zoo. The week before, they had stopped at a small playground and he had hung back in alarm, watching the other children clambering up the play fort and down the slide. He did not know what to do, Marina had realised. She lifted him up and hauled him to the top of the slide. A look of amazement had come over him as he slid down, clutching her hand tightly all the way. It was the closest thing she had seen to pleasure on his face.

When they reached the Museum of Natural History, Marina stopped and turned to Constance. 'Would you like to go in? It's a museum.'

The girl stared at her uncomprehendingly, her lips slightly open. With hardly any shared language between them, how would Constance know what a museum was? In a way her world was just as limited as her child's.

'There are elephants,' Marina said. 'And lions. Lots of animals from Africa.' All these relics of another world, possibly the one Constance had lost. Were there elephants and lions in Rwanda?

How little she really knew about Constance's country. On all the maps it was so tiny that its printed name barely fitted inside the sliver of colour.

The three of them walked up the stairs and into the cavernous entrance hall. Gabriel stared in bewildered wonder at the enormous dinosaurs looming above them, their tapering spines arcing elegantly towards the ceiling of the atrium. In the intricate traceries of their skeletons the spirit of the creatures could somehow be felt. They were beautiful and terrifying at the same time. How Ben had loved these dinosaurs. He once climbed beneath one, lying on his back and staring up, transfixed, at the solid casing of its ribs. A little boy encased in a great ship of bones. He loved most of all knowing that his father had come to see them as a boy – this seemed to him more miraculous than the dinosaurs themselves. On one outing to the museum Ben had stood solemnly before each display and asked the same question: 'Did my father see this giraffe? Were these elephants here when my father was little?' She could see in him the fascinated awareness of lives that existed before he did, his delight in the symmetries between his father's childhood and his own. Sometimes he still stopped by the museum, he had told her not so long ago, just to look at the dinosaurs. She wondered if he would ever bring Alma here, if he would offer up his childhood to her like some secret, tender gift. She hoped so.

Constance followed them as they walked through the museum. The girl always acquiesced to Marina's suggested itineraries when they were out on an errand together. A café, a shop, a visit to the playground, she never refused anything. Marina would like to have seen this as an agreement of trust between them, but Jacob had pointed out to her that Constance might not feel she was able to say no. By casting herself as the girl's benefactor, had Marina removed any agency Constance might have had? What if she detested the hot chocolates in crowded cafés, the shopping trips to buy sensible shoes, the visits to parks? How could she ever express this?

There was something unnerving about the painstakingly constructed dioramas in the hall of African animals. Behind each glass window was an entire world, the animals carefully arranged to look as if they were in the wild. A pride of lions grouped around a waterhole, a baby zebra nestling against its mother's side, an ostrich raising its wings. All of this against elaborately painted backdrops. The hall was dim and hushed, each tableau lit up with its own simulated sunlight. It was as if the ghosts of the animals were watching them.

If there was any flicker of recognition in Constance, she revealed nothing. Standing before the animals in their counterfeit wildernesses, her face remained impassive, as though nothing she saw had any power to make an impression on her. Perhaps another kind of woman could have befriended Constance more adeptly than Marina had, coaxed her under an assured wing. Someone stronger or jollier might have drawn her out in a different way. It was impossible to describe the precise nature of their relationship, if indeed it was any sort of relationship. My friend, she called Constance to doctors and officials and shop assistants, but in truth it was not a friendship. Just an existence in the same space of waiting and uneasiness, the contours of their own folded lives unknown to each other. Then there was their shared currency. Gabriel.

The little boy stood solemnly before one of the more elaborate dioramas, his face very close to the glass. Marina crouched down behind him and pointed to the animals, telling him their names.

He leaned back, making a place for himself against her. He did not speak, but his lips moved as if he were testing out the shapes of words. Looking up, Marina saw that Constance was watching them. The girl's arms were clasped behind her back, a pensive air about her.

On the second floor, Marina led Constance and Gabriel into the Hall of New York City Birds. She wanted to show them creatures that they might see here in the city, birds she could point out to them in Central Park. It seemed important that they learned the names of things, a form of knowledge that could locate them. An antidote to everything that had been lost. She had been rereading *A Passage to India* and she thought suddenly of the scene where Ronny and Adela try and fail to identify a strange green bird they see in a tree. To know the bird's name would somehow have solaced their hearts, Forster had written. A lion or an elephant might seem too large and abstract a notion for Gabriel, but she could find him a wren or a sparrow here in the city. She wanted him to come to know New York as his own place. His home.

The room was dim and hushed. There were no elaborate dioramas, no attempts to create the illusion of life. The birds were arrayed in rows in long glass cabinets, small cardboard tags tied to their feet. Study skins, Marina remembered they were called. Preserved for scientists, not to entertain museum-goers. The birds seemed unbearably melancholy, pinned neatly to cardboard. They were so inert, so irretrievably dead. She had not been here for a long time and she had forgotten how macabre the display was, how gruesome the birds looked. It was not a place to bring a child.

Beside her Constance lurched away from the cabinets, her hand to her chest. The girl looked stricken, a deep and terrible surprise crossing her face. She gave a rending, guttural wail. Marina was stunned. She put her hand on Constance's shoulder.

'I'm sorry, it's awful. We can leave.'

But Constance leaped away from her touch as if she had been scalded, and turned and ran out of the room. Marina watched her disappear down the empty corridor, her plastic sandals slapping against the floor. She picked up Gabriel and hurried down the stairs after her, but when they reached the ground floor there was no sign of Constance.

Surely the girl would come back. Marina sat for a long time in the entrance hall of the museum, waiting for Constance to return. Gabriel ran up and down the room, seemingly unconcerned by his mother's absence. A panicked sense of shame engulfed her. How could she have taken Constance into that gallery? All those rows of tiny bodies. The unmistakable presence of senseless death. It had been artfully disguised with the animals downstairs, but the still, slick bodies of those birds seemed horrifying. Marina found it difficult to keep from crying, and her sorrow had a confused, amorphous nature. She was not sure whether it was the birds or Constance she wanted to weep for. Perhaps, she thought, it was herself.

A museum guide touched her on the shoulder. 'Excuse me, ma'am,' the woman said. 'Your little boy has gone into the butterfly exhibit.'

Marina jumped to her feet. How could she have let him out of her sight for even an instant?

In the conservatory Gabriel was standing completely still in the middle of the walkway. Around him, like a strange halo, was a cloud of brightly coloured butterflies. Against the greenery, the yellow of their wings looked even more improbable. It was like an image from a dream, or from a fairy tale. After the grimness of the dead birds, the butterflies felt like a miracle of redemption. Such unforeseen abundance. Gabriel was staring up, transfixed, his hand outstretched. It was the first time, Marina realised, that she had seen him smile.

At home later that afternoon, Marina sat in the armchair by the windows with Gabriel asleep in her arms. He had cried and clung to her when she had tried to put him down on her bed. She could feel the rise and fall of his small chest and the quick, steady beating of his heart. She put her hand against his cheek. He seemed to her to possess the most singular beauty, a kind of hypnotic perfection. She could stare at him for hours. All mothers believe their children to be the most beautiful in the world, Rose had told her once. But Gabriel was not her child. No matter how swiftly she had fallen for him, he did not belong to her. She thought of the way he had sobbed when she had deposited him on the bed just now, the frantic scrabble as he had thrown himself against her. All of this was fraught with danger, but the greatest peril, she realised, was for this damaged child sleeping in her arms.

When Marina moved her legs Gabriel moaned quietly in his sleep and pressed himself closer to her. He tucked his head into her neck and she rested her cheek against his soft hair. The pale curtains moved slowly beside them in the faint afternoon breeze. She was making a promise to the little boy, Jacob had told her, that could not be kept.

Marina had waited a long time at the museum for Constance to return. Eventually she walked north through the park towards Harlem, Gabriel beside her, his hand in hers. When they reached the projects Marina climbed very slowly up the stairs. She was afraid, she realised, to face Constance. She kept thinking of the flinch that had moved through the girl's whole body, her cry as she fled the room. Marina imagined a descent into a grief that she would not be able to rescue Constance from. Or, worse, that the girl would stand before her in some sort of angry accusation; that she would blame her for the birds and never want to see her again. So often with Constance, Marina felt that the girl had sized her up and found her wanting. Here was another example of her own ignorance, her failure to understand anything important. Perhaps this would be the end of whatever relationship they had forged these past weeks.

When Marina knocked on the door to the apartment there was no answer. She pressed her ear to the thin plywood, listening for movement inside. She knocked harder on the door and called Constance's name. A large Puerto Rican woman emerged from the next apartment, a red scarf tied around her glossy wig. There were small droplets of sweat on her forehead. She stared suspiciously at Marina.

'You from Children's Services?' she asked.

Marina wondered later why the woman had asked that. If it was only because she was white, or if there was some other reason for her question. Had Children's Services been involved with Constance and the child? They led such unnoticed lives she found it hard to believe that anyone would intervene in them. But she thought of the times she had seen Constance strike the child, or push him away roughly. Perhaps someone else had seen this.

'No,' she said to the woman. 'I'm just looking for Constance. I'm her friend. Have you seen her?'

The woman gave her a hard stare but said nothing, stepping back into her apartment and closing the door with a bang.

By the time Jacob came home that afternoon, Gabriel had woken and was sitting at the kitchen table eating an apple she had cut into quarters for him. Jacob had never met the little boy before. He knew of him only from Marina's descriptions. He frowned when she told him what had happened at the museum. He had read her a quote from Lionel Trilling the other day. Something about being aware of the dangers that lie in our most generous wishes, about kindness turning inadvertently into a form of coercion.

Jacob watched her pouring Gabriel a glass of milk. He was unusually quiet. It was Friday evening and soon they needed to set out for Rose's house. Marina slipped her arms around Jacob and rested her face against his neck for a moment. 'I thought we could bring him to your mother's house with us and then take him back to Constance on the way home.'

Jacob frowned. 'The child should be at home with his mother, not out late at night. And what if she's not there after dinner?'

'I'm sure she'll be back by then. She can't stay out all night. Perhaps she just needs some time to gather herself.'

'If we can't find her, we'll have to call the police or Children's Services.'

Marina stared at Jacob. His mouth was set in a firm line but he looked faintly stricken, as if he knew he had said something unforgivable.

'I don't know how you could even suggest that. It's not like you to be so heartless.'

Marina could barely stop her voice from s⌇ ⌇ moment she imagined Gabriel being wrenched ⌇ handed over to an officious social worker or brusque po⌇. There was something chilling in the idea that they would deposit him with strangers. She was furious at Jacob, she realised, for even contemplating such a thing. For having understood so little that it was possible to see Gabriel as an anonymous waif. To believe that he was not in any way their responsibility.

Jacob stepped back and held up his hands as if he were admitting defeat. 'Okay, okay. Let's just hope she's home after dinner.'

Marina thought angrily of all the kindness Jacob doled out to his patients, his careful, cultivated empathy. Perhaps that was the problem. His empathy was circumscribed. His care always had a limit to it. He was not required to really feel anything himself. It was a necessary skill that his profession had instilled in him, but what if it had made his heart somehow smaller?

Gabriel was staring gravely up from the table, a look of concern on his face as if he could understand everything passing between them. Marina went to him and kissed him on the top of the head. 'It's okay, sweetheart,' she said to him. 'You're coming with us.'

Jacob turned away and went upstairs to get ready for dinner, closing the bedroom door behind him.

On the way to Rose's house, Gabriel let Ben take one of his hands and he and Marina swung the little boy between them, his legs kicking up into the air. Ben was so kind to Gabriel, and gentle with Constance, too, despite her refusal to speak to him, her blank stare when he greeted her the handful of times he had come across her at the house. Ben simply accepted that they needed to make allowances for her.

Gabriel gave a delighted crooning sound as they swung him, close to laughter. There was such a raw, hungry surge in her love for him. This was what alarmed Jacob, Marina knew. Already this excess of feeling.

After dinner Rose found some old crayons and a sketchbook, relics from Ben's childhood, or perhaps even Jacob's. She put a crayon into Gabriel's hand, curling his fingers around it. She stood behind him, guiding his hand. Then Rose took his hand and placed it down on the paper, drawing an outline of his fingers. The boy stared in amazement at the marks on the paper. Marina thought of Constance printing her name on the form at the Public Assistance office. Her bewilderment at seeing the letters she had formed. Watching the deep concentration on Gabriel's face as he scribbled, Marina saw the possibility of the child he might have been. The child he might still become. It was easier, that night, not to think of Constance and what she could be doing.

The evening slipped away, darkness falling slowly, impurely. There was always a pallid orange haze to the night in the city. Gabriel climbed on to Marina's lap and folded himself into her, his thumb in his mouth. Rose sat beside her and touched the child's hair. 'He's a beauty,' she said, staring intently at his face. 'A serious little soul.' From the kitchen Marina could hear the clink of teacups and the low hum of Leah and Ben's conversation. 'It's a long shot,' Leah was saying. 'These asylum claims can be so messy. But of course we'll try. Of course we'll fight.' Leah had brought cakes of powdered cacao back from Guatemala, spiced with cinnamon and cloves, and she was making hot chocolate for all of them. It was such a calm encircling, this reconstituted family.

Across the table Marina saw that Jacob was watching her, something guarded and thoughtful in his eyes. Some years earlier they had tried to have a child. Jacob had always imagined that he would have several children, had always wanted a daughter. Months passed and she had not fallen pregnant. It became a consuming disappointment, a cycle of hope and despair. She began to feel exhausted by it, tired of the endless calculations, the enormous effort required. There was nothing explicable about their failure, a doctor told them eventually after rounds of tests and investigations, nothing that was obviously wrong. They would simply need to try fertility treatment and hope for the best. At home she lined up the vials of drugs, the plastic-wrapped syringes. The bathroom felt like a small pharmacy.

In the end, she could not do it. It was a kind of visceral rebellion against the extreme level of intervention required for something they had expected to come easily. It felt wrong to meddle so intensively with their particular fate, as if she would be tempting some form of punishment for such a concerted summoning. It seemed that a child would not be a gift given to them after all. They had each other, the great good fortune of their marriage. Their work. Ben. It had always felt like consolation enough. It did not seem right to want more than all this, so miraculously offered.

Ben carried Gabriel on his back as they walked home, his arms linked through the little boy's legs. They all walked to the projects together. Jacob followed them up the stairs, his discomfort obvious. This time when Marina knocked on the door of Constance's apartment the girl answered. She seemed composed. There was no sign of whatever grief or terrible memory had come over her at the museum; it was as if it had never happened. When Marina asked her if she was all right Constance said nothing, once more stared fixedly at the floor as if she had not registered the question. She would not permit it to be spoken of, Marina realised.

Gabriel had fallen asleep, his head resting on Ben's shoulder. When he woke and saw Constance he began to wail. Ben set him down on his feet and he ran to Marina and clung to her legs, his crying growing louder. She bent down and held him for a moment and he scrambled to climb into her arms, screaming now and flapping his hands in agitation. Constance stood in the doorway of the apartment staring somewhere beyond them. Eventually Marina had to peel Gabriel away from her, wrenching herself free of him. The little boy collapsed to the floor and lay there crying, his whole body heaving. Constance made no effort to comfort him. It was like that first day on the street when she had turned away from the child's tantrum as if he had nothing to do with her. When they walked away down the corridor, Gabriel picked himself up from the floor and ran after them. The little boy stood at the top of the stairwell, gasping through his sobs, tears pouring down his face. Marina felt her own heart pounding, her hands shaking. She wanted to turn back and go to him. They could still hear his screams as they walked down the stairs. Then the sound of the door closing, and silence.

Back at the brownstone, Jacob came and stood in the doorway of the bedroom as she undressed. She could feel him trying to gather himself before he spoke, trying to weigh up how much he might say.

'Marina, that scene was appalling. You're on incredibly dangerous ground here.'

'What am I supposed to do? They need my help.'

'But you're not actually thinking of their needs. You're thinking of your own.'

'That's not true. They don't have anyone. Would you rather I just abandon them to their fate?'

'It's too murky. The whole thing is too murky. Bringing him along to dinner. You can't just pretend that he's part of our family for a night. What does that do to him?'

She could hear the strain in Jacob's voice. How rarely they argued. She used to think that it was a sign of their compatibility, but now she wondered if perhaps it was because they were too afraid to bring any trouble upon themselves.

'Life is murky. Human relationships are murky. You of all people should know that.'

'You are doing damage. You have to leave space for her to love her own child.'

'But that's the thing. She's not capable of loving him. Should he just be sacrificed because it's unwise for me to love him? Because it's murky?'

Jacob sat down on the bed beside her and took her hand. She felt so unreasonably angry at him. They sat together in silence for several minutes before Jacob spoke again.

'Look, I know it's sad. Of course it's sad. But you need to examine your motivations. Have you considered that perhaps you're trying to rescue this child because he reminds you of yourself? I really think it might be good for you to talk to someone about this. I know you've never wanted to see a therapist, but it could be really helpful. For lots of reasons.'

Marina pulled her hand away and stood up. Such a look of concern on Jacob's face as he stared at her. It was worse somehow, this considered, reasonable line of thought, this sensible advice. This professional position. She picked up her book and walked downstairs, standing at the kitchen counter while the kettle boiled. Her hands, she realised, were shaking. She thought of Gabriel's distraught face at the top of the stairwell, the way that his screams had echoed through the building. Was he still crying now, she wondered? Would Constance comfort him? She could not imagine it. Standing there in the darkened kitchen, Marina felt completely unmoored. She had forgotten, it seemed, how a reasonable adult would act in this situation. How to protect herself and how to protect the child. She sat there for a long time at the kitchen table, staring out at the garden beyond her.

Later that night she lay in bed awake beside Jacob, listening to the soft rush of his breath as he slept. She knew that some part of what he had said earlier was true. When Gabriel had turned away from his mother and clung so fiercely to Marina, she had felt a tiny glimmer of satisfaction. She could not deny it, this small thrill that the child had chosen her to love over Constance.

Harlem
August, 1997

In one of the books that Marina had taken out from the library about the Rwandan genocide, there was a line she could not stop coming back to. 'In villages all over the Bugesera, fathers threw their children into the river as a last gesture of love.' Running from the Hutus with their machetes, spears and clubs, mothers and fathers had chosen to drown their children to save them from slaughter. Singing as they went, the assassins wore manioc leaves like crowns in their hair. 'They laughed with all their heart. They struck with swinging arms. They cut anyone, without choosing.' The words were lined up on the page like some kind of terrible poetry, but still she found it hard to believe that such things could be written. That such things could be done.

In the last weeks of the summer Marina began to read about Rwanda. In a carrel at the library on 96th Street she read as if everything written about the genocide must be known, as if this was the only way she could enter the terrain of Constance's life. A hunger for details. The lists of names, the numbers slaughtered in each region. People trying to explain or analyse what had happened, their words wrenched forever into horror. The words of the survivors all had the same stunned quality, the same sort of bewildered disbelief. The Hutus became obsessed, one woman said, with burning the photograph albums left behind in looted houses, so that the disappearance they sought was truly complete. 'To be safer,' she said, 'they tried to kill people and their memories, and in any case to kill the memories when they couldn't catch the people.' Such a profound eradication had been sought, such a vigorous erasure.

Marina would look up and find that hours had passed, that the sun had shifted or summer rain had begun to fall without her noticing. It was terrifying to her to read this way, leaving everything behind. At the end of the day she would walk slowly home through the ordinary living of hazy August streets, and they would seem mysterious and full of violence to her. The smell of hashish, the hot blasts of air from the subway grates, the scratchy blare of a radio, papers plastered to a bodega wall. All this carrying on through those terrible months in Constance's country, and still here now.

Rwanda. Even the country's name was like a code. A word that had to be murmured, the long, low sounds of it running along the tongue. Constance had given her nothing to piece together, no hint of a narrative. Only the name of her town typed on that piece of paper, the birthday that someone in an office far from her home must have invented for her: there were rarely ever official records of births and deaths, Leah told her, so dates were estimated. Officials in refugee camps guessed ages by looking at people. Some could say that they had been born in the time of the rains, or in the dry season, so the month of their birth would be estimated based on seasons. The true date of Constance's birth would never be known.

Marina knew that Constance had come from a part of the country called Nyamata. It was a place of hills and marshes. Small churches perched on hillocks, fields of yams and pale-green banana groves, gardens planted with beans. High flowering hedges and mango groves. Mud roads thronged with bare-chested boys poking goats with long sticks. One of the pictures showed a straggling soccer field, a pair of slanted goalposts.

After the president's aeroplane was shot out of the sky and the killing started, thousands of people in Nyamata town ran to the parish church. 'It's part of Rwandan custom,' one of the voices in a book of survivor testimonies explained, 'to take refuge in God's house when the massacres begin.' Throughout the book were these gracious notes of explanation. 'Umunzenze are giant trees. The masu is a big club studded with nails. There had always been killings and house-burnings in the region, but each time we told ourselves that it would end no worse than usual.'

The small villages of Constance's district were framed by marshland waterways and papyrus swamps. The bogs of Butamwa, the Akanyaru River, the swamps of Nyamwiza, Lake Cyohoha and the Murago marshes. For the weeks of the genocide, many Tutsis from Nyamata hid in the swamps, concealed by the thick reeds, the cold mud. At night, when the killers had gone home, these Tutsis wandered among abandoned huts, crept into empty houses to hide. To rest. To eat what they could forage. And the next day at first light, the same again.

In the morning we all decided to hide in the marshes. That's what we did every day, for a month. Each morning we went to hide the littlest ones beneath the swamp papyrus. When we heard the interahamwe arrive, we ran to spread ourselves out in silence, in the thickest foliage, sinking deep into the mud. They stripped her to take the money knotted up in her pagne. They chopped both her arms off first, then her legs. Mama was murmuring 'Saint Cecile, Saint Cecile,' but she didn't beg for mercy. You must understand that we fugitives, although we lived all for all in our evening camp, were forced to live everyone for himself during our flights through the swamp. Except, of course, for the mamas carrying their little ones. I called one of the children to help me. She was a girl of about nine. She replied that she couldn't help me because they had cut off her arms. In the beginning, deep in the papyrus, we hoped help would come. They found me, holding my child in my arms. That was the rule in the marshes: anyone who was seriously cut had to be abandoned, for safety's sake.

I heard later that a small number of people committed suicide. Especially women, who would feel their strength fail and preferred the rushing river to getting hacked up alive. They said they were going to rape us, but they used the word 'marry'. They said they were going to marry us until we stopped breathing. The Hutus would follow the faint cries of tiny children, who couldn't stand the mud anymore. An interahamwe, when he caught a pregnant Tutsi, he began by cutting into her belly. Not even the spotted hyena imagines that kind of viciousness with his fangs. I saw a nursling sleeping forgotten on his mama, who had been cut down. Soaking wet, we'd set out to hide the children in small groups under the papyrus. We used to tell them to be as good as fish in ponds.

Marina must have read a hundred such testimonies. More, perhaps. The reading left her dazed and sickened, but she could not stop. Later, she found it hard to remember which books she had read and which she had not. Always she found herself searching the accounts, the survivors' words, for stories she might tell herself about Constance. She did not know if the girl had been in the marshes. Some had hidden in the eucalyptus forests, or in abandoned buildings. Others had managed to cross the border to safety in Burundi. Marina had no way to know which story belonged to Constance. The girl would never entrust that knowledge to her and she could never ask.

She photocopied a page of the testimony of a survivor named Innocent. There were times, he said, when he found himself at the genocide memorial at the Nyamata church. 'Sometimes, when I go to the memorial with a visitor, I look at the skulls lined up on the shelves and catch myself studying little details, like the teeth, as if I were hoping in spite of myself to recognise those of my wife or my son, who were cut down in the church.'

A man standing before a row of bleached skulls, imagining the deaths of his wife and child. How did Constance gather her ghosts, Marina wondered?

At the end of her days in the library, at home Marina would lie down on her bed. On those afternoons she often fell into a thick, oppressive kind of sleep. Waking, the things she had read would come back to her and she would struggle out of sleep, remembering that the voices were not from her dreams, but from the books she had read at the library.

'When I meet a stranger's eyes, I fear for my child,' one of the women said. 'In my bed, I turn away from the shadows; on a path, I glance back at forms following me.' In one book there were black-and-white portraits of each survivor. Each face had the same look of mute incomprehension, the same blank stare. It was the look that Constance bore.

Narrowsburg
January, 2000

When the cold came, the stream at the bottom of the valley began to freeze. Once, Sister Vera had walked out on to the ice, all the way down the stream to the small bridge. Constance watched from the banks. She could see the water moving under the ice, a dark-green swirl. In the summer it was a gurgle, as though it were pouring down a drain, but now the flowing was silent. She had been worried that the ice would crack open and Sister Vera would fall through. That she would disappear into all that cold. She had made her way slowly back down the river, her hands stretched out on each side for balance. She knew the strength of the ice, she said. Knew when it would hold a person and when it would not. She knew how to be safe. When she was small she had skated on lakes sealed closed by ice. This was in her own country, where rivers turned to ice in the wintertime, too. People brought lamps at night-time and lit fires on the banks of the lake, Sister Vera told her. It was like a kind of flying, the soaring across the ice in the darkness. It was something so beautiful it made you forget the cold. Still she dreamed of it.

When Sister Vera told her this story about the frozen lake and the lamps in her childhood, Constance was afraid it would mean she would want Constance to talk about her own country. But Sister Vera never asked her. She did not wish to learn what Constance did not want to tell. Their talking was about the garden, the clothes that needed mending, the things they would plant in the spring, the worms that had got to the apples in the small orchard. Most of it was Sister Vera talking and Constance just listening.

Constance stands by the front door with her coat on. It is the first day for a long time that it has not snowed. In between the snowing has been a hard, low rain. But now there is a pure blue sky. This morning, while the nuns were eating breakfast, a great sheet of snow slid from the roof, startling them. There is sun in the sky now, too, but not the warming kind. It will be many weeks before she feels that kind of sun on her face.

When she leaves the house she dips her fingers into the small wooden bowl of holy water by the door. She doesn't know how the water comes to be holy. What makes it so. A priest blessing it, Sister Vera told her once, but no priest has come for a long time. Now it is just water they fetch from the stream. Holy water put the devil to flight, Sister Cecile believed. When she was dying she asked Constance to sprinkle her with it. Sister Cecile had many holy things. A bottle of water from a magic spring that could cure you from sickness. Another glass bottle full of red sand from the place where Jesus was born, the country in the Bible. The Holy Land, they called it, which meant that the sand was holy, too. Sister Cecile had been there once many years before. Now that she is dead, Constance has the bottles, as well as Sister Cecile's wooden rosary beads and a book of prayers that was hers when she was a little girl in Ireland. The book is very old and the pages are very fine, like the wings of the moths that cluster on the windows in the summertime. Cecile wanted her to have all these things, Sister Vera said, though Constance isn't sure why. She has put them in the small wooden cupboard beside her bed. Sometimes at night she takes out the little book. A strange thing to think of Sister Cecile being a child and that book being there with her in Ireland so many years ago. And then here in Constance's hands. In another country.

All around outside is the feel of things melting. A trickle and seeping everywhere. Snow falls from the branches of the trees, hitting the ground with loud thuds. There is a brightness to the day, a hard white sparkle. Constance holds a plastic container full of the special food she has made for the birds. In the small library next to the room they used for a chapel she found a book called *How to Attract and Protect Wild Birds*. She can read now. Sister Vera said she must learn, made her write the letters out over and over until her eyes felt dizzy and her head ached. Most of the books in the library are holy books, but there are some books of poems sent to Sister Vera by her brother. A poem didn't have to tell anything or mean anything, Sister Vera told her. It was just words made to sound pretty. She can't find any sense in the poems, but she likes the book about birds. Birds can perish in winter from want of food. 'Kind-hearted people have always taken pity on our feathered winter guests,' the book said. There was a special kind of food you needed to make – a mix of melted fat and seeds, millet, dried meat and breadcrumbs. The paste should be painted over the branches of trees for the birds to find.

The book gave very detailed instructions on how all this should be done, and there were pictures too.

Sister Vera told her that this kind of feeding would spoil the birds. They would no longer be able to do their work in nature. Humans should not interfere with the lives of wild animals. It did them no service. But to Constance it seemed like a good thing to help them like this. The feathered winter guests. She wanted to do something for them.

After she has painted the lower branches of the trees at the bottom of the path, she stands very still, watching to see if any birds will come. She can make herself stay quiet like this for a long time. If she does not move or speak it is as if she is not there at all. She could stay there longer if the cold were not so stinging. Still now she is not used to it. Sister Vera has shown her how to heat a brick on top of the stove and wrap it in a cloth so that she can put her feet against it in bed at night. That is another thing from Sister Vera's childhood. Hot bricks in your bed.

Constance wonders if this is something Marina does for the child, to keep him warm in the winter. If it is something all people do in cold places, or just in Ireland. She did not know to do this when they lived in the city. No one showed her. It was always too cold in the apartment. Mornings in winter she could see her breath in the air. When it was cold she made a nest out of blankets for the child. He slept under the small table in the kitchen, wrapped up, with not one part of him visible. Perhaps there was a safety he felt there. A hiding place. Sometimes she thought it was her he was hiding from. The second winter they slept buttoned into the thick coats that Marina bought for them. She still has that coat, though the child would be grown too big for his now. He would have another one, Constance is sure of it. He would have everything that he could need.

⌐

No birds come for a long time. A drift of snow falls from a branch above her, brushing her shoulder. She hears Sister Vera calling her name from the window on the second floor. When she looks back towards the house she sees that every window is alight and the sky is dark already. The darkness looks like it is tucked in around the house. She can see herself in the glass of the downstairs window. There is a ripple to her face, like when she peers over and looks into the stream and sees herself there in the water. Sister Vera is calling her name again. They are going to make jelly from the last of the summer apples. Sister Vera is going to show her how. These are things her own mother taught her in Ireland: how to preserve fruit, make candles, roll pastry.

Constance turns and picks her way slowly back along the path to the house. Behind her the snow starts again, covering over her footsteps on the path.

Harlem
September, 1997

Harlem softened in the fall, the blankets of leaves and the blue dusk muting the sharpness of the streets. The chill in the early mornings seemed miraculous after the long months of heat. Marina stood by the back door, imagining the glass branching with frost, the small garden glittering under snow. Ben had been downstairs before her and left a pot half-full of coffee on the stove.

Once, Marina had spent a month at a writers' colony in the south of France, not far from the Spanish border. It was Christmas time and she and an Australian essayist were the only writers-in-residence. The writers' colony was housed in an enormous old *manoir* and she rarely crossed paths with the essayist. They each had their own floor of the house, meeting sometimes in the kitchen, or once on the path by the stream at the bottom of the valley.

Every morning the Australian writer would make a pot of coffee and leave half on the stove for her. He was always awake before her, out walking in the mountains when it was barely light. He had spent that summer in northern Lapland, he told her during one of their conversations. He had lived for many years in London and longed to go somewhere there was always enough light: he wanted, just for a time, to escape the fretful bleakness that came with the late rising of the sun and its early disappearance. He looked very melancholy when he told her this and she wondered what sorrows his life had held. None of us is unscathed, Marina thought then, listening to the essayist speaking about the light in Lapland.

It was a lovely kind of caring, the coffee made for two, a reminder that she was not entirely alone. In the mountains around the writers' colony the walking paths were carefully marked with stripes of paint on trees or rock faces to show the way. Divergent paths, the ones that did not lead the right way or came to dead ends, were marked with a yellow cross to signify that the wrong fork had been taken. You could walk for miles following the small signs. This tending of the paths seemed to Marina to be another form of distant care. It sustained her through the long days of work, the only sound the peal of church bells, or a dog barking across the valley. Sometimes she could hear the Australian walking around the room above her, or his chair scraping across the old tiles.

They did not keep in touch after their month together at the writers' colony, but he became quite renowned in the years afterwards. She often saw his name in literary journals and newspapers. One year he came to the Brooklyn Book Festival to read from a new collection of essays. Marina was too shy to line up at the signing table after his reading, but she bought his book. The essays were beautiful, tender pieces, following the sweep of his wide-ranging thoughts. One was about that time in France, about the walks to the floor of the valley and the carefully marked paths through the mountains.

⌒

Jacob was away for two months that fall, teaching a child psychiatry course at Harvard, and Marina fell into a pattern with Ben that reminded her of the time at the writers' colony. Ben would leave for work early in the mornings, coming home when she was out walking, or at her desk. Several days might pass when they did not see each other. Late at night she would listen for the murmur of voices from upstairs. Ben brought Alma home more now that Jacob was away. Marina was not entirely sure if it was intentional, but he was withholding his relationship from his father. The one time that Jacob's path had crossed with Alma's on the front steps, Ben introduced her simply as 'my friend'. Uncharacteristically, Jacob had not asked questions.

One evening Marina cooked dinner for Ben and Alma, and they sat around the dining table with a bottle of wine. There was a calm attentiveness to the girl that appealed to Marina, a serene sort of watchfulness; her face looked so very young, though she was three years older than Ben. Besides the brother who had come with her to America, there were three younger sisters, all of them still in El Salvador.

'Look at them,' Alma said shyly, passing a photograph across the table. 'Just look.' Marina took the picture and examined it; Alma was watching her face very closely, she thought. It was as if by making Marina look at these children, Alma was forcing her to acknowledge their existence. Their peril. It reminded Marina of the way Gabriel would sometimes take her face between his hands if he sensed she was not paying full attention to him. He would twist her face around to look at him, holding her gaze for a long time.

In Alma's photograph three small girls in white dresses stared solemnly into the camera, as if they had been instructed by the photographer not to smile.

'The little one,' said Alma, 'she has only four years. Her name is Providencia.'

Marina wondered for a moment if the little girl was actually Alma's own child. There seemed too large an age gap for her to be a younger sister. Marina had heard terrible stories from Leah. Children left behind while their mothers made risky journeys across the desert. Sometimes these women never saw their children again. 'They are very beautiful.' Marina handed the photograph back to Alma.

'Yes,' said Alma quietly, still watching her. 'Very beautiful.' She pressed the picture to her lips before putting it back in her bag.

Alma and Ben took out the Scrabble board and plucked their letters from the velvet bag. Alma always insisted on the game – it was the best way for her to learn more English words, she said. She was sharp and diligent; insistent on perfecting her English, always asking questions about the particular meaning of a word or phrase. The girl's presence sometimes made Marina feel a failure of nerve in herself. Alma was in peril. A different kind from those little girls back in El Salvador, but her situation here in New York was tenuous. She had no immigration status, she could not work legally or study. She could be deported at any time if she was discovered. It was easy, gathered around the dinner table or playing Scrabble together, to slip into the pretence that Alma was just another one of the bright, lovely friends that Ben had brought home over the years, their futures full of promise. But this was not so, and Marina could not help feeling that they should be doing more to help her, though she was not sure what kind of help they could offer. She had given money to Ben for the immigration lawyer Leah had organised, but the outcome of this was uncertain. Marina had not told Jacob about the money for the lawyer, just as she had not told him about the money she gave

Constance. It was not the money itself that would alarm him; it was what he felt was, again, the recklessness of this involvement in the precarious lives of others. It was not their responsibility, he would say.

That September Constance started a literacy program at one of the non-profit migrant agencies near the East River in Spanish Harlem. Leah found the course; she was always looking for ways that they might help Constance. Counselling, parenting classes, an art therapy course – everything that Leah suggested Constance refused with her usual indifference. She would barely glance at the pamphlets Leah brought over, placing them aside as if they were not meant for her. But, to Marina's surprise, Constance had listened with what seemed to be a rare flicker of attention when she read the flyer about the literacy course to her. 'Three mornings a week, beginners welcome, coffee and tea provided, childcare available.' When Marina asked her if she would like to go to the classes, the girl made no reply, but before they had parted that day Constance had paused for a moment. 'I do the lessons for writing,' she murmured before she disappeared into the foyer of her building.

Marina was trying, after her argument with Jacob, to make a more concerted effort with Constance. She needed to create a space for the girl to love her own child, Jacob had told her, and she was trying to do this. At the hospital she made Constance hold Gabriel while the doctor gave him a needle; on the train she placed him on his mother's lap. But none of this made any difference. If anything, Constance seemed more detached from the child than before. She carried him on her back less and less, barely ever reached down to hold his hand. Constance expected

Gabriel to follow her, and if he did not keep up, she would not wait for him.

Marina collected Constance from the projects on the first morning of the literacy class. The course was run by elderly nuns, Leah told her. They would be kind to Constance. Marina was hopeful about the classes. She was doing what Jacob had suggested – helping Constance find her own way. This unexpected desire to learn could be the beginning of something; the girl's first step back into the world.

The tall brown cinder blocks of the projects loomed up above Marina, rusty air conditioners balancing in the windows. The place had the look of a shell-scarred fortress. The old men sitting in folding chairs outside the lobby seemed to be almost motionless, like some kind of decrepit sentries. They stared silently at her as she passed them. A slim boy in a puffy jacket pushed past her and ran up the stairs, his sneakers flashing silver and red. '*Blancita,*' he called back to her in a low, jeering lilt, his laughter echoing in the darkness of the stairwell. She had been here several times now and still the place appalled her – the squalor of it, the reek of urine, the pressing sense of danger. She wished that she could find somewhere else for Constance and Gabriel to live.

The girl and the child were both wearing the new coats Marina had bought for them. Gabriel tore towards her as soon as Constance opened the door, his small body pushing against her legs. She picked him up, his arms around her neck, the soft fuzz of his hair against her chin. When she kissed his cheek she held her lips there for a moment. The warmth of his skin, the weight of his body in her arms – it still shocked Marina, the fierceness of this hunger for him.

211

Marina sat on the old flowered sofa as Constance fed the child breakfast. Brisk and efficient, the toast chopped into squares, Gabriel's face scrubbed with a damp cloth. Always silence between them. The clink of a spoon, the hum of traffic, muffled shouting from the apartment above them. Constance slapped Gabriel's hand when he reached out to pick up the knife, and took his plate away.

They walked the nine blocks east in silence. A rainy wind blew in across the Hudson and the roads looked tarred, water flicking up at them when a bus or a truck lurched in close to the sidewalk. Gabriel pulled the hood of his red coat over his head.

The waiting room of the agency was filled with young Mexican women, strollers and shopping trolleys jammed against the walls. There were small clusters of commotion, conversations in rapid Spanish, a child crying. Through an open door several women knelt on the floor, piecing together a brightly coloured quilt.

It was food pantry day, the elderly nun at the front desk explained. Every Tuesday morning. Constance could take food, too, if she liked; bring a basket or a trolley next time she came. Rice, beans, oil, flour – they always had staples, sometimes fresh fruit. Marina saw the glint of a gold cross at the woman's collar as she looked over the enrolment forms she had filled out for Constance. Had there been nuns in Constance's country? Was this something that the young girl could understand, that would seem familiar to her? These sensibly clad, sturdy women on their missions of mercy.

'Rwanda,' the nun said, looking up at Constance. 'We had sisters in Kigali once. And an orphanage in the south. Not for a while now, though. Where was your village?'

Rwanda. Kigali. There was such a casualness to the names in the nun's mouth. Not stones between them, only words, released from all their malevolent meaning. 'South or north?' the nun tried again, but Constance said nothing. She stood there beside Marina, her coat still on despite the warmth of the room. She was holding the blue notebook that Marina had bought for her the day before. Constance had chosen the colour herself, standing solemnly in the stationery aisle at one of the dollar stores near the projects, her tongue between her lips like a serious child. It was a small moment of hope, Marina thought, the choosing of a notebook. The unexpected agreement to come to these classes felt like an acquiescence to something outside her small world of strictly necessary things. Had Constance been to school? Marina could not imagine the other life the girl must have had, that disappeared world of villages and goats and banana groves. In the warmer weather Marina watched her walk down the street in her brightly patterned wrap and wondered if it was something from her old life. But, no, nothing could have been salvaged. It must have been allocated to her in a refugee camp, or bought cheaply from one of the African shops here in Harlem. What could Constance own that would hold any meaning, any memory?

The nun led them down a corridor to the crèche. A room full of children, mostly Mexican, one African girl with elaborately braided hair. The spin and clatter of them was overwhelming: an older boy launching himself off the top of a plastic climbing fort, a baby crying in a stroller in the corner, a young woman reading a book to a cluster of little girls on a rug. The nun bent down beside Gabriel, her grey head close to his. 'Would you like to come and play with the other children?' Marina heard her say to him.

Constance stood in the doorway, staring into the room. She reached out for Gabriel, wrapped her fingers around his upper arm. There was a look of panic on her face as she turned to Marina. This is a first, Marina thought. Later, she would try to remember other moments like this, times when something in Constance unbuckled and there was some glimmer of feeling for her child.

Gabriel began to cry. Constance looked stricken, touching her throat with her fingers as if she was trying to summon the words she needed. She would not leave her child with strangers, Marina realised. She would not turn away and leave him to be cared for by people she did not know. Gabriel broke away from Constance and pressed his head into Marina's legs, his arms around her thighs. When she picked him up he wrapped his arms so tightly around her neck that she could hardly breathe.

'I'll keep him with me,' she said to Constance. 'I'll take him home and you can come and get him when the class is finished. You don't have to leave him here.'

She wondered if Constance would allow Gabriel to stay with her this time. She had never witnessed this protective surge, this instinct in her for her child's safety. When she was walking home with Gabriel, she realised that, apart from the day that Constance had left him with her at the museum, this was perhaps the first time that the girl had ever been apart from her son. A year in a refugee camp, a year in the city, the child tied to her back, trailing her as she walked to shops, to hospitals, to the subway station, never more than a few feet away from her in that tiny apartment. Who could she ever have left him with?

At times that fall, the image of Jacob's face would rise up unbidden, often accompanied by a qualm of guilt and regret;

214

a feeling that she had failed him in some important way. After Marina had helped Jacob load the car on the morning he had left for Harvard earlier in the month, he held her for a long moment, his hands resting on her hips, his lips on the top of her head. He wanted her to come to Boston with him. It would have been possible, now that she was not teaching. There was the colleague's elegant apartment in Cambridge, near the university. The small study she could use there, with a view over the charming square. The walks they would take together by the river, the cafés, the museums, the quiet decorum of the city itself. Jacob had described the shape of the journey eagerly, hopefully, as if he were trying to sell something to her.

'Say yes. It will be an adventure. A vacation.'

He was standing in the doorway of her study when he put the proposal to her. She closed her book. He looked so hopeful. So youthful, somehow. Part of her wanted to say yes. To gather up her work and go with him. To take long walks around Cambridge and cook dinner for him each night. But she suspected that his desire for her to come to Boston was not entirely pure. He would like her to be away from New York. Away from Constance and Gabriel. He wanted her out of their orbit so that the ties between them might loosen. So that she might come to her senses. Several times these past weeks she had caught him gazing at her with a kind of perplexed concern, as if she had suddenly become errant and unknown to him. Did he wonder whether the whole sturdy scaffold they had built so carefully might turn out to have been shoddily constructed after all? He gazed at Ben in the same way these days and she suspected that his sorrows and fears for both of them had come together in a cloud of concern that threatened to overwhelm him. Sometimes we have to learn new truths about people, she had said to Jacob the week before. That their priorities and dreams are not always the ones that we had imagined for them. She had been referring to Ben, but staring at her husband as he stood before her, she wondered if perhaps she had been speaking about herself, too.

'Darling, I'd love to come,' she said, 'but I have so many interviews lined up for the book these next few weeks. And I want to keep an eye on Ben.'

Marina knew that Jacob could not argue with this. That he would be grateful for her watchful care, her presence in the house with his son.

'You'll come back down for Rosh Hashanah in a couple of weeks, and maybe I can come up for a few days. We could go to Nantucket for a weekend,' she said. She felt, even as she said it, that she was offering him some kind of consolation prize.

When he had let go of her that morning, Jacob turned back suddenly. 'You know, we could still try.' At first Marina was not sure what he was talking about. 'To have a baby,' he said. 'It's not too late. We could go back to the clinic.' It was early and the street around them seemed strangely quiet – all the customary noise and clatter winnowing down to just the two of them standing there on the front steps of their house. 'I love you, Jacob,' she said quietly, taking his hand in both of hers. He kissed her, then. A proper kiss, his mouth opening into hers, her tongue meeting his own.

After Jacob had driven away, Marina stood for a long time in his study. His desk looked as if he had just stepped out for a moment. A black-and-white photograph of a peregrine falcon soaring above a valley. A ceramic bowl full of sea-smoothed glass. A miniature painting of a palm tree that they had bought together from an artist at a temple in India; a picture where the brush-strokes were so fine that a magnifying glass was needed to see the cross-hatched beauty of the leaves. A collection of Montaigne's essays left splayed open on top of a pile of academic papers. A framed picture of his father. A mug still half-full of coffee.

The clock above the desk ticked. It was a cuckoo clock, made by Jacob's father. An exact replica of the one from his own childhood that had been lost to fire in Poland. Rose had given it to Jacob when they moved to this house. The clock fascinated Gabriel. Several times Marina had stood with him in her arms waiting for the hour to strike and the small wooden bird to appear from behind its door. Each time it was as if it were the first, the startled delight on the boy's face undiminished. She smiled thinking of it. If Gabriel were their child, the cuckoo clock would become part of his own history. The story of the clock and its echoes of other lives would be bequeathed to him, as it had been to Ben. But would it be a kind of false inheritance, a plastering of other memories over his truer ones?

She did not want another baby, Marina realised. She only wanted Gabriel.

By Jacob's abandoned coffee cup there was a pad of writing paper. On the blank page she could make out the faint imprint of letters, the ghostly impressions of his handwriting like a secret watermark. Who had he been writing to? How well do we ever know another person, she wondered? How much of our real selves ever manages to rise up to the surface of our lives? We live beside a person year after year, and yet we so often fail to understand the most fundamental aspects of their nature.

When they were children she and Dov had often rifled through their mother's drawers when she was away from the apartment. They were searching for a pile of letters bound with a ribbon, a tin of photographs, a volume of poetry – anything that might provide them with some clues to Gizela's past. They had been obsessive amateur historians, she and Dov, unshaken in their belief that if only they could line up all the facts of her history they would somehow understand their mother.

Most children want their parents to dwell only in the present, in the life that contains them, but for Marina and Dov the opposite was true. Gizela's insistent inhabiting of a completely ahistorical present unnerved and alarmed them. Never once did she tell any story that veered into her past. This fastidious withholding must have needed terrifying discipline, Marina thought later.

She and Dov had only a handful of details, a truncated outline of her history. An old passport, official letters, a travel document: these were the only guides for their imaginative reconstructions of their mother's life. Gizela was born in Prague in 1933. In the summer of 1939 she was sent, along with a group of other Jewish children, to England. She stayed with an English couple on a small farm in Suffolk for the duration of the war, and then for nearly a year longer until a relative could be found who was willing to take her. Eventually a great-aunt was located in Brooklyn, an elderly woman who had left for America many years before Gizela was born.

Marina often thought of the train journey that her mother had taken in 1939, when she was six years old, from Prague through the German Reich and the Netherlands to the Hook of Holland, where she was put on a ship to Harwich and then a train to Suffolk. How the loud roll out of the station and the thunder of the train through the Czech countryside must have terrified the little girl. The flashing fields and rooftops, the faint curls of smoke from trackside towns, the wailing of the other children around her. That two-day train ride away from everything known to her always struck Marina as being the poison at the heart of her mother, the terror that had so deeply unbalanced her. Though she knew that it was summertime when her mother left Prague, Marina always imagined it as a journey through a winter landscape, drifting cloud and a low sky, the Bohemian mountains swathed in grey and the cold creep of frost on the windows at night. She imagined a small girl sleeping upright in her leather-seated compartment, her hand still clutching her suitcase. Gizela had never spoken one word to them about that journey, or about her years in England, but Marina and Dov had traced it on maps, reconstructed every step of its arc, filling in the gaps with their own imaginings. It became a kind of earnest game for them, this invention of possible histories for their mother.

The further into Gizela's past they ventured, the fewer details were available. There was an impenetrable silence around her early life in Prague; everything about that world had to be imagined. Of the English years they had a scant collection of verifiable details, a handful of dates and names from the documents they had found in the drawer beside her bed. They knew that she had been sent to Suffolk, and as children the very name of the place had taken on an almost mystical resonance. It was a secret code between the siblings. A stray fragment of detail that they clung to because they had so little else.

Several years earlier, after a conference in London, Marina had caught a train to the small village on the edge of the East Anglian broads where Gizela had lived during the war. It was the beginning of winter and the clothes Marina had brought were not warm enough. Her shoes were soon swollen with water after she had walked through the fields, and she had to buy a woollen scarf and hat from a small shop in the town. The streets of the village seemed to be almost entirely deserted. She could see lights behind the drawn curtains of the houses but there were no other signs of habitation. In the yard of one of the houses a dog was chained to the verandah. As she walked past, it hurled itself against the fence, making Marina jump back in fear.

The husband and wife Gizela had lived with were long dead, but she hoped she might find someone who had known them. Or someone who remembered Gizela. Marina had always wondered why the English couple had not kept Gizela with them after the end of the war. She was thirteen years old when she was sent to America; she had lived half of her life there in Suffolk. The distant aunt in Brooklyn was a stranger, Gizela's existence had been unknown to her. Surely it would have been possible for Gizela to stay in Suffolk? Perhaps the English couple felt that their duty was done and were relieved to deliver her into someone else's care. The child might have been a source of anxiety; an unwelcome burden, the trouble compounded by her foreignness.

A woman in the village had known the couple, had run errands and done some housework for them in the years before their deaths. She agreed to talk to Marina, and they sat in the formal parlour of her small house with cups of tea before them. The armchairs were draped in plastic slipcovers and an enormous black-and-white dog lay at the woman's feet. The house felt damp and rank, full of the stale smell of animals. A scurrying could be heard in the roof above them. Dusk fell very quickly in the town, Marina noticed, the windows darkening though it was not yet three o'clock. She kept her coat on while they talked.

They were an odd pair, the woman had told Marina, with their own ways. They had kept to themselves. They were not from these parts so their histories were unknown. They had no children of their own and there were no other relatives. Apart from the minister, she herself had been the only person to attend their funerals. Yes, she had heard that they had taken in a Jewish child during the war, but the woman found it very hard to imagine this. It was not a household that she thought could ever have accommodated a child. She did not elaborate on this, except to say that the couple had been very religious and perhaps that had led them to take the child in the first place. Some notion of Christian piety. She drew Marina a map showing where their house was, on the very outskirts of the town. Of course it was much changed now with the new owners, she said, foreigners who had moved there from France.

The house stood much further away from the village than Marina had anticipated, past a dense stand of trees and a small lake. She walked along the side of the road, a dull trail of pink clouds in the sky above her, the scattered shapes of sheep in the fields beyond the lake. The trees beside the road creaked like the masts of sailboats at night. A cold, watery wind blew in. The shadows of the trees seemed very dark and precise. Marina thought of the deep woods in the fairy tales of her childhood. Was this the place Gizela had thought of when she had read to Dov and her? She must have walked this road each day to the small village school, though her name did not appear on any of the enrolment records.

The woman who answered the door looked flustered and exhausted, a baby on her hip. The crying of another child could be heard in the hallway beyond her. She was reluctant to admit

Marina to the house. The children were unwell, she was trying to get them down for a sleep, she said. And the house was completely different – it would not be recognisable as the place it had been fifty years before. It was in a terrible state when they had bought it a few years earlier. Nothing had been modernised, not for many decades. The toilet was in a wooden outhouse at the bottom of the garden. Another English family had owned the house before them – they must have been the ones to buy it from the elderly couple. She had heard in the village that the old woman had died here in the house and that her body had not been found for several days. She had not wanted to live in a house where someone had died, the woman told Marina, but her husband said she was being ridiculous. The price had been very good and that part of the house was gone now anyway, torn down when they did the renovations.

Eventually she said that Marina might as well come in if she really wanted to, it was no good to stand there in the cold. The owners before them had tried to conceal all the problems with the house, the young woman said as she led Marina down the hallway to a large barn-like room that opened on to a garden strewn with children's toys. They had put cheap linoleum over the rotting floorboards, and layered wallpaper over mould and cracks. Can you imagine, the woman said, there was even wallpaper on the ceilings. In France we call it *cache-misère*. Did Marina know the expression? It meant, quite literally, 'a cover for misery'.

The woman showed Marina the original floorboards, which she and her husband had restored. At some time in the life of the house, meat had been hung to cure from the ceilings, and the old boards were covered with animal fat. The walls underneath the cheap new wallpaper had been blackened with smoke from a hundred years of fires. It was terrible, all the things they had discovered behind the *cache-misère*. Unimaginable, said the Frenchwoman, that people could live like that.

Marina wanted to see the bedroom that her mother might have slept in but it was not possible. All the rooms that had been bedrooms had been torn down to make way for the large room at the back of the house. The wooden outhouse was still there, the woman told her, as if this might be some kind of consolation. They used it as a garden shed, though she did not like to let the children near it because it was full of mice and spiders. She and Marina stood by the windows at the back of the house, looking out at the tiny shed. Marina tried to imagine Gizela as a small girl, crossing the garden in the darkness, but it was impossible. She could see her mother only as she was during their life together. Tall and quiet in her blue coat, her hands tucked around her elbows, her gaze fixed somewhere in the distance.

As Marina walked back along the road towards the town it started to rain. The lake and the sky seemed to merge into one silvery expanse. When she turned to look at the house all its windows were lit up. It looked like a besieged ship in the middle of the dark fields.

She had planned to visit the small doctor's surgery the next day to see if there were any records of Gizela, but instead she walked to the station and caught the early train back to London. She wanted only to leave the town.

Gizela's life in Brooklyn after the war was more available to them, because the great-aunt she had lived with was known to the Jewish community of Crown Heights. Marina and Dov had grown up among people who remembered Aunt Sura and had known Gizela as a girl before she had left America for Israel. Even so,

nothing Marina and her brother uncovered was particularly satis-
fying. Sura and Gizela seemed to have existed in isolation from the
insular Hasidic neighbourhood, their lives floating, unnoticed.
Some scandal had placed Sura outside the circle of the community, and she had abandoned any kind of religious observance,
which had cast her further beyond the pale. There were things
that people would not tell them because they were children, but
they managed to decipher that Sura had conducted an affair with
a married man and this had brought disgrace to his family and
to Sura. No amount of detective work could uncover who this
man was, but it was generally believed that he had given Sura the
apartment in the brick row house on Union Street where Marina
and Dov had later lived with Gizela. There seemed no way that
Sura could have bought the apartment herself. She had no family
in America and her only work was taking in sewing. She had
done less and less of that as the years passed, and no one knew
how she and Gizela had lived. There was no doubt that they had
been destitute. Gizela had not attended any of the Jewish schools
in the neighbourhood, nor had she ever come to shule, so her
life had very few points of intersection with the community.
People remembered her, but no one seemed to know anything
about her.

The reluctance to discuss Sura, Marina later realised, had to
do not only with the fact of the scandal, but her instability. Many
years afterwards, a rabbi from Crown Heights told Marina that
Sura was profoundly unhinged. That it had always been so, but it
became more evident as she grew older. There would be a better
understanding of it now, perhaps, he said, but in those days it was
brushed away as a kind of eccentricity. He did not know exactly
what form her illness had taken, but remembered her shouting
in the street once. Sura was not capable of caring for a child, he

224

said. It was wrong that the little girl had been left with her, but no one had seen fit to intervene.

Sura died in 1952, the year after Gizela left for Israel. Gizela was her only relative and the rabbi wrote to tell her of the death, but there was no answer. Gizela did not come back to attend the funeral, and the apartment on Union Street remained empty for many years until she returned to Brooklyn one winter with her two small children.

Marina often wondered what it would have been like for Gizela to come back to that apartment, where nothing had changed since she had left it nearly a decade before. The dark, heavy furniture, the enamel dishes on the kitchen shelves, the small collection of books in the glass-fronted cupboard, the brown velvet curtains – all of these were from Gizela's childhood and yet, for Marina, they never seemed to swell with any particular meaning. They were simply objects that Gizela lived among, just as she and Dov felt that they, too, were incidental to her life. Sometimes Gizela would emerge from Sura's bedroom in the mornings and stare at them with mild surprise as they sat at the kitchen table, as if she had not expected to find them there at all. They had the sense that she kept them with her only because she could not think of anything else to do with them.

Gizela had never lived with Marina and Dov before, never bathed them or cooked for them or put them to bed – all of that had been done in the Children's House on the kibbutz. Very early on they had been taught to be independent, like children in an orphanage or a boarding school. When they moved to New York with Gizela she did not know them on any intimate terms, and there was an odd formality between them. Marina remembered

225

Gizela asking them what they usually ate for breakfast, as if they were house guests whose preferences she must ascertain.

Ben told her once that when Leni came home from London when he was six years old she greeted him with a formal handshake and said, 'You've grown very tall.' She called him buddy and gave him a toy that was intended for a much younger child. It was as if she were some distant aunt returned from abroad, not the vanished mother who had loomed so large in his remembering. Her absence, and the hush that surrounded her name, had transfigured her and it had amazed him that she was a flesh-and-blood person after all. She seemed uncertain and he could feel her nervousness, Ben said, the effort she was making to sound casual. Leni sat down on the floor with him and they took the toy she had bought out of its box. Leni applied herself with great earnestness to its assemblage. It seemed extraordinary to Ben that this very beautiful woman with her long curled hair and her soft white cashmere coat had consented to sit there with him and build castles out of blocks. He realised that she was trying hard, and the very fact of her trying made him feel tenderness for her, and pity, too. Leni did not know how to be a mother, Ben said. She did not know what she was supposed to do. But he had his grandmother's example and his father's unwavering love. He could help her.

Sometimes Marina and Dov would walk from Crown Heights to Prospect Park after school had finished. Often they would stay in the park until it was dark, or too cold to be outside any longer. On one edge of the park there was a playground that was always full of women and children. She and Dov never played on the children's equipment, they preferred the parts of the park that

were still shrouded in wilderness – the lake wi⸱
and the tangled thickets beyond. But one day tn⸱⸱
railing of the playground and watched the mothers pusn⸱⸱
children on the swings, helping them to climb up the ladder o⸱
the fort. One little girl had fallen down and she sat there in the
sand, an expression of bewildered despair on her face. She could
not see her mother and she began to cry. Just then a woman came
running across the playground and knelt down in the sand by
the child, folding her into her arms. Dov and Marina both saw
the terror on the little girl's face when she was casting around
for her mother, and the instant relief when she saw her dashing
across the park towards her. They watched this small unfolding
drama of despair and rescue with bemused interest. They had
never imagined that this sort of comfort might be available to
them. For if Gizela did not know how to be a mother, they did
not know how to have a mother.

After Dov died and Gizela had gone, Marina was left with the
strange archive of their childhood: the boxes full of maps and
notes and photocopies, the pictures of Prague and Suffolk they
had cut out of magazines, the imaginary family trees they had
constructed. All of it seemed so accidental, so marginal and
inadequate. No detail they had uncovered had ever mitigated
Gizela's distance from them. They were children who had spent
their whole lives watching their mother, waiting and hoping
for her to turn back and take their hands. By their vanishing,
Dov and Gizela had turned everything that was left behind into
a ruinous sort of clutter, a false history. Standing there in the
dark apartment, Marina felt like she was the last survivor among
the wreckage. That if she did not leave, she too would plummet

disastrously beneath the surface. When she cleared out the apartment to move to California, she threw the boxes of papers into the garbage along with everything else. Gizela had forgotten her pale-blue coat and Marina left it hanging limply from the hook behind the front door.

At first Constance kept to the hours of her classes, returning to collect Gabriel soon after midday. She never spoke about what she had learned. Once, Marina showed her a child's book of letters that Rose had given her for Gabriel, but Constance displayed no glimmer of recognition. She looked at the letters as if they were something far from her. One of the women in a book on Rwanda that Marina had found in the library had spoken of suffering because she was tied to a life that was not the one she was supposed to have. When she watched Constance trailing down the street towards East Harlem, Marina thought she must feel that, too. How terrifying it must be for Constance to have been transplanted here, into a life she could never have imagined. How had the things she needed to know been passed on to her when she first arrived? Marina had asked her once what it had been like when she first came to New York and Constance only considered her with an inscrutable expression. Marina was not sure if it was because she did not understand the question, or if she could not think of any way to answer it.

One day Constance did not arrive to collect Gabriel until nearly two hours after the appointed time. Marina had made lunch for the little boy and he was playing in the garden when Constance finally knocked on the door. She said nothing about her lateness and Marina thought it would sound like a scolding if she mentioned it. She wanted to ask Constance anyway if she could keep Gabriel longer the following day so she could take him to the Central Park Zoo. Rose was going to walk across the park to meet them and they had planned a picnic for lunch. It was something that Rose had done with Jacob and Leah, and then later with Ben. She still had the old picnic basket and the set of enamel dishes her own children had eaten from on camping trips and holidays. Rose had accepted the presence of the little boy in Marina's life with great delight, although there was a thread of anxiety there, too. She had started knitting him a sweater for the coming winter. She would make a sweater for Constance as well, Rose said, so that the girl would feel that she was in the circle of their care too. She had always imagined, Rose had told Marina once, that she would have many grandchildren, and it was a great sorrow to her that Leah had never had children. She did not say it, but Marina knew that Rose also grieved that she and Jacob did not have a child together.

Marina felt guiltily that perhaps she should invite Constance to come with them to the zoo, but she did not. She thought of Jacob's advice about giving Constance the space to love her child. But she could not imagine the girl sitting on Rose's plaid blanket with them under the trees. It would be a relief to Constance not to be asked, she told herself.

She asked Constance if she could come for Gabriel at four o'clock the next day, and after that she always arrived in the late afternoons to collect him, usually waiting in the entrance hall while Marina gathered up Gabriel's things and fastened his shoes. She could never be persuaded to stay for a cup of tea or something to eat. Marina had no idea what Constance did in the hours between the end of her class and the time she collected Gabriel. There was nothing she could imagine the girl doing.

The first few times Marina looked after him, Gabriel had dissolved into screaming tantrums when Constance arrived to collect him, sliding to the floor and kicking his legs. But then this stopped and he went home with his mother without complaint. Marina wondered if Constance had threatened him or if he had simply resigned himself to the order of things. She would stand on the front steps and watch the two of them walk down the street together, Gabriel a few steps behind Constance. Sometimes when they reached the corner, the little boy would turn and look behind him before hurrying along after his mother.

In the afternoons Marina would often lie down on the couch by the windows with Gabriel while he slept, his body curled into hers. The force of her feeling for him terrified her at times. It was something akin to falling in love; the same consuming surrender, the same vast tenderness. What she felt for Gabriel was more capacious and potent than her love for Jacob, for Ben, for anyone else. There was no reservation, no part of herself that it was possible to withhold. She wondered, as she held Gabriel in her arms, was it ever possible to love anyone but a child in this way? Sometimes she thought that Jacob was right, that she should have made a greater effort to fortify herself against this. Humming away behind her love for Gabriel was the vertiginous fear of loss. Perhaps that was why it was easier when Constance was not with them – there was no reminder that the little boy belonged to someone else.

She had not told Jacob that she was taking care of Gabriel so often now. It was easy enough to disguise it. When they spoke on the telephone each evening she filled their conversation with other things: the book chapter she had finished, the new Mexican restaurant that had opened on the corner, the film she and Ben had watched together. She always felt a guilty sense of withholding when they spoke, a small kind of treachery. Was this what it was like to have an affair? To hold a secret world inside you and to pretend that it did not exist?

Gabriel would turn three in February. His papers said he had been born on Valentine's Day. The poignancy of this struck Marina: his life had contained so little love until now. Another term of literacy classes would begin in the new year and Marina had been thinking about nursery school for Gabriel. When she returned to work after the Christmas vacation she would no longer be able to take care of him during the week. There was a very good nursery school at Columbia; several of her colleagues sent their children there. Marina liked the idea that he would be close by her. She knew that Jacob would say that she should find a Head Start program for him in the neighbourhood. Somewhere that Constance could take him and collect him. It would not be the cost of the fees that he would object to, but that she was pushing the child's mother to the edges of his life. He would say that providing Gabriel with the expensive kind of private education that Ben had received would be a terrible displacement for him and for Constance. It would be another one of those conversations that would end with Jacob looking pained. She wished, Marina realised, that Jacob could share her love for Gabriel. That he would not see it as something errant and misguided, some foolhardy form of trespass.

Marina often thought in these days about a story that the dean of her faculty at Columbia had once told her about her daughter. She and Marina were at a conference in Phoenix

together and, because of an error made by the hotel, needed
to share a room. The two women were not close and Marina
initially felt alarmed at the prospect of such proximity for four
days, but they slipped into an unexpectedly easy companionship. One evening they stayed up long into the night, drinking
wine and talking. The dean showed Marina a photograph of her
daughter, who was the same age as Ben. She and her husband
had adopted the child. The baby had come to them when she
was only a few days old, but the adoption could not be finalised
for six months. This was because the child's mother had abandoned her at the hospital and a stretch of time was needed in
case she changed her mind and returned for the child.

The baby was sickly and unsettled, as if whatever trouble had
come into her mother's life had been passed on to her. The dean
sat up through each night rocking her; the little girl would only
sleep if she was pressed against her chest. It was a terrifying time,
she told Marina. Even so many years later this woman could not
look back on it without being seized by an awful anxiety. After
the first week she had known she could not possibly relinquish
the child. Her claim on the girl might not have been recognised
by a judge if the mother returned, but she felt that it was the truer
claim nonetheless. If it had come to it, the dean told Marina, she
would have taken the child and run. To South America or some
other place where they would not be found. Each night for those
uncertain six months she would walk up and down the hall of
the apartment with the baby in her arms and plan their escape.
The things she would take with her. How she might obtain false
papers. She didn't talk to her husband about any of this, the
dean said. He would have thought that she had lost her mind.
But she would have left him behind if it had come to it.

During those fall days Harlem seemed transformed. The heat of the summer had dissolved and the light seemed clear and luminous. It was the light of mountains and green valleys. The sky felt high and pure, the afternoons very still. In the mornings when Gabriel was with her they would walk across the road to Mount Morris Park. The little boy loved to climb up the great craggy rise of rocks, or to play on the swings on the eastern side of the park. He did not know how to play with other children, Marina realised. Sometimes he would approach a cluster of children and stand on the fringes staring at them with a bewildered sort of fascination. He always hung back, holding on to her skirt, his thumb in his mouth.

One day Ben and Alma came to the house carrying crates full of plants. There were plastic pots of herbs and lettuces, small chilli plants bent over under the weight of their fruit, tiny trays full of marigolds. They had been discarded by the grocery store and he had retrieved them, Ben told her. He and Alma wanted to plant a garden. It was not the right time of year for planting but they thought that if they could get the seedlings into the ground they might be strong enough by wintertime to survive the frost. Their seriousness and their careful attention to the task warmed her. What could be more hopeful than planting a garden?

Marina sat with Gabriel while they dug out a square in one of the flowerbeds for a herb garden, another for lettuces, earnestly discussing the best arrangement of plants. Alma wore one of Marina's straw hats, her hair hanging in a thick braid down her back as she bent over the plants, pressing marigolds in among the green seedlings. Ben knelt beside her, tying the chilli plants gently to tiny stakes with scraps of fabric.

When Ben was fourteen, Marina and Jacob had taken him to Philadelphia. Jacob was at a conference, and she and Ben spent

233

the weekend wandering through the city together, slipping into museums to avoid the frequent rain. At the Rodin Museum she loved watching Ben stare intently at each sculpture, silent and absorbed. He bent over every plaque, reading the accompanying information attentively, his hands folded behind his back. Watching him now, Marina could see the same absorbed attention, the same watchful love for the world. She tried to think of a way that she could let Jacob know that Ben had received all the good he had meant for him. That things would be put right somehow.

In the early mornings a silvery light hung over the backyard. When Marina looked down from her window the garden was mapped out into small squares of green, like a landscape seen from high in the air. A careful patchwork. The plans for the garden grew more elaborate, all of them slipping into the work. Marina went with Ben and Alma to the nursery and they bought more herbs: sage, mint, chives and thyme. Alma chose tomato plants and they staked them against the far wall, beside the nuns' abandoned grotto. Ben found an old gardening manual in the library and he sat on the steps with the book open on his knees, reading out loud to them about methods of natural pest control and the benefits of mulching with pea straw.

Working in the garden felt necessary and important, almost a kind of restitution. It made Marina think of her brother, the letters that Dov had written her from Poland during the summer he had spent there cleaning graves in the Jewish cemetery. What he was doing was *avodat kodesh*, Dov told her in his long, fervent letters. Holy work. He slept on a camp bed in the small house of the village priest and the life he described was spare and monastic.

Early risings and long days of hard work in the cemetery, cutting back vines and cleaning the gravestones. The graves had been neglected for decades, some of them had been vandalised and covered with graffiti. Dov had abandoned his religious observance by then, but this felt to him like a truer form of faith. Small, unnoticed works of mercy were what interested him now, he wrote to Marina. No longer for him the fanfare and ceremony of organised religion – it had too much of the performance about it. He wanted nothing false. How Marina wished Dov could have been there with them, crouched in the soil among the plants.

In her telephone conversations with Jacob at night, Marina told him about the things they had planted that day. The flower seeds they scattered among the herbs, the little tents of muslin that Ben had constructed to protect the kale from bugs. She tried to imagine Jacob sitting in an armchair in the borrowed apartment in Cambridge, a glass of wine beside him, his feet resting on the coffee table. Ben's footsteps sounded on the floorboards above her. A soft laugh, a door closing, then the house fell quiet.

When she woke from a dream hours later, the whole room was awash in a pale shaft of moonlight. She reached out for Jacob, forgetting for a moment that he was not beside her. Rose had once told her that for many months after Max died she surfaced from sleep believing he had been returned to her. Every morning there was the fresh grief of waking to find his side of the bed empty. She had worried that this was a sign that she was not steady in her mind. She felt his absence so piercingly, she told Marina, that she had truly feared she might go mad. That some essential part of herself would remain forever unhinged. She went walking a great deal in the weeks after Max died and she would look in at the lighted windows of the townhouses on the streets around her, thinking that she would always now feel cast out of her own life. She had entered into some other element and she was not sure how to inhabit the world anymore. This was what it would be like for her to lose Jacob, Marina thought now, staring across at the pile of books scattered on his side of the bed. It was a devastating thought. Rose was only a few years older than she was now when Max died. So much life still before her.

Marina had read a story once about the Aleut people that she had found strangely comforting. When an Aleut man's wife died, the tribe would gather around him to brace his joints against grief. It was a literal swaddling – hide bindings wrapped firmly around the knees, the ankles, the elbows and shoulders. All the vulnerable points of bone. The Aleuts believed that if they did not take this precaution it would be possible, in your grief, to go to pieces; that the body could fall apart from sorrow. It seemed right that grief could take such a physical form. And a comfort to think it could be guarded against.

One afternoon when Constance arrived to collect Gabriel she came out to the garden. The girl stood there framed by the door, her canvas bag clutched in her arms, watching them all at work. Marina could not look into her face anymore without remembering all the terrible things she had read in the books about Rwanda. Of all the possible histories she imagined for Constance, the story of the marshes was the one that Marina most often inserted her into. She found herself searching Constance's face sometimes for traces of the young girl who had hidden herself beneath the water. Waiting, watching in the cold mud, some desperate instinct for preservation conquering her terror. Marina agonised over the things she might have seen during those long weeks, the ways that she had been hurt.

Ben waved exuberantly to Constance. 'Come and see our splendid kale,' he called out to her. He simply filled in Constance's silences, carrying on a conversation with her as if she had responded after all. To Marina's surprise, Constance came over to the garden bed and crouched down in the dirt next to Ben. She reached out and touched one of the new kale plants, running her finger over its knobbly leaves. Ben passed Constance a tray of parsley seedlings they had bought at the nursery that morning. 'Here. Help us get these planted,' he said casually.

Constance looked down at the tray of small plants. A silence hovered over the garden; it was as if they were all holding their breath. Gabriel stood very still beside Alma, a small watering can in his hands. They were watching Constance, Marina realised, to see what she would do.

Constance placed the seedlings down gently and picked up a trowel that was lying in the garden bed beside her. She slipped off her shoes. Deftly, she dug out several small holes and pressed the plants expertly into the ground. When the parsley was planted, she set to work on a tray of silverbeet, bending silently over the plants, the soles of her feet pale in the sunlight. Something must still remain in her after all, thought Marina, from her life before this one. Someone had taught her about turning soil and tucking seedlings into the earth, about the space to leave around each plant. She contained such submerged histories. Not only the things that had happened to her during the genocide, but the life she had lived before that. Had she been married? She most likely would have been only seventeen when the genocide began, but perhaps that was old enough for marriage where she came from. Or had she lived with her parents? Were there brothers and sisters? But even if she asked her these questions, Marina knew, the girl would not answer her.

The next day Constance arrived just after midday. She must have come straight from her class in East Harlem. She went to the garden, where Alma and Ben were pulling up weeds from around the nuns' old grotto. They wanted to plant bulbs there so that in the spring there would be tulips and daffodils. Constance joined them, hitching her wrap above her knees and taking a small hoe. She did not speak to them, but a different air came over her when she was working in the garden. There was something less formidable about her, something softer. She worked carefully, bent closely over the plants. Sometimes she stopped to examine her work, a faint glimmer of satisfaction on her face.

For Gabriel the garden was a place of fascination. He scratched away in the dirt with a stick, scavenging for hidden shells and dead beetles, his mouth pursed in fierce concentration. Marina plucked sprigs of rosemary and wild thyme, and crushed them for him to smell, found feathers and the skeletons of insects for him. One day she came towards him holding her hand out in front of her and let a ladybird circle from her wrist to his small cupped hand. He stared as the tiny speck made its way down his arm, brightly red against his skin. He leaned into her, taking her arm and placing it around his waist. Since the very beginning there had been this hunger in him for touch. This need was something she felt constantly and sharply, as if the only way he could truly know her love was when he was in her arms. Of course it made sense, Jacob said when she told him this. The mother's body is our foundational experience, the relationship that tells us what a relationship is. The child was looking for something that would bear the trace of his mother's body.

Marina thought of Gizela. If her history was remote to her children, then her body was just as unavailable. They had watched their mother with a stunned awe; even as children her beauty was evident to them. It seemed incomprehensible that they had come from her body. There were no photographs of Gizela when she was pregnant. If Marina and Dov had not looked so like her, they could have convinced themselves that they were not her children at all, that they had somehow been deposited into her reluctant care. Once, Gizela had caught a brooch in her long hair and asked Marina to untangle it. The sensation of having her hands in her mother's hair felt like the most illicit of thrills, and Marina lingered over the task for as long as possible, until Gizela grew impatient and told her to hurry up. Marina and Dov were always dreaming up scenarios in which Gizela might need their help: illnesses that they would nurse her through, hospital stays when they would keep vigil by her bedside. They would save her from terrible accidents and she would turn to them with love and gratitude.

Gizela did go to hospital one year. Marina was seven years old, Dov eleven. Their mother refused to tell them what was wrong, only that she needed to have something done and she would be gone for two days. They could not visit her, she said when Dov asked, because the hospital would not allow children. They watched her from the window, walking down the street with a small suitcase in her hand. At the corner she paused and looked back towards the house for a moment before setting off again. The apartment seemed darker than ever with Gizela gone. They missed the clatter of her typewriter from behind her bedroom door, the sounds of her feet on the floorboards as she walked around her room.

She was gone for twelve days. For all this time Marina and Dov continued to pack their lunches and go to school and do their homework at the kitchen table in the evenings. Dov bought loaves of sweet challah from the bakery around the corner and they ate bread and butter for dinner. They stayed up late reading, often falling asleep on the old velvet sofa, the reading lamps still burning when they woke in the cold winter mornings. Each day there was a growing, unspoken fretfulness. Some sense of dread stopped them from speaking to one another about their mother or where she might be. It was as if by naming possibilities they might conjure them into being.

But after a week passed they wrote down the names of all the hospitals they knew in Brooklyn. Gizela's name was not listed at any of them. Marina watched Dov as he stood at the counter of one hospital, leaning in and carefully writing their mother's last name on a piece of paper for the clerk. She and Dov had not once spoken about what they would do if they could not find Gizela, if she failed to return to them.

Several days later, the door opened and she walked into the apartment. She put her small suitcase on the floor and sat down at the kitchen table where Marina and Dov were playing cards. She looked pale and gaunt, her hair dull and unwashed. She said nothing to them about where she had been for so long, but she drank the cup of tea that Dov made for her, gazing at the two of them as if they were strangers. She sat there with them for a long time, still wearing her coat, her elbows resting on the table.

Those fall days in the garden of the brownstone were like brief, hopeful flares. They took on an enchanted cast. The liquid afternoon light, the modest flourishing of the vegetables, the shared effort. Constance joined them every day, coming to the house even when she did not have class. Ben would race home after his shifts at the supermarket, bursting through the back door into the garden. Sometimes they kept working until the sky darkened. How safe they all were there in the garden. As if the walls had been built to shelter such peace.

Late in the afternoons Marina made a pot of tea and they all sat together on the terrace, surveying the work they had done. The blue teacups lined up on a tray, slices of dark fruitcake that Rose had made – they were the strangest of tea parties. They talked then, too. Alma would describe the countryside of her childhood or the particular way her mother had cooked tamales. Ben once told a long story about an elusive Japanese mathematician and the particular beauty of the theorem he had discovered. Marina found herself speaking about Frieda, the young Satmarer woman who had left the community, and whom she found herself writing more and more about. 'You should invite her for Shabbat sometime,' Ben said. 'She must be lonely.'

Constance remained silent, but sitting there beside her, Marina could sense an attentiveness that she had never seen in her before. Once, she caught her staring hard at Alma as she spoke about her younger sisters. Constance was trying, Marina thought, to be there with them in the best way that she could.

In November Jacob returned from Boston and soon afterwards the weather changed with an alarming swiftness. Within the space of a few days winter was everywhere. A frost spread over the garden and the lettuces and tomatoes succumbed. Their wilted remains felt irretrievably sad to Marina. It was too cold to be in the garden any longer. The nursery where they bought all the plants offered Ben a part-time job, and he and Alma spent long hours there learning how to propagate seedlings. Constance stopped coming. They returned to the old pattern. She brought Gabriel to the house before her class, sometimes walking away down the street as soon as she saw Marina open the front door, leaving the little boy standing bundled up in his red coat at the foot of the steps. She returned in the late afternoon, always refusing Marina's invitation to come in for a cup of tea. It was as if those days in the garden had been dreamed, their strange companionship dissolving as quickly as it had formed. By the time the first snow came, the only thing that still survived out there was the rosemary.

Harlem
November, 1997

Marina walked west through the park to Columbia. The sun hung low in the sky, hidden by a gauze of clouds. She tucked the ends of her scarf closer around her neck. It was not yet December and already the city had succumbed to what felt like the bitter cold of midwinter. She had agreed to give a lecture in the School of Journalism about her research process for the Romani book. The students were learning about the art of the interview, her colleague told her; it would be interesting for them to hear about her experiences with the Romani community. When she was preparing for the lecture the day before she had taken her book from the shelf and turned it over. 'An ambitious panorama of European Gypsydom', the publisher had written. 'A penetrating study of the world's most elusive people'. She hated the word panorama. There was something false and smug in it, something against the whole spirit of the work. It was the same feeling she had about the idea of teaching students how to conduct an interview. What could she tell them? That very little of what they needed to know could be taught. That it took time and long silences and quiet, attuned listening. That they should throw their earnest lists of questions away. It was not what they would want to hear.

After the lecture, Marina walked to her office to collect her mail. She stopped to make herself a cup of tea in the staff kitchen. Strange to think that she would be back at work in a few weeks' time, that her days would no longer be her own. The sky had turned dark and she saw the first few taps of rain as she sat down at her desk, the soft roll of it against the dusty window. There was a book that had finally come in on an inter-library loan, a pile of letters. One of the envelopes was handwritten; an unfamiliar scrawl. She sliced open the envelope carefully with the letter opener shaped like a feather that Ben had given her one birthday.

The letter was from a man called Patrick Stone. Marina's mother had been his neighbour, he wrote. They had lived side by side for nearly twenty years in a small seaside town called Truro in Cape Cod. He was writing to tell her that Gizela had died. It was cancer, diagnosed at the beginning of the summer. Terrible but swift. By the time it was found there was nothing that could be done. In any case, Gizela had refused all medical intervention. She had died at home, in her house by the ocean. It had happened just after dawn, which, as Marina might know, was her mother's favourite time of the day. Gizela had given firm instructions, the letter went on to say, that Marina was not to be told that she was sick. That she was not to be told of her death until afterwards. He had not felt able to defy her in this.

Gizela had been cremated, Patrick wrote, another thing that she had insisted upon. She had not wanted any ceremony, any gravestone or memorial, only for her ashes to be thrown into the

244

Atlantic Ocean. The ashes had come back from the funeral parlour now and he wondered whether Marina might want to come to the Cape to be there to scatter them into the sea. She might also want to come to her mother's house and see if there was anything of Gizela's she wanted to keep. He understood if this was not possible for her, but had wanted to extend the offer. He would wait to hear from her. At the bottom of the letter he had written his address and telephone number.

Marina sat there with the letter in her hands. Everything seemed to close around her, as if the air had been sucked from the room. Here it was, all her old hunger for her mother slipping into something so terrifying that it turned her stomach, made the edges of the room rise up, and recede. Her shaking hands, a lurching sea-sickness, tightness in her ribs. She looked at the date on the letter. It had been written nearly four weeks earlier. Marina struggled to line up the facts: Gizela's death, this life by the ocean in Cape Cod. Impossible to fathom any of it. The distant sound of voices in the courtyard, the faraway hum of traffic, the catch and drip of the rain against the glass, the cooling cup of tea in front of her: the whole episode seemed suspended, out of time. She didn't know how long she sat at her desk after she read the letter, her hands clasped around the mug on her desk to keep them from shaking, the tight twist of fear in her stomach. She laid her head down on the desk and closed her eyes.

Jacob came to bring her home from the university. He picked up the telephone when she called his office, and half an hour later he was there in the doorway, his coat slick with rain, a wrench of worry on his face as he crossed the room and put his arms around her. Suddenly she was weeping against him, his hand stroking her hair. *Darling, darling.* He murmured it to her like an incantation, a good spell to keep her from harm. She let him lead her home through the park, his arm looped through hers, the wide spread of his big umbrella encasing them so that she could barely see the world before them.

Back at the house he made her a cup of camomile tea, with a sliver of lemon on the saucer and a dissolving clod of raw honey. Marina sat at the kitchen table watching the rain mist over the garden. Had this man named Patrick cared for her mother in this way? Had he brought her tea when she was sick or sorrowful? Had Gizela allowed this sort of solicitude? Who had looked after her in her illness? Jacob draped their scarves and gloves over the radiator to dry and the sight of them hanging limply there made Marina dissolve into tears again.

In the days that followed, a grief more consuming than Marina had ever imagined set in. And something more than grief, something awash with horror and fear. A clawing at her throat. A loss had been lit in her that was too large for anything rational to appeal to. There was no consoling conversation she could have with herself, no way to hope that this grief, like others that had come before it, would someday merge into the past. Her mourning for her mother had slipped past any defences she had.

In the weeks after Dov died and Gizela disappeared, Marina had imagined her mother dead too. A crumpled heap by the guardrail of some far road, spidery glass in her long hair. Or a shifting darkness beneath the frigid winter river, stones in her pockets like Virginia Woolf. But Gizela was not dead. Her clothes were missing from her shelves, her hairbrush gone from the bathroom. Her leaving was deliberate and planned. Marina had been waiting for it her entire life, she realised on that first night alone in the apartment. Every moment of her childhood and Dov's had been lived in the shadow of their fear that their mother would not remain with them. In a way it was a relief when it finally happened.

Two months after Gizela left, an envelope arrived, addressed to Marina in her mother's slanted handwriting. There was no note and no return address, just the title deed to the apartment, made out into Marina's name. The envelope was damp when she took it from the mailbox and the postmark had bled so that she could not decipher it. It was the day before her eighteenth birthday.

It was the only time she ever heard from her mother, and in the years to come it seemed to Marina that Gizela must be dead. That she could not possibly exist out there in the world. Just as she and Dov had never been able to imagine a credible past for their mother, Marina found herself unable to conceive of any life that Gizela could be living after she had disappeared. She did not have the heart for speculation after Dov had died. Gizela seemed to have cast herself adrift in the most irretrievable and complete of ways. She did not want to be found so Marina would not look for her. Yet all along she was living by the ocean just a few hours north of the city.

They had been to the Cape three summers before. It was for Ben's former girlfriend Isabel's eighteenth birthday. Her parents had arranged an extravagant party at their house in Wellfleet, and Marina, Jacob and Ben drove north for the weekend. Marina remembered the clapboard inns and sea captain's cottages, and the luminous cast of the afternoons. Edward Hopper's light. They had driven through Truro on the way to a lunch in Provincetown;

she remembered seeing the sign for the town and thinking about the ways that in exile we layer the names of the familiar over the new places we find ourselves. We reach for the known, hoping that it will help us to inhabit what seems too large, too strange. Marina suddenly felt seized by a wrenching sort of homesickness. She could have met her mother walking down the main street of the little town with its English name.

In the mornings she lay in bed with her knees curled to her chest to still the dull churn of her stomach. She could see Jacob moving about in the bathroom, hear the buzz of his shaver and the low hum of the radio as he listened to the early news. She watched him – the familiar lines of his body, the surprising slenderness of his legs as he stepped into the shower. It was one of the purest pleasures of her life, this daily revelation of his body. They kept between them a sweet shyness that was at odds with the live coal of desire that sprang up in bed. When she slid beneath him in the darkness it was all sensation. The weight of his chest, the sound in his throat, her lips at his neck. But in daylight there was a tentativeness with their bodies, a closed bathroom door, a towel around the waist. It was one of the spaces they left each other. And so this morning ritual, this secret glimpsing of his body, became even more laden. Her eyes half-closed, the pretence of sleep, Jacob's unconcerned gaze at himself in the bathroom mirror.

Now there was no desire left in her. She didn't want anything. When Jacob came to sit beside her on the edge of the bed, she rested her head against his shoulder and he stroked her hair as if he were soothing a small child. He had always comforted her like this, the wise, kind weight of him propping her up, his hand against her shoulder on a sleepless night. It was something she had to learn to give in to, a yielding she had never allowed herself with anyone before him except for Dov. But something in her had gone awry now. Everything felt like false consolation. The wide rooms of all the books she might have read; Ben's clutch of flowers from the nursery; Jacob lying down for a moment beside her in the morning before work, her face against his suit jacket. No weeping after that first day, just an inward dissembling. She didn't even feel capable of seeing Gabriel. She would dissolve if she held the little boy in her arms. It would not be fair to let this kind of grief come near him; he had enough sorrow in his life. She had asked Ben to walk to the projects and tell Constance that she was unwell; not to bring Gabriel to the house.

Jacob sat on the edge of the bed beside her, wearing a shirt they had bought together years before in Paris, a film of rain on the window behind him. The fine linen of his shirt was the watery blue of airmail paper. She remembered unbuttoning that shirt in a hotel room in St Germain, the faint click of the small horn buttons as it fell to the marble floor. A tight knot formed in her throat as he picked up her hand.

'I'll book a table at Balthazar tonight. Come down and meet me after work.'

She tried to imagine it. The long judder of the subway, the jostle of umbrellas on the street corners downtown, the swerve of cabs in against the sidewalk, the crowded restaurant, the sure-footedness of it all.

'I can't.'

Marina could feel the sigh in Jacob, the slight pulse at his temple. She felt suddenly as if she were one of his patients, sitting in the armchair by the window in Chelsea. The benevolence of him, the reasonableness, that considered gaze across the room.

But there were no words to contain a sway of elusive meaning, nothing that could be deciphered or reasoned with. A heartsickness, that was the only name for it. A sickness, yes.

Later that morning she pulled back the curtain and watched Jacob walk down the street towards the subway station. He was slightly bewildered, she knew, by the extremity of her grief. When his father died Jacob's sadness had been a sweeping but manageable thing, an anguish that could be spoken to, and turned eventually into something else. How many times had she listened to Jacob speak about the father he adored, narrating the long curve of a known history. Max at six scratching his lessons on a slate in the coal-heated schoolrooms of his Polish childhood. His parents' escape to America before the war. The unlikely jobs they found as caretakers of a sprawling Victorian guesthouse in the seaside town of Cape May in New Jersey, all the rooms and suites named for members of the English Royal Family. Ten-year-old Max and his younger brother hiding under carved four-poster beds; learning English by reading adventure novels; playing cowboys and Indians in the guesthouse gardens. The tiny muslin sacks just big enough for one clove of garlic that his superstitious mother had sewn and hung around her children's necks; fragrant necklaces that were supposed to ward off sickness. All the trips to the Museum of Natural History that Jacob and Leah had taken with their father, the afternoons at the library, the holidays to Cape May.

Marina had no narrative like this to unspool, no consoling memories. What could she have said about Gizela, had she been given the chance to speak at her grave? She did not own even one thing that had belonged to her mother. She was like a miserable bird, locked into experimental darkness by scientists and turning wretchedly towards some lost north when the seasons shifted. So many years, and Gizela's power to wound her was undiminished. She imagined her mother walking by the edge of the sea, her head down, her long braid between her shoulders. Dawn had been her favourite time of day, the man who wrote the letter said. Marina had not known this. Gizela had never communicated any preference for anything; it stunned Marina to know that her mother had any feeling for what time of day it was, what season. She had always seemed so impervious to the world around her.

More than anything Marina wanted to go to Cape Cod, the slim stretch of land where Gizela had lived for close to two decades. 'The outermost shore', someone had called it in a poem, the distant edge of America. Such a small spread of space between them all those years. Suddenly it was the only place she wanted to be.

Several days after Marina received the letter, she dialled the telephone number at the bottom of the page. 'Oh, yes,' said the man who picked up the phone, as if he had been expecting her call. There was an unusual lilt to his voice, an accent that she couldn't quite place. No, he had not scattered the ashes yet, Patrick told her. He had not been able to bring himself to do it.

'I thought I might come and spend some time in Truro,' she said. There was a long pause. 'I'd like to see where she lived.' Marina could hardly bear to speak her mother's name to this stranger. 'It had been so long since I last saw her. Twenty years. You know this, perhaps.' She was not sure what this man had been to Gizela, how much of her story he knew.

'You should come,' Patrick said. 'You can stay in Gizela's house. I can order a load of wood for you.'

It gave her some consolation, to think of a fire burning against the great night.

Jacob sat quietly across from her at the kitchen table when she told him that she needed to go to Truro. He had just come in from work and he looked very tired, his hair silvered by the soft afternoon light. He picked up her hand and stared at her palm as if there were something he could decipher there, some secret and important clue.

'If you need to go ...' *If you need to go.* It was the same thing he said to her all the times she had struck out and away from him. To the writers' colony in France for those quiet weeks of work, a conference in Lisbon, a research trip to London. These small, necessary departures made her feel the weight of her love for him all the more, as if her life made more sense when she looked at it from the outside. It was a kind of punishment she inflicted on herself too, sick with longing for him after three days sleeping alone in a hotel bed. Their conversations trailing into the night, across the country, across the Atlantic, the days counted before she turned around and came home to him.

But this was different. What she wanted was not a clean sallying out into the world, a circumscribed journey. This was like a sad trick she needed to play: stepping away from all of them and turning herself into someone who did not belong anywhere.

The evening before she left for the Cape she and Jacob took a long walk through Central Park. The rain that engulfed the city for days had stopped at last and the world had a damp, gauzy feel. Marina was packing her suitcase when Jacob came and took her hand and led her out of the house. The night was cold and still, not even the tiniest rip of wind in the trees. They sat together on a bench near the top end of the park, their shoulders touching. Marina slipped her hands under Jacob's sweater. There were so many intuitive gestures between them, such a vast bodily knowledge. Her eyes were full of tears. That knot again in her throat, like the beginning of illness.

'I'm worried about leaving Constance and Gabriel,' she whispered. She could feel the sigh move through Jacob's body. She had not seen them since she had received the letter. It felt to Marina like the cruellest of betrayals, but she did not know how to explain it to the girl. What was her loss against Constance's? How could she explain that she had been undone by the death of a mother she had not seen for twenty years? And Gabriel. Marina missed the little boy with a longing so forceful that it threatened to overwhelm her. She thought of the way that he would turn and look back towards the house when he was walking home with Constance.

'They'll survive,' Jacob said firmly. 'They did for a long time before you came along.'

That night they made love, their bodies curved around each other. Marina listened for the catch and gasp in Jacob's throat as he collapsed against her, then the slowing of his breath as he drifted into sleep.

Truro, Cape Cod
December, 1997

The early winter light in Truro was pale, insufficient. Marina lit the fire in the afternoons, coaxing the twigs into life when she sensed the shadows shifting. On her knees in front of the old wood stove, the flames cast a small diameter of warmth around her. Outside, the dusk was fine and powdery; the next time she glanced up at the windows, night had fallen. She crouched by the light of the fire, listening to the calls of the gulls in the distance as they coasted above the winter beach. At the end of the curve of land the Truro lighthouse could just be made out. She could see the beam of light suspended and secure above the night.

Gizela's small cottage stood on the great bay of Cape Cod, perched on a narrow sand spit with meadows and marshland at its back. Along the western side the windows opened emptily to the sea. From outside, the place had the look of a besieged country house, with its peeling shingles and shuttered windows. The wind hissed over the grasses behind the house.

⌐

On her first night in the house by the sea Marina found an old bottle of whisky in a cupboard under the sink, and each evening she poured herself a few fingers in a glass and carried it to the table by the window. It took on the air of a ceremony. Here on the Cape these rituals gave a shape to her days; they were a kind of map. The armfuls of logs carried in from the wood shed, the tending of the fire, the walks along the shore – they all formed a pattern that was comforting to her in its circumscription. Was this how Gizela had lived, tucked away from the world here on this slim promontory? How had she even found this place?

At night Marina lay awake in the high wooden bed listening to the slow heave of the ocean. Stacked in a small pile on the windowsill behind her bed were the letters Jacob had written her, one for every day of her absence so far, dropped in the mailbox at the end of their street. Sometimes just a poem, or a few lines from an essay scrawled on a sheet of his letterhead. They had always brought each other these gifts from books they had read, lines slipped between them like codes that became part of the private language of their marriage. A vast, secret museum.

There were no words of consolation or sensible advice in Jacob's letters. He knew her better than that. He wrote about the shape of his days, the cake a patient had brought him, which he and Ben had devoured in one evening. 'It's so good to see him display some appetite again,' Jacob wrote, his relief almost singing out of the lines. Ben was eating cake, shovelling the sidewalk after an early snowfall, reading botanical textbooks. The two of them sometimes watched the documentary channel together in the evenings. Ben had brought Alma over for dinner one night. The girl was clearly very bright, Jacob wrote, and her situation was so very difficult. Marina wondered how much Ben had told Jacob about Alma. There was no mention of Constance

255

or Gabriel in any of Jacob's letters. Even if he had seen them in the neighbourhood he would not say anything to her about it. She wanted to write and ask him to check on them, but she did not. Tucked inside one of the novels she had brought with her was a photograph of Gabriel. He was running along the path in the garden, turning back to smile at her. His whole face was illuminated, a pure kind of joy in his expression. He looked like an ordinary child. Like a child who knew love.

One of Jacob's envelopes held a sprig of green from the garden. 'This was rosemary when it left me,' he wrote. She pressed the dried leaves to her nose; that sharp, sweet smell.

Marina lay in bed in the mornings watching the light seep into the world. There would only be a handful of hours of daylight before the sky began to empty again and the world returned to darkness. She remembered the Australian writer in France who had wanted to be somewhere the light was always sufficient, where there was no looming dusk. We are always, she thought, trying to ward off the darkness in one way or another.

Every morning she put on her coat and scarf and walked out along the winter beach, staring down at the stones and the wet kelp. The placid lap of the bay made her think of rivers. Sometimes she saw a single line of footsteps. The sand was criss-crossed with the light tracks of gulls. Birds and their brief, physical lives. If she came across gulls or terns nestling on the edge of the shore, they rose up in a half-hearted flapping as she approached, coasting out on to the waves or settling back on the sand as soon as she was safely out of reach. Once, she saw an enormous slick-feathered bird standing on a clump of mossy rocks. A lost osprey, she thought, or perhaps an albatross. She had never known the names of birds.

Further along the beach the dunes rose up steeply and the cottages at their crests tilted above the long wooden staircases that cut down through the scrub to the sand. All the houses were closed up for winter, boards nailed neatly and firmly across the windows. There was a care in this that she found strangely touching. It was hard for her to think of these houses in any other season, open and unshuttered, full of people, canoes and deckchairs dragged down to the water's edge. In the warm months the whole place must take on a completely different cast: summer lavender and wild ducks, the mild golden light of the afternoons. Marina imagined bringing Gabriel here in the summertime, teaching him to swim. She could see the little boy crouched by the water, collecting shells. They could walk to the lighthouse together. Nowhere in her imaginings, she realised, was Constance.

The day she had left New York was icy, the streets swept by river wind, the briny gusts coming at them as they stood on the steps of the brownstone. A crack of light opened the clouds as Ben packed her bag into the trunk of the car. Jacob stamped his feet on the sidewalk, his grey scarf covering his mouth. Marina's mind was already on the journey, the hours of light she still had left to reach Truro. The map of Massachusetts was spread out on the passenger seat. Ben had highlighted the route in yellow for her, recited all the names of the towns she would pass through on her way to Truro. Bourne, Barnstable, Yarmouth, Eastham, Wellfleet. Villages lined up along the narrow curved arm of the Cape. Grey shingled rooves and the leaking smell of fir. Gizela's house.

Jacob and Ben stood side by side on the front steps of the brownstone, something bewildered and bereft in their faces.

Marina could still feel the close press of Jacob's arms around her, the prickle of Ben's stubble as he kissed her cold cheek. They were what she had to stand against her doubt, her sadness. The throbbing, holy heart of whatever home she had created in the world. She tried to imagine them there in Truro, their voices breaking the bleak, solitary hush of the house, their winter coats hanging on the hooks by the door, their boots warming by the fire.

She was glad to be alone. After trouble this was always how she felt safest. She had enough food to last for days. Tins of tomatoes, dry pasta. Some fruit, some cheese. When she needed more she could take the car and drive the ten miles to the supermarket in Provincetown. She avoided the small seaside town in the afternoons. The shimmering Christmas lights against the blue dusk and the fast firm steps of couples walking their dogs along the narrow streets seemed unbearably sad to her. The town itself, so quaint and charming when she had visited in summer, had taken on a kind of menace. The clapboard inns with their Christmas wreaths and brass doorbells, the narrow-fronted shops and the lobster restaurants along the boardwalk – all of it seemed cold and turned in on itself.

The way that the hours drifted made her think of the time after Dov died and Gizela had gone. The months alone in the apartment, the sharp shiver of her grief keeping her awake into the night. Sometimes in the evenings she ran a bath and lay for a long time in the cooling water, the ridge of the tub pressing against her neck, the fire cracking and shifting in the room beyond her. There was no depth to submerge herself in here, no high waterline to hide the body. Her knees were folded to her chest, her mouth resting against the bare flesh of her arm. She blew out the candle that she had placed beside her. Such pure darkness. It seemed then like a comfort to her; the absence of light, the soft dark chill pressed in around the small house. The great vastness of the night.

Birds, she knew, had a perfect memory. More than memory, perhaps – something so deeply ingrained that it brought them back season after season to the lands they had left. A path in her own memory would always lead her back to the day that Dov had died. She had been the one to identify his body, to say, 'Yes, this is him.' She remembered signing her name at the hospital morgue, her hands shaking. It had felt to her that by writing her name, Dov's death was sealed forever. She had signed him away, cast him into a realm where she could not follow him.

Leaving the hospital, Marina had taken a wrong turn and walked down a long corridor that stretched between the small wards. Through the open doors she could see patients in their beds, watching television, reading books. A nurse wheeled a dinner trolley down the hall. A woman poured a cup of tea for her mother. Life continued, safe and oblivious. A cup of milky tea, a lighted window, a cool hand against the forehead. It seemed impossible to Marina then that she would ever find any comfort in the world again.

Four months later, when the school year was over, she had caught a Greyhound bus west to California. She had a scholarship to Berkeley, had sold the apartment on Union Street to the Zelman family. Their oldest son had his own family now and they wanted him to be close to them. Eked out carefully, the money was enough to sustain her throughout her studies and into graduate school. It had occurred to Marina that the apartment was the closest thing she would ever have to a family legacy. It had harboured both Sura and Gizela; made their lives in the city possible. It was the place where she and Dov had grown up. And yet it had not felt like a home. It had housed them, yes, but the four walls had never given any of them refuge. Now the money from the apartment would make another life possible for her.

It was deliberate, the drawn-out journey across the country to California, through dust-bowls and ancient sea beds, the taut line of the road spinning endlessly out ahead. The hasty meals at truck-stops, the smell of diesel, the cold press of the window on her forehead; she needed a long journey to feel that she was putting enough space between herself and Brooklyn and everything that had happened there. A swift plane ride would not have been sufficient. She barely slept in all those days of driving west, the bus trundling through brief bouts of night-time rain, the lights of towns slipping away into the distance. It was a world in itself, that journey. A book in her hands, a cooling thermos of tea, the other passengers sleeping around her. It felt final; a necessary departure.

Until she met Jacob nearly a decade later she had never believed that it would be possible for her to return to New York.

In the mornings the winter tide narrowed the beach to a glistening sliver, a stretch wide enough for a solitary walker. Marina followed the path towards the dunes, her hand above her eyes to shade her face. The morning was pure and airy, a rare blaze of sun touching every cold blade of grass. Further along the shore she saw a figure moving towards her, a man with a pair of binoculars around his neck, a backpack hanging over one shoulder.

As he came closer she could see the coarse wool of his sweater, the faded corduroy of his trousers. A tall man with a gingery beard. Patrick Stone. When she had arrived at Gizela's house several days earlier he had been there to meet her. He was just about to go to Boston for a few days, he said, but would call on her when he returned. There was a bottle of milk left in the refrigerator for her, a loaf of sourdough bread on the kitchen counter. Kneeling down in front of the wood stove that first afternoon, Marina found that a fire had been laid in the grate ready to be lit, the twigs neatly layered over twists of newspaper. At first she thought that Gizela had made this fire, but the date on the newspaper was too recent. It must have been Patrick. When she put the logs on, it had burned long into the night, the glow of the flames reflected in the darkened windows.

She and Patrick were a few metres away from each other when a flock of small birds rose up suddenly from the dunes, dipping and swinging noisily. A constellation fragmenting and closing in again, shrieking loudly and then disappearing into the freezing air. They stood together in the quiet. The air was very cold, too cold to be outside for much longer.

'It always seems strange to me,' Patrick said slowly, 'that a sound like that evaporates.'

He was looking into her face with a bemused scrutiny. There were tears in his eyes.

'I'm sorry,' he said, bowing his head, embarrassed. 'It's just that you look so very much like her.'

Marina pulled her coat closer around her. 'Yes. I always have.'

Patrick was quiet. He looked at her again, his head tilted to one side. There was something tentative but kind in his expression.

Had Gizela loved him, Marina wondered? It seemed impossible to imagine her mother succumbing to anyone. But she must have once loved Yoav. She had married him and lived with him for ten years, however unfathomable the fact of that marriage had always seemed to Marina. Perhaps it was possible for Gizela to love someone else. Marina felt immensely sad, and somehow envious, too. What might this stranger have unlocked in Gizela that her own children could not?

'Stop by for a cup of tea after your walk if you like,' Patrick said. 'It can get lonely out here in winter.'

Marina stared at him. She had seen no one since she had arrived in Truro. She noticed the smear of paint on his green sweater, his fingers winding themselves through the leather straps of his binoculars.

An hour later she walked along the narrow path that led back from the beach towards the two houses, Gizela's set high above the sea, Patrick's cabin at the foot of the dunes. They were built with a gracious respect for privacy, she thought, far enough apart to allow for space and silence. She hesitated at the front door. It was the hour of light that felt kindest to her in this place, the dusky early afternoon softness. She stood watching the dune grasses swaying lightly in the wind and wished that Jacob were with her, his hand on her back to steady her. She thought of him sitting in his office in Chelsea, listening to a patient, reaching out for the mug of coffee he had placed on the windowsill. If she took the car right now and drove seven hours south she could be back in New York before he was asleep, could take off her coat and crawl into bed beside him, her cold feet against the familiar, drowsy heat of him.

Patrick's house was full of books; they sat stacked haphazard piles on the floor and the old velvet couch. A glassed-in porch faced the ocean; there was a desk there with a view out over the dunes to the water. Marina hung her coat on the back of one of the bentwood chairs at the kitchen table. Something about the place appealed to her; its seemingly perilous closeness to the edge of the sea, perhaps.

He lit the fire, crouching in front of the stove with an old pair of leather bellows. Marina saw how carefully he arranged the kindling, his skilful coaxing of the fire to life. An old tabby cat sat on its haunches near the stove, ducking its head to wash itself. The smell of wood smoke and cedar filled the cabin. On the windowsill was a collection of smooth stones, arranged according to colour and size. The sea was in those stones, Marina thought, and the particular colour of the light here. On the table beside her was a jam jar full of feathers. She reached out and picked up a stippled brown one, holding it to the light.

'Have you ever seen an owl?' Patrick asked her, closing the door of the wood stove and rising slowly to his feet.

Marina looked up at him. 'Yes. In Israel. A long time ago.'

'Ah, an Israeli owl. I was out hunting for owls on the wing today. I haven't seen an owl all winter. Only this,' he pointed to the feather in her hands.

'They used to frighten me as a child,' said Marina. 'So wild and ruthless. Those strange painted faces.'

'Last year on Christmas Day I saw one up on the spire of the old Methodist Church in town.'

'An observant owl.'

'Yes, seeking atonement for all those mice and rabbits.'

She watched Patrick fill a teapot from an old kettle. That tipping gesture of his wrist was familiar. She couldn't remember the

263

person who tilted a kettle like that. Not her mother. Perhaps one of the other women on the kibbutz. Those old days arrived back in the strangest of ways. The high clear air of the desert, the Children's House with its rows of iron beds, the call of jackals at night across the fields. She wondered how much Patrick knew of her childhood, how much of their lives Gizela had unspooled for him. A bare reckoning, knowing her mother, a few taut details.

When Marina had first stepped inside Gizela's house, she walked slowly through the rooms trying to imagine the shape of her mother's life there. Thick beams held up slanting walls and the roof pitched wildly upwards. The cabin had been built mostly from the salvage of shipwrecks, Patrick had told her when he had let her in. Driftwood lugged back from the beach, planks washed white and smooth. How well he knew the house, Marina had thought, watching him walk down the narrow hall, pointing out a thick beam above a doorway that had come from an old whaling ship wrecked on the beach below. Once it had been the home of a sea captain, Patrick said. A proud old man who had wanted his house to have the echo of a ship at sea, so he could feel that he was still aloft above the waves even when his seafaring days were over.

The cottage held a sense of absence. It was more than just the quiet of a winter house, the windows glazed with frost. There was so little there. A canister of Earl Grey tea on the kitchen counter, some cans of soup in the tiny pantry, three white mugs on a shelf above the sink. On the wall of the living room hung a small watercolour – a pure blue sky over a field. In a wardrobe in the bedroom beside the kitchen she had found clothes hanging – a black dress with fine white spots, a woollen coat, a linen shirt. Marina had taken each piece of clothing out and held it up to her chin in front of the mirror on the inside of the wardrobe door. A mirror that must have held her own mother's reflection. She remembered the day when Gizela asked her to help untangle the brooch from her hair, how she had stood behind her mother at Sura's old dresser. Both of their faces had been reflected in the glass; for a moment mother and daughter had stared up at their twin images. It had filled Marina with a strange elation – the closeness of her mother, the way that the mirror held their faces. It seemed to her that Gizela was looking at her for the very first time, that her usual abstracted expression was replaced by a quiet consideration of her daughter's face. How fiercely she had wanted to lean forward and kiss her mother's cheek. Where does such longing come from, Marina wondered now, staring at herself in the mirror. How do we know to yearn for the things that we have never had? She was not a child who had ever been kissed or held by her mother and yet she had burned so piercingly for one gesture of love – a hand against her cheek, an arm around her shoulder. Even a tender look would have been enough to sustain her. She thought of Dov slipping away from the Children's House and walking through the night fields to find his mother; of Gabriel and the desperate way he pressed himself into her arms. We long more, not less, Marina thought, for the things that we have never had.

While Patrick was making the tea, Marina stood up to look at the watercolour. It was a beautiful work, a quiet, contained grace in the lines. Not a seascape, but a field, trees stretching into the distance. It was the same artist, Marina realised, who had painted the work on Gizela's wall.

'My wife's,' Patrick said as they stood looking at the picture together. 'She lived for forty years by the ocean, but she couldn't stop painting fields. She grew up in Kentucky.' He handed Marina her tea, the cup trembling faintly in the saucer as she took it from him. 'I think the lucky ones are those who belong to the places they are born,' Patrick said. 'They don't have to go searching.'

Marina was silent. She had not expected a wife; he seemed so solitary. There was so much she wanted to ask him about Gizela. For much of her life, she had longed for someone who might be able to tell her something about her mother. She had given up after that visit to Suffolk all those years earlier, but suddenly the old, unanswered questions seemed to rise up again.

'Ellen died four years ago,' Patrick said. Marina had to struggle to bring her attention back to him. Ellen must have been his wife, the painter of the watercolours. 'It was early-onset Alzheimer's,' said Patrick. 'A ghastly thing. But she remembered Kentucky to the very last.' Patrick stopped and took a sip of his tea. 'Gizela helped me when Ellen was ill,' he said quietly. 'She was very capable.'

Marina stared out the window. The sun was low in the sky, a darkening shadow across the beach like a chill presentiment of something. Even the sunset felt pallid here; a faint orange leaching and then the long night. She thought of her mother's look of wary surprise, her distracted presence in the world. She could not imagine her for one moment as someone who might be thought of as capable.

Marina learned from Patrick Stone that Gizela had come to the Cape twenty-one years ago. No one knew where she had come from, and in all her years there she made no friends in the town. She did not seek out company and she made it clear that she wished to be left to herself. She worked shelving books in the small library in Provincetown. It was a job that suited her because

266

she was not required to speak to the customers. She was good at the work, quick and methodical. She also did some typing for the writers staying at the writers' colony in Provincetown, where Patrick was the director for many years. She lived at first in a small room in a lodging house in the town, and then in the cottage by the sea. Patrick owned the cottage, it transpired. He and Ellen had been good friends with the sea captain and had cared for him in his old age. When he died, the house was left to them. The cottage at the top of the dunes came with a large tract of land that included the marshlands and the ponds behind it. Patrick and Ellen could have sold the house and the land, but they had not wanted the sea captain's cottage razed to the ground and some towering mansion built in its place. It would have seemed like a desecration of his memory. And then Gizela arrived.

The light was already gone by the time Marina walked back to her mother's house. She knelt by the fire, coaxing it into life. The twists of newspaper flared into brightness and subsided as she prodded the fire with the poker. From the corner of the living room she could just see the faint glow of light from Patrick's cabin at the foot of the dunes. The lights of Provincetown were hidden by a gauze of clouds. Marina sat cross-legged in front of the fire, the woollen blanket from the bed wrapped around her shoulders. Gizela had been befriended; something in her had loosened enough to allow her to accept Patrick and Ellen's restrained benevolence. Just the three of them on this sandy promontory for all those years. How well Gizela must have known this shore, this hidden corner of the world. Each morning she went walking by the sea, Patrick told her. In the warmer months Gizela walked at night. He knew this because he was a poor sleeper, a night

•

walker too, and sometimes they met each other coming back up the path to the dunes. Both of them had loved those late walks – the thin clouds and the damp sand, the sea only a sound, the lovely pale flare from the lighthouse against the briny darkness. One summer night not long after his wife had died, Patrick told Marina shyly, he and Gizela stayed on the beach until sunrise, watching the light swell gently over the smooth dunes and the bright green coils of sea grass. Marina tried to imagine Gizela walking home along the dune path in the early morning, her coat holding the night air. A cup of coffee, a heel of bread, her solitary breakfast.

It was almost the winter solstice. Truro seemed to Marina a place of perpetual winter – she could hardly imagine the days becoming longer again. She stood by the water, watching the ducks drifting in their safe clusters of sleep. The scalloped edge of the surf was almost at her feet; further out to sea there were curls of foam and sombre whitecaps.

Her days here in Truro seemed to be unmoored from the normal order of time. It was the lack of light, she thought, and the long nights. And the bewilderment of her grief. Often she would look up at the windows to find that the sun had shifted, that darkness was battening down. The days she had spent with Gabriel had the same timelessness. Whole mornings hurtling past, watching him playing in the leaves, lying on her bed with him, a book resting on her knees and those huge eyes fixed on her, his fingers in his mouth. A tilting joy would flood her in those moments. Such an ease to it, after all, this loving of a child.

Dov believed that it was the Children's House which had made it impossible for Gizela to love them. That if she had cared for her own babies, had held them and fed them and rocked them to sleep, she would have loved them. Some door in her would have opened. Proximity, Dov believed, would have made things different. Once, Marina had spoken to a woman from their kibbutz who left with her children when they were toddlers. She realised, the woman told Marina, that she could not recognise her own child's cry. She could not help feeling that this was a necessary knowledge, the woman said. The sound of her baby crying.

Marina thought of Constance. As far as she knew, Gabriel had been with her from the very beginning. She knew the sound of his cries, the weight of him against her back, the smell of his skin. And this had made no difference.

They were coming to Truro, Constance and Gabriel. It seemed impossible to believe, but in a few days they would be there. 'We want to come to you for Christmas,' Rose had written to her. 'All of us. Please let us come.' Marina's eyes pricked with tears when she read Rose's letter, slipped in with a package of chocolate, a box of tea, a thick pair of socks she had knitted. She, Ben and Jacob would have discussed this one Friday night, clustered around the table after dinner. Rose would have been elected as the emissary. It was a tradition to band together for the holiday: the lunch at Rose's apartment, the walk through Central Park afterwards, the evening watching old films. She tried to imagine Gizela's house full of the bustle of them. Leah making her famous cranberry sauce, Ben chopping firewood, Jacob reading the paper in Gizela's armchair by the window.

The day after Marina received Rose's letter she drove to Provincetown and called Ben from a telephone box. There was no telephone in Gizela's house. Ben was full of news of his work at the nursery. People had been grafting plants for thousands of years, he told her. It was a form of alchemy. A hybrid rose grafted on to the root of a tougher variety. An apple tree that could produce two different varieties of fruit. Small botanical miracles. He and Alma were thinking of starting their own gardening business in the spring, he told her excitedly. It would be a kind of urban farming. They would teach people how to make gardens in their backyards or in pots on terraces.

At the end of their conversation Marina asked Ben if he would bring Constance and Gabriel to Truro for Christmas. 'I don't like to think of them being alone,' she said. 'She doesn't know anyone else to go to.'

Yes, Ben said. He would walk to the projects and ask Constance that afternoon. If she agreed to come, he and Alma would catch the bus to the Cape with her and Gabriel.

Marina walked slowly to her car and drove the short distance back to Truro. Every radio station was full of Christmas carols; the soft hush of them filled the car as she drove along the shore in the dense, shadowless light.

She had asked Ben about Jacob, too. 'He's fine,' Ben had said. 'Busy. Missing you.' There had been a faint twist of guilt when she and Ben were planning the Christmas visit. She knew that Jacob would not approve of Constance and Gabriel coming to the Cape. That at the very least she should discuss it with him before asking them. But it was not a conversation she wanted to have with him.

On the beach one afternoon a gale blew in across the dunes, the grasses lashed by wind. Marina held back the whipping strands of her hair with one hand, watching a single gull coasting above the waves. Further north, the emptiness of the shore was broken by the outline of a figure kneeling down on the sand. Patrick, Marina saw as she walked closer, digging for clams. His hands were bare and streaked with dark sand, his legs encased in rubber boots. He looked sturdy and competent, thrusting his spade into the wet sand, focused on his work. A green bucket stood beside him.

'There's something I want to show you,' Patrick said as she approached. 'Look out to sea.' They stood together looking at the wild, rushing sheets of water, the wind meeting the breakers. White foam, made brilliant by the afternoon sun, streamed behind the waves.

'There,' said Patrick, touching her shoulder and pointing to a dark shape in front of them. 'A seal.' Marina saw the smooth black head breaking the surface. 'You hardly ever see them here. He's just a winter traveller, out foraging. Looking for a flock of ducks.'

For a long time they watched the great dark heft of the creature tumbling through the waves. Gusts of wind swept in from the ocean and Marina pulled the hood of her jacket over her head. It was the woollen coat she had found hanging in Gizela's wardrobe. The first time Marina had worn the jacket she slipped her fingers into the pockets and found a dried stalk of lavender. Gizela must have plucked this. There were lavender bushes on the path leading into town. Marina pressed the flower between the pages of one of the books she had brought with her.

The seal disappeared beneath the waves and Patrick picked up his bucket. 'I have cake if you'd like to stop by. From the Portuguese bakery.'

They stepped into friendship cautiously. During the days they kept between them a charming formality, but in the afternoons

271

Marina would sometimes walk over to Patrick's house and sit on the sofa by the window while he lit the fire and the kettle rattled on the stove. Their pots of tea by the window in the last hour of light acquired the seriousness of a ritual. Patrick was gentle and watchful, a touching shyness to him. Perhaps he was the kind of friend that Gizela had needed all along. One evening he left a box of dry kindling on Marina's doorstep after a day of rain; another time she found a note pinned to the door warning her of a fierce gale that evening. Patrick's light often burned late into the night, she noticed. Lying awake in Gizela's bed she tried to imagine what he was doing. Reading in the pool of light from the cracked Bakelite lamp on his kitchen table. Standing staring at his wife's painting of the fields of her childhood. Writing a poem. Had Gizela stared out at Patrick's lighted windows against the vast night? Had it been a comfort to her?

They had not spoken yet about the scattering of Gizela's ashes. Patrick must have the urn somewhere. He was the one who had made all of those arrangements after she had died. Patrick was waiting, Marina sensed, for her to raise it.

Later that afternoon snow began to fall slowly and soundlessly. Marina and Patrick were sitting together drinking tea, and they both turned to watch the drift of white at the window. What would the shore look like covered in snow, Marina wondered. She remembered Jacob telling her about Sibelius's sixth symphony – how the composer had said that the music always reminded him of the scent of the first snow.

Patrick stood up and walked into his study and came out with a book in his hands. 'I wasn't sure when to give you this. I should have done so before.'

It was the first American edition of Marina's book, a picture of a Romani girl in profile on the cover. She flicked through the pages; they were covered in careful pencil markings. Words and paragraphs had been underlined, pages turned down, asterisks marked by certain sections. Next to one paragraph describing the sorrowful face of a Romani musician, the word 'beautiful' had been written and underlined several times.

'It was Gizela's copy,' said Patrick. 'She lent it to me because I was writing a poem about a Gypsy singer. That book was never far from her. I don't know how many times she must have read it.'

Marina felt a sudden tightening in her chest. Her mother had found a copy of her book, had read her words over and over again. Gizela might have sat at the kitchen table in her cottage, the book open before her, a pencil in her hand. Marina's eyes filled with tears.

There was a photograph of her on the jacket of the book, sitting in a grey armchair in front of the bookshelves in Jacob's apartment on Park Avenue. Marina remembered the day so clearly: Ben's excited direction of the publisher's photographer, his earnest suggestions for props. A teacup, an open volume of poetry in her lap, the neighbour's tortoiseshell cat in her arms – all of these things would make her look more serious and literary, Ben insisted. Jacob and Ben had sat side by side on the bed earlier that morning, advising her what to wear. The blue dress, Ben had declared. Marina was twenty-eight when the photograph was taken. Ten years after Gizela had last seen her face.

Had her mother scrutinised the photograph, tried to make out the titles of the books on the shelves? Had she imagined the apartment outside the edges of the frame, the unknown life surrounding the daughter she had abandoned? Could she have speculated about Marina's life the way Marina and Dov had about hers? In all of these years shadowed by longing for her mother, Marina had never once considered the possibility that her mother had also longed for her. She leaned her face against the side of the old flowered armchair and wept.

That evening Patrick walked Marina to the door of Gizela's house, carrying a slab of cake he had wrapped up. He waited while she opened the door. The snow was still light; it dissolved as soon as it touched the shoulders of Patrick's coat.

'Gizela almost never spoke to us about her other life. And we did not ask her. But there is one thing she told me many years ago,' Patrick said. 'When she left Israel after your father died, the kibbutz wanted her to leave you and your brother behind. They wanted you to remain Israelis, to be brought up in the Children's House. You belonged to the kibbutz, they told her, not to her. It was your home. It was what her husband would have wanted, someone said. She could turn away from her country if that was what she chose, but why send her children into exile too? It was very hard for her, but she did not feel that it was the right thing to leave you behind.

'After your brother died, she felt that she had made a terrible mistake. That something in her had tainted both of you. She was convinced that she was responsible for his death. That if she stayed with you she would only do more damage. She tried to explain to me once how, all her life, she felt some terrifying deficiency in herself, a lack of something profound at her very core. As if she were simply occupying the shape of herself.

'When she told me this, I thought of Pablo Casals. Practising Bach's neglected cello suites every day for more than a decade before performing them in public. And then his silence. First,

274

his refusal to play in countries that mistreated their citizens; and then, after Franco came to power, his vow never to perform again. I don't think it was a conscious choice for Gizela, but it was the same kind of withholding. The same removal from the world.'

They stood together in the snow for a long time, silence between them.

'If I have learned anything,' he said to her at last, 'it is that sometimes all we can do for someone is to wait with them. And I know you might not feel this as a comfort – that it might not mean so much after everything that happened – but she loved you. I do believe that is true.'

There was no moon that evening, but the snow on the ground seemed to glow. The night was very still, not even the faintest rattle of wind. Marina sat at the kitchen table with a glass of wine in front of her. She wondered if Gizela had told Patrick about Dov's art exhibition at Cooper Union. Remembering the look on her mother's face when she had walked into the gallery that night, Marina could not imagine that she could ever have spoken about it to anyone. But to feel that she was responsible for Dov's death. Yes, she could understand that.

It still seemed strange to Marina that Gizela had come to the opening of the exhibition. For all their lives she had absented herself from any event that involved her children. Marina could not remember Gizela ever setting foot in any of the schools she had attended. She never came to a school play, a parent evening, a graduation ceremony. Always Marina and Dov made excuses for their mother. She was unwell, they would say. She was working. She was in bed with a migraine. Once, one of Dov's teachers came to their apartment. It was during Dov's first year of high school, when he had become errant and stopped going to classes. Marina could still remember their panicked fear when the woman knocked on the door one summer evening. Gizela was not home. They did not know where she was or when she would return, but Dov told the teacher that she had gone to collect Chinese food for their dinner. It was something that a mother might do. The teacher said she would wait and sat down at the kitchen table, her legs crossed neatly at the ankles.

An hour passed, the teacher looking at her watch, fingering the handle of her handbag. This is very irregular, Marina remembered the woman saying. Dov looked stricken, walking to the window and peering out the curtains again and again. Gizela had never voiced it to them, but it was understood among them that no one must know how frequently she was absent, how often they were alone. Marina was not sure what had terrified them more: that Gizela would not appear, or that she would return to find the teacher sitting there at the table.

Eventually it grew dark. She could not in good conscience leave two children alone in an apartment at night, the teacher said at last, rising to her feet. She did not know where their mother was but it was well past dinnertime and something needed to be done. He had forgotten, Dov said suddenly, that Gizela had told him she was going to look in on a neighbour who was unwell. She must have needed to stay with the old woman. They would go downstairs and wait with the Zelman family, he said. They were good friends of Gizela; she could collect them from there when she returned. The teacher seemed content with this arrangement – the burden of responsibility for them had been shifted to another adult.

Mrs Zelman warmed up soup for them and sat with them while they ate. When she rose to clear their bowls, she placed her hands briefly on Marina's shoulders. Even this most casual of gestures seemed enormous. Lying in bed that night, Marina could still feel the gentle pressure of those hands on her shoulders.

The exhibition was Dov's final art project at Cooper Union. All through their childhood he had sketched and painted, but it became a serious passion for him during his last years of high school. There was a teacher who encouraged him to apply for entry to art school and he received a scholarship to Cooper Union. The scholarship included housing in the college dormitories, but Dov stayed on in the apartment with them, catching the train to Manhattan every day. He was intensely private about his work – it was the only thing that was not shared between him and Marina. She had not even known the subject of his final exhibition until she saw the title printed on the invitations.

An intensity of purpose emanated from him the whole year he was immersed in creating the works that would form the graduation show. It was something that transcended the zeal of his other passions; there were times when Marina was frightened by the depth of his obsession. There was something too desperate in it. Dov would stay at his studio until late every night, often sleeping there. Always thin, he grew almost skeletal that year. His face took on an alarming, starved expression. There were many days, Marina suspected, when he forgot to eat.

Sometimes Marina caught the train to Cooper Union after school and forced him to come to a café with her. She watched the tremble of his fingers as he held his cup of coffee. It seemed that the tremor moved through his entire body, something that he could barely contain. When he leaned close to her she could smell the stale reek of cigarettes. All the art students smoked, Dov told her. It was impossible to avoid it.

Dov's final exhibition was called 'Children of the Gods'. It was a chronicle of his obsession. Every work in the exhibition was an echo of displacement and deprivation. A series of fourteen enormous canvases depicted each aspect of the Children's House, rendered in the most meticulous detail. The rows of beds, the hand towels on pegs along the corridor, the dining hall, the shower room. When Marina saw the paintings she could hardly believe how detailed Dov's memories of the place were. They had no photographs – everything had been reconstructed from his memory. The paintings themselves seemed ominous and fore-boding, a terrible chill hanging over each one. In all the works, a tiny depiction of a pair of children could be seen. A boy and a girl, hand in hand. The figures of the children were dwarfed by the scale of the paintings; they appeared lost and adrift, their faces always in shadow.

Dov had found an old official black-and-white film extolling the virtues of communal child-rearing as it was practised on the kibbutz. Clips from the film were projected on to the walls of the gallery, sometimes over the paintings themselves. Children danced in circles, their hands held by women in nurses' uniforms. The children beamed up at the camera as they clustered around sinks brushing their teeth. Rows of tiny boys and girls, no more than three or four years old, lined up outside a dining hall hand in hand, singing in Hebrew. One scene showed a dormitory full of sleeping children. Again and again a clip of a man speaking was played, cut in between every scene. 'We will always be foreign-ers,' he said. 'But they are the children of the Gods.'

Spliced into these scenes were clips from another film, a documentary Marina had seen before, made by a young man who had grown up on a kibbutz. The man had conducted a series of interviews with the children of the kibbutzim, now adults in their twenties and thirties. All these men and women had been terribly wounded; their quiet, serious voices spoke in Hebrew as the camera moved through the rooms of an abandoned Children's House. The place had fallen into ruin: doors hung off hinges, broken furniture was piled in the corners of rooms. English translations of their words were projected over the images of empty rooms. One woman spoke of feeling as if she had no skin on her body, living in such close proximity to hundreds of other children. Another spoke of her terror of the communal showers, her shame at the daily revelations of her changing body to a room full of other girls. 'I'm not sure who is more of a mother to me,' one woman said, 'my own mother or the space that was always around me.' Even on the crackling audio of the film, the tremble in her voice could be heard. Several times she turned from the camera to wipe away her tears. Another man spoke about how his greatest pleasure was to say goodnight to his own children. 'Sleep is when they leave the world for a little while,' he said. 'And even before they were born I knew that I would want to be there with them each night when they slip away.' Another man spoke the same phrase repeatedly, his voice full of bitterness. 'They called us children of the Gods, but really we were small offerings to the Gods of ideology.'

The scenes from the films and the voices, repeated over and over, formed a kind of echo chamber, a strange and disconcerting symphony. Down the centre of the gallery, hanging from the roof, were fourteen enormous silk screen images. Each one was the same image of Gizela. Her face, rendered in black and white, loomed. Dov had caught her expression with an excruciating

279

exactitude: the huge eyes, the distant, abstracted gaze. Her hair was braided around her head like a crown, her arms folded across her chest. It was the most intimate of portraits. Across every image were emblazoned the Hebrew letters for mother.

Gizela arrived late to the opening of the exhibition, just before the speeches were about to begin. Sitting with a cluster of Dov's friends on the other side of the room, Marina saw her walk through the door and stand there stunned for several minutes as she took in everything around her. For a moment Marina feared that her mother was going to cry. People always looked at Gizela: it was her beauty, and something fierce and singular about the way she held herself. But that night Marina watched as people in the audience began to notice that Gizela was the woman in the pictures. She was instantly recognisable – that crown of hair, that gaze. Perhaps it was only her flawed recollection of that night, but Marina remembered a hush over the room and whispers. And Gizela's face. That terrible look on her mother's face.

Gizela walked through the room, all the way to the front, where Dov was standing beside the art critic who was to give the opening speech. Standing in front of her son she raised her hand and slapped his face. The crack of it rang out across the room. Then she turned away and walked out of the gallery. Marina jumped up to follow her but when she stepped into the street it was empty, not even the sound of footsteps on the pavement. By the next day, Dov was dead and Gizela was gone forever.

When Constance stepped down from the bus in Hyannis, it struck Marina again how unprotected she was. Constance looked around her uncertainly, her eyes huge in her narrow face. She seemed thinner than ever. Ben and Alma emerged from the bus, Gabriel in Ben's arms. As soon as he saw Marina waiting there, the little boy struggled free of Ben and came running to her, flinging himself against her legs and starting to cry as she picked him up. She had been away from him for nearly a month. He could only have felt her absence as a terrible betrayal. He sobbed against her shoulder, his tears running down her neck, his hands twisted in her hair. Marina was glad that Jacob was not there to witness this.

Constance hung back, a plastic shopping bag clutched in her hands. She permitted Marina's embrace, leaning in against her briefly. Driving back to Truro from the bus station, she caught sight of Constance's face in the mirror. The girl needed a mother, a wise uncle. Someone from her own country. The car wound around the road by the shore, the band of sea glimmering beyond the dunes.

After so many days of silence it felt strange to Marina to have the house full of people. Her only company for the last month had been Patrick; those hushed conversations in the last afternoon light, the pots of tea by the fire. They were all there now: Jacob had arrived with Rose and Leah late that afternoon. When he stepped out of the car, Marina fell into his arms in the same way that Gabriel had dissolved against her earlier that morning. She felt the sharpest tenderness for him when she rested her head against his chest, his arms around her as they stood together in the gathering dusk.

The hum of voices, the smell of coffee brewing, the clatter of dishes as Leah and Jacob cooked together; the cold silence

281

of the house was suddenly gone. It was as if it were a different place altogether, barely one she recognised any more. Marina sat at the kitchen table with Gabriel on her lap, pointing out the gulls perched in the swaying fir trees beyond the window. The noise of the waves was all around them. Rose and Alma sat beside her, bent over a pile of wool. Rose was teaching her to crochet. Marina smiled to see them – Alma's serious absorption, Rose's quick fingers, her gentle instructions like an incantation. The girl had been befriended, just as she herself had been so many years before.

Through the window she spied Patrick walking up the path, rubbing his hands together in the cold. He had offered his spare bedroom for Rose and Leah to stay in and they had insisted that he come to the cottage to join them for dinner. The day before, he dragged two mattresses to the cottage for Alma and Ben to sleep on, and they made the beds together, fluffing up the pillows and piling on extra blankets. He was going to make a plum pudding for Christmas lunch – a very un-American tradition, he said.

'We love him already,' Leah whispered to Marina as they watched Rose and Patrick deep in conversation at the end of the table. He was telling her about frigate birds. Those great regal creatures with their sweeping feathers and sun-drenched lives in islands full of mild evenings and clear water. Sometimes, Patrick said, whole flocks were swept up in hurricanes and carried thousands of miles through the gale to other countries, not knowing where they had come to, or how far a distance they had travelled. The miracle of the birds, Patrick said, was that they could pick themselves up and intuit home. The birds found food and water, gathered their strength in hiding, and began the long flight back to their own lost lands, their sweet white beaches and shady palms. Home was a trace laid deeply in them, Patrick said, a kind of true north that they always knew to navigate towards. Where they belonged was never in question and return was always possible.

Marina wondered if he was thinking of his wife's watercolours, those yellow fields of her childhood. Or perhaps of Gizela, who had never belonged anywhere. She noticed Alma listening very closely to Patrick's story, her chin resting in her hands. What happens, Marina wanted to ask Patrick, when there is no possibility of return? No way for the wanderers to find a path home.

Constance had disappeared almost immediately into the small bedroom at the back of the house. She refused a cup of tea, an extra blanket, only emerging reluctantly when Rose went to fetch her for dinner. She sat silently at the table beside Ben, staring at her plate. Perhaps it was too much for her, Marina thought, to be here among all these people. The slow banter, the bursts of laughter, the crowded table. It was as if those days in the garden that fall had been dreamed. Constance seemed to have retreated even further into herself now; to be marooned entirely by her despair. Sometimes there is a kind of damage to people's inner lives that can never be rectified, Jacob had once told her. He had been speaking about Gizela, but it was true for Constance too, Marina thought, watching the girl's face.

That night the sound of thunder woke Marina, the rumble of it loud and close. It was raining, a sudden hard spatter against the window. She heard the horn of a ship out at sea, a cold, disembodied sound; mournful and ominous. For a moment, she thought it was the cry of a child. Surfacing from sleep, she was confused briefly to see Jacob there beside her. She could see his face clearly in the shaft of moonlight that spilled into the room. Sleeping, he looked younger, his lips open slightly, his cheek resting on his hand. How deeply he cared for those he loved, for those who had been granted admission to the circle of his protection. Marina turned towards him and he moved to make a space for her against his warm body, his arms reaching around her, his lips pressed into her hair.

On Christmas morning they walked slowly in single file along the path through the dunes, a silent procession. The first breath of light was in the sky, the cold so sharp that Marina could feel it in her cheekbones. A whisper, the call of a bird, the crunch of their boots on the sand; the morning was still and hushed. They had left Constance and Gabriel asleep in the bedroom at the back of the house. Patrick put his hand on Rose's arm to steady her as they walked over the top of the dunes down towards the water's edge. In his other hand he held the small wooden box that contained Gizela's ashes.

It had troubled Marina at first, this burning of her mother's body. It was something forbidden by their faith. A desecration of the flesh that had housed the spirit and the breath of God, had housed her own holy soul. The dead must be buried in the earth. But Gizela had cast all that behind her long ago. She didn't want a brass plaque under a salt-blighted rosebush, would not allow her name to be carved on a stone in the cemetery. It was how she had lived her life. Marina believed Patrick when he said that this was what Gizela had wanted.

They stood in a line along the edge of the water, watching the light creep slowly into the sky. The ocean stretched away beyond them, still and black. There were no speeches, no words about Gizela as they scattered the ashes into the waves, but as they stood there together Patrick began to sing. It was a high, strange tune, the words bending into cadences Marina could not identify. Later, he told her that it was a Gaelic love song, that as a small boy he had watched his father sing it above his mother's grave, tears streaming down his face. One of them should have said Kaddish for Gizela there by the shore, Marina thought at first, but no, Patrick's song was right. So often consolation was unexpected; so often it came in a language not one's own.

An arc of grit, her mother's body out there on the waves. The ocean that she had loved. These ceremonies of sustenance. Beside Marina, Jacob touched her cheek gently; she had barely realised she was weeping. Patrick swayed slowly as he sang, the notes rising up high and pure in the cold morning air. It seemed a hymn not just for Gizela, but for Dov too, and for Constance. For all the lost and the uncommemorated. Beyond them a drift of pale pink cloud trailed across the dawn sky. The black motes of distant birds circled and turned above the waves, taking up a cry among them with a single voice.

Gabriel
December, 2018

The Christmas Day my mother disappeared there was a particularly savage winter storm on the Cape. The winds were so fierce they peeled back the sand from the dunes, and the blackened skeleton of an ancient ship that had been buried for over a century lifted itself free. There's a newspaper clipping about it – a photograph of the old ship perched on the dunes as if it were cresting a wave, its hull a giant ribcage. When I first saw the picture, it reminded me of the dinosaur skeletons at the Museum of Natural History – those ancient arcs of bone. After the weather had cleared, the townspeople of Truro made their way down to the beach to exclaim over the old ship, to climb through its hull and take photographs of each other standing by its prow.

At the same time, a small search party was combing the town for my mother. The Coast Guard, the Truro police; men who had left their Christmas lunches to look for a woman who would never be found. Later there were dogs. A pond was dredged. For some reason this collision of stories seems to be important, as if the resurrected ship is somehow connected to my mother, as if the two things are part of the same story.

There was no photograph in the newspaper of my mother, because no image of her existed. She wasn't the sort of person you took photos of, Marina said. Seven months, she knew her: a summer, a fall and part of a winter before Constance disappeared. Barely any time at all.

I've divided the pictures of me as a small child into two piles: the ones I know were taken while Constance was there, when I still lived with her in the projects, and the ones taken in the years afterwards. I suppose I'm looking for a trace of her in me. Not in the sense of any physical resemblance, but a feeling I must have held for the life I had with her, the life I went back to at the end of each day. Marina took so many pictures – me playing in the leaves in Mount Morris Park, squatting over a bed of seedlings, sitting on Ben's lap. She's a relentless archivist, Marina; a chronicler and a recorder. My face gets older in the pictures, but there's no shift that I can see. No before and after. Living in an apartment in the projects; living in a brownstone on the park. A ghost mother; a real one. Nothing in that little boy's face to register those shifts.

'Yes, yes,' Marina says when I ask her, 'of course she held you. She bathed you and fed you and brushed your hair and carried you on her back.' But there's a catch and a pause in the things she tells me; something that she can't bring herself to say. She did all these things, but she did not love you.

When they were searching for Constance – along the water's edge, by the Truro ponds and then later through advertisements in papers, traces on her bank account, notices in post offices all over the north-east – Marina was terrified that she wouldn't be found. Then, as the years passed, I suspect, although she never said this to me, her terror was that Constance would return.

That Marina would have to give me back. But no word came, no sighting was ever reported. There's no pressing rewind, no miraculous reversal or return.

Last Christmas at the Cape, Patrick told me a story about the Nauset tribes who first inhabited the dunes there. Living on a sandy promontory, they had nothing with which to build monuments, so they marked the sites of important events by digging ceremonial holes in the sand. They kept these sand holes well dug out, year after year, returning to them through the seasons.

So life forms around an absence. We have almost nothing to remember Constance by. No photograph, no letter. There's the blue exercise book from the literacy classes that she stopped attending after the first week, but only three pages are filled. The letters are firmly drawn – clear, squat forms, large and awkward like a child's. They remind me of my own workbooks from my first days at Calhoun. I take the blue book with me when I travel, tucked into my suitcase. It seems the only tangible proof that my mother existed.

Marina took a few things from the apartment in the projects when she went to clear it out after Constance disappeared: old pots and pans, a grey blanket, three drinking glasses, a mismatched set of cutlery. She wrapped each item neatly in butcher's paper and packed everything into two cardboard boxes. They're still down in the basement of the brownstone. Everything in the boxes seems anonymous; nothing of Constance clings to them. She must have cooked with the pots, slept under the blanket, perhaps poured me a drink in the plastic glasses, but they all seem tired and anonymous. Hand-me-downs doled out to her, things that had passed through many other hands before hers.

Marina has told me that there was always a strange force-field around Constance, something about her that prevented anything from the world from penetrating. I know that she used all these things in the boxes, washed them, put them away, but none of them bear a trace of her.

I once read a book written by a man who was sent to England on a kindertransport during the war. Marina gave it to me when I was in high school – because of her own mother's story, but I think also because she wanted me to know that she too had lost things, and that what we lose remains in us as a slow burn.

Then of course there was everything that might have happened to Constance in Rwanda. 'We could go there,' Marina has said a few times over the years. Visit the region she came from, search for anyone who might have known her. See if there's family. 'One day,' I say. One day, perhaps. But it's not a gulf I think I can bridge. I'm not sure how useful these kinds of excavations are. Constance never let a word of her story spill out – what right do we have to go searching for what she didn't want to be known?

The man in Marina's book was four years old when he left his own country, a year older than I was when Constance disappeared. He described the faltering of his language, the way the sounds lingered in him for the first few months of exile and then slipped beneath the surface, with all that went with them. He wrote about the echoes of his childhood language coming back to him, scratching or knocking, then falling away into silence as soon as he strained to hear it. My feeling for my mother is something like that. I don't have any memories of her, but she's in me like a door banging a little in the wind. Or perhaps I just think she's there because she should be there. A mother should be there.

Every year we return to Truro for Christmas, converging on the winter beach. Ben and Alma and the girls fly up from Arizona; Jacob and Marina and I pile into the car with Rose, all talking over each other as we drive up the expressway, Christmas carols playing on every radio station. Patrick and Leah are waiting for us when we arrive, the fire burning, the kettle on the stove. There's spiced brandy with cloves in the evenings, morning walks along the shore, visits to the Portuguese bakery in town.

All through my childhood the year seemed to revolve around those two winter weeks by the sea. That house is where I spoke my first word. It's become a story now: four years of silence and then my first word sung out across the dunes.

Once on the Cape I dreamed of my mother. In my dream it was dawn and I was alone by the ocean. Constance walked towards me from further up the shore. I can't remember her face in my dream but I knew it was her. She couldn't tell me what she knew and I didn't know what to say to her, but it didn't matter. We watched the light rise up from behind the water and we kept quiet there together, the morning sun on our faces. We sat there for a long time, not touching but very close.

Acknowledgements

Many hands have guided this work and I am deeply grateful to all those who have helped me in so many ways. Thank you to Brenda Walker, whose friendship, editorial wisdom and enduring belief made all the difference. I am indebted to Ilana Sharp, Catherine Therese, Stephanie Bishop and Leah Kaminsky, who have inhabited the world of this novel with me for many years and whose steadfastness and solidarity made it possible to write it. Thank you to David Carlin for being such splendid and inspirational company for those weeks in France when I was finishing the book. For showing me a way through the story when the path did not seem clear, I am very grateful to Barbara Hewson Bower. Thank you to Peter Bishop for Sibelius, the perfect poem and many other gifts of literary friendship. Enormous thanks are due to Dietra Gamar, who has offered so much to me over so many years since those days in the brownstone in Chelsea. For her unwavering support from the very beginning, I am very grateful to Anne Day. Thank you to Hayley Katzen, Amanda Webster and William Yeoman for their editorial acuity and friendship. Thank you also to Alison Manning for her practical assistance and encouragement, and to Carol Major, novel whisperer and generous soul.

I am enormously grateful to Meredith Curnow for championing this book with such passion, and also to the whole wonderful team at Penguin Random House. Special thanks to Catherine Hill, editor extraordinaire. I am indebted to Emma Paterson at Rogers, Coleridge and White for her unfailing support and belief.

This book was written in many extraordinary houses and some of them have seeped into the story. To all those who have offered me space to write and a quiet room when I most needed it, I am deeply grateful. Thank you to Varuna, the Writers' House in the Blue Mountains, for various residencies over the years. To Sister Annette Allain and all the Little Sisters of the Assumption, who have always opened their doors and hearts to me in Harlem and Walden, New York. To Lis Sur Mer Artists' Cottages in Truro, Cape Cod, for the cottage above the dunes. Thanks to John Fanning and Kerry Eielson at La Muse Artists' and Writers' Retreat in the Languedoc in France for the gift of space and time in one of the most beautiful parts of the world.

Writing this novel led me into many different worlds and I thank all those who shared their knowledge with me and patiently answered my many questions. My sincere thanks to Rabbi Beryl Epstein for helping me to understand so much about Hasidic life in Crown Heights. Thanks also to Daphne Bondy for all her assistance in Israel; to Blair Nikula for the advice on birds; and to Father Claude Dumas, former national Gitane Chaplain of France, for sharing insights about the culture and history of the Gitane community of France. I am indebted to Jenny and Les

Shub for generously sharing their experiences in Israel with me and providing me with a wealth of information, as well as much support and encouragement.

The greatest thanks are due to my family for their enduring love and care and, above all, to Danny, who makes everything possible.

Sources

Many texts were important to me in the research for this novel. I would particularly like to acknowledge Jean Hatzfeld's books on the Rwandan genocide, *Life Laid Bare: The Survivors in Rwanda Speak* (Farrar, Straus and Giroux, 2007) and *The Antelope's Strategy: Living in Rwanda After the Genocide* (Farrar, Straus and Giroux, 2009). The testimonies of the Rwandan genocide survivors included in the novel on pages 195 to 200 are taken directly from Hatzfeld's recordings of survivors' stories in these two books.

Intended Consequences: Rwandan Children Born of Rape (Aperture Foundation, 2008), Jonathan Torgovnik's collection of photographic portraits and testimonies about the use of sexual violence as a weapon of war during the Rwandan genocide was also particularly helpful in my research, as was the comprehensive documentation of the genocide produced by African Rights, *Rwanda: Death, Despair and Defiance* (1995).

The documentary *Children of the Sun* (2007) by Ran Tal and the film *The Children's House* (2005) by Tamar Feingold were both enormously useful in my research on early life on Israel's kibbut-zim. I have drawn on both these texts to inform this invented narrative, and some of the elements of Dov's art exhibition are adapted from them.

The allusion to the Australian essayist writing about the love between mothers and children refers to Helen Garner's reflections on Elizabeth Jolley in her essay 'Dreams of Her Real Self', published in the collection *Everywhere I Look* (Text Publishing, 2016).

Mrs Zelman's thoughts on the Jewish sabbath are inspired by Abraham Joshua Heschel's text *The Sabbath* (Farrar, Straus and Giroux, 1951).

The line of poetry that Jacob quotes in his lecture is from 'Land in Sight' by Anne Michaels, originally published in her collection *Skin Divers* (Bloomsbury, 1999). Thank you to the Wylie Agency, London, for permission to quote this line. The Jose Angel Valente quote is from the poem 'Be My Limit', published in *Landscape with Yellow Birds: Selected Poems by Jose Angel Valente* (Archipelago Books, 2013), translated from the Spanish by Tom Christensen. Grateful thanks to Archipelago Books for permission to use this.

After university in Australia, Alice Nelson lived and worked in Harlem, living in the brownstone on 120th Street in which *The Children's House* is set. While studying in New York, she worked at a non-profit agency run by an order of nuns as a case worker with refugee and undocumented migrant families. Alice was named one of the *Sydney Morning Herald*'s Best Young Australian Novelists for her first novel, *The Last Sky*. The novel also won the TAG Hungerford Award and was shortlisted for the Australian Society of Authors' Barbara Jefferis Award and for the *Australian/Vogel*'s Literary Award. Alice's short fiction, essays and reviews have appeared in publications such as the *Sydney Review of Books*, the *Asia Literary Review*, *Southerly* and the *West Australian*. Alice now lives in Perth.